"I will not play Russian roulette with Garry Channing's life!"

For one terrible moment, Elaine and Paul stared at each other. Then Paul strode to the desk and grabbed the sack that held the incriminating items on Keith's list.

Hot tears stung Elaine's eyes. A prison term would destroy her brother, and the truth would cost her her job at the bank. She had to stop him any way she could.

She leapt at Paul and jammed her thumb into the loop surrounding the trigger of the rifle he held. The gun barrel swung crazily toward the ceiling, the floor, the window.

Suddenly, their macabre dance was halted by three ear-splitting explosions. Elaine heard a quick expiration of breath as Paul's body jerked against hers. All of a sudden, he was holding her against him in a crushing embrace.

"Yes..." she whispered.

ABOUT THE AUTHOR

The psychological twists and criminal complexities of *A Time for Trust* stem from the author's work with a psychologist who tested prisoners indicted for crimes of violence. Its page-turning drama can be traced to her childhood love of mysteries. With this, her third Superromance book, Karen Field has turned her grade-school nickname, the Storyteller, into reality.

Books by Karen Field

HARLEQUIN SUPERROMANCE
244–TIME WILL TELL
331–JUST SAY THE WORD

A Time for Trust

KAREN FIELD

Harlequin Books

TORONTO • NEW YORK • LONDON
AMSTERDAM • PARIS • SYDNEY • HAMBURG
STOCKHOLM • ATHENS • TOKYO • MILAN

This book is respectfully dedicated to the many
'500' Festival volunteers who help to make the
'500' Mile Race a racing spectacle with a
community's heart.

Although the '500' Festival events depicted in the
story are real annual events in Indianapolis preceding
the '500' Mile Race during May, all the characters in
this book are strictly the imagination of the author,
have no relation whatsoever to anyone accidentally
bearing the same name or names, and are not
inspired by any individual known or unknown
to the author.

Published May 1991

ISBN 0-373-70450-X

A TIME FOR TRUST

CHAPTER ONE

ALTHOUGH TRAFFIC MOVED steadily past him, Paul Cooper kept to the speed limit as he traveled Interstate 65 south from Indianapolis. The concrete surface glistened, wet from late-April rain as a torrent of raindrops pummeled the windshield of the silver Chrysler LeBaron. The raindrops slowed to a patter, then finally ceased altogether, revealing a sky layered in gray, the breaks in the clouds proving the storm had passed. Calm azure eyes behind conservative glasses squinted against the unexpected glare of the sun as it descended in the west.

Paul looked up from the wide three-lane ribbon of road ahead to see a delicate band span the sky. The arc of a magnificent rainbow gleamed in iridescent pastels—red, orange, green, blue, indigo and violet. He shot a dour look in the direction of the spectrum of colors. Madeline Pruett had loved rainbows.

Madeline... Her name surged into his thoughts against his will and gave him a momentary pang, distracting his attention from the highway ahead. He rubbed his broad forehead and ran his long fingers through the dark blond hair that had a slight wave at the brow.

A warning rumble sounded behind the LeBaron, bringing Paul to full attention. Glancing into the rearview mirror, he saw the huge round headlamps of the cab of a semitrailer that was hugging the bumper of his car. Paul refused to speed up.

The driver of the truck gave a Change of Lane signal and pulled out into the middle to pass the LeBaron. Paul cast a withering glance at the rectangular metal mountain as it moved around him. Riding in its wake was an aged white Buick, a four-door sedan filthy with road dust, its fenders and doors nibbled by rust. As the Buick passed, too, Paul caught a glimpse of a young male driver, brown hair blowing in the wind from the lowered windows. A thick, oily smoke, wafted by the wind, streamed in an upward spiral from a rusted tail pipe; a Save the Whales sticker was spread across the rear bumper. The car had a Brown County, Indiana license plate, he noticed.

An accident waiting to happen, thought Paul uneasily. The smoke from the Buick's exhaust spread like a malevolent cloud, hovering over the windshield of the LeBaron, making it difficult for him to see.

As his gaze fixed absently on the rear view of the white car growing smaller in the distance, he was lulled by the strains of a tune from Gershwin's *American in Paris* coming from the LeBaron's stereo speakers. The white car raced ahead, and his mind moved back in time to that assignment in Paris for the

Wall Street Sentinel. Madeline had met him there on a weekend holiday. . . .

The familiar large green sign loomed just ahead.

SOUTHPORT ROAD—1/2 MILE
SOUTHPORT HOMECROFT
NEXT RIGHT

Then it happened. In one heart-stopping moment Paul saw the old Buick shudder as the car rounded the curve and veer to the right of the wet roadway like a stone released from a slingshot. It plummeted through a reflective boundary marker and careened down a slight grassy depression, a part of the berm. Then it hurtled toward trees that towered sixty yards from the base of the tall embankment that supported the overpass. A chain-link fence stretched along the field, just in front of the trees.

Horrified, Paul applied his brake as swiftly as he dared, his gaze fixed on the out-of-control vehicle as it lunged toward fence and trees. He saw the car strike and crumple the fence, before it smashed into the wall of trees. The momentum sent it spinning round, worn tires skidding along wet grass, until it was heading back in the direction from which it had come. The battered hood jutted upward and a huge spiderweb of cracks in the windshield glistened in the golden sunlight. The horn blared—a loud, unremitting cry for help.

Paul skidded as he pulled the LeBaron onto the narrow strip of gravel at the right side of the road. He came to a stop close to the exit ramp beyond the overpass and twisted in his seat to get a better look at the scene of the accident.

Traffic continued to pour past, but there was no sign of life from the stricken car—except for the thin line of smoke streaming upward from the engine. A tingle ran along the hairline at the back of Paul's neck. *Get the hell out of there!* he yelled silently to the youthful driver inside.

Trying to remain calm, he reached for a small directory in his glove compartment and looked up the number for the Indiana state police. He picked up the receiver of the mobile telephone mounted beneath the dashboard and heaved a sigh of relief when a voice answered promptly. Paul gave his name, license number and the highway location, describing in terse sentences exactly what he had just seen. He recited the license number of the old car and gave a brief description.

"The car appears to be on fire. I'm going to try to get the driver out," he said, trying to mask his fear. A coolness was beginning to settle over him, as though he had already accepted what he knew he must do.

"We'll get help to you, sir," answered the male voice on the line.

Paul replaced the receiver, released his seat belt, and turned on the LeBaron's Hazard lights. He exited the car at a run, cursing himself silently for failing to purchase that emergency fire extinguisher for the trunk he had thought of buying just two weeks before.

The column of smoke from the overheated engine was growing thicker and darker. As he neared the other car, Paul saw that it was leaning a bit to the right, as though a tire had collapsed. Then he detected something that made his stomach tighten. The acrid smell of burning plastic and rubber intermingled with the pervasive odor of gasoline. As a dull flicker of tiny flames began to dance in the fractured engine, he realized the gas tank at the rear of the car must have cracked.

Paul hesitated and almost drew back. *That gas tank could go any second.* He felt an overwhelming urge to escape. Then he thought of the young driver inside. Maybe there was a passenger as well! He fought down his rising panic and drew close. Leaning down, he looked through the window on the driver's side. The only occupant was slumped forward, face and chest against the steering wheel. His eyes were closed and blood streamed down his face. He appeared to be in his late teens, perhaps, and had the hefty build of a football quarterback.

The deafening, shrill cry of the horn was what galvanized Paul into action. He jerked on the car door, which all but came off in his hands. Acting on instinct alone, the tall, lean runner reached down and released the seat belt that stretched tightly across the upper part of the unconscious driver's sturdy legs. Paul grasped the young man under the arms and tugged with all his strength, pulling him away from the steering wheel and through the opening left by the sagging door.

The shrill sound of the horn ceased.

The driver's legs hit the wet grass with a perceptible thud. Paul bent down at an angle guaranteed to break a back and wrapped his arms around the inert figure, grasping the victim's left wrist with his right hand, and pulled. Pulled hard. The gut-wrenching odor of gasoline was filling his nostrils and the sweat of terror streamed down his face, steaming his glasses so he could hardly see and soaking his dress shirt.

The task appeared impossible. The youth's passive bulk seemed to weigh a thousand pounds, yet fear lent Paul a strength he couldn't explain. He was thankful his training for the "500" Festival Mini-Marathon had kept his muscles toned. He concentrated on dragging the man along the ground an inch at a time, away from the burning car.

Dimly he became aware of a truck's bright headlights rounding the curve, although the sun was still in the sky. He heard the hiss of a diesel engine, the sound of brakes, the crunch of huge tires scattering gravel. Vaguely he sensed that the truck had come to a halt just ahead of the LeBaron, its red taillights blazing. He was more aware of a police siren wailing in the distance. Then two. They seemed to be coming from different directions. This was the help Paul was counting on.

He heard the pounding of leather soles hitting gravel. "Here!" Paul heard a male voice behind him at the same moment as he felt large hands grip his shoulders. "You take his feet and legs. I'll get under his arms." The voice had a melodious Southern accent.

Paul was glad to obey. The truck driver wrapped muscular arms around the unconscious youth in a kind of Helzheimer hug, while Paul grabbed the kid's legs at the knees. The two men lifted their burden between them, and broke into a trot, putting distance between themselves and the abandoned car, where ripples of flame were now visible through the open door.

They ran toward the overpass while the sound of police sirens drew ever closer. Gently the two men laid down their burden in the grass at the foot of a tall embankment, and Paul straightened, breathing hard, his heart pounding and muscles aching. The cool wind drifted across his sweat-dampened clothing, chilling him. He looked back at the burning car.

An explosion ripped through the tranquil countryside, sending up a shower of sparks and an eerie flare of light. Paul recoiled, throwing a hand over his face.

"Lord have mercy!" the truck driver muttered, staring at the ball of flame, his thumbs hooked into the pockets of his jeans.

Suddenly feeling weak, Paul wiped his glasses with a handkerchief from his hip pocket and stumbled to the LeBaron, removing from the trunk a clean army blanket that he kept for winter snow emergencies. *The kid might be going into shock,* he thought.

He returned to the still-unconscious youth, and the two men gently wrapped the blanket around him, cushioning his bloody head with part of it.

"Thanks for stopping! I wouldn't have made it without your help," Paul declared fervently.

The contract hauler nodded and gave Paul a solemn smile. The name of the company for which he drove was painted across the side of the trailer. "I was going back to Atlanta empty, or I couldn'ta stopped in time when I saw the trouble. I figured you could use some help. Dragging passive weight like that is more than one man can handle."

"I couldn't get a good enough grip on him to hoist him over my shoulder," said Paul.

Another set of headlights loomed bright and large as a police cruiser pulled off the highway and onto the grassy berm, a safe distance from the blazing Buick. A uniformed trooper quickly got out. His relief was evident as he hurried toward them.

"Are you Mr. Cooper? The one who phoned in?"
Paul nodded.

"Are you burned?" the trooper asked Paul in a tense voice.

Stunned, Paul stared at his hands as if seeing them for the first time. He felt his face and inspected himself for injuries. His new tan suit jacket was streaked with black, his maroon silk tie marred with streaks, his trousers were grass-stained at the knees. They looked as though he had slept in them. Yet nothing hurt except his muscles.

"I don't think so, Officer. I was so scared, I hosed down beforehand, as you can probably tell." Paul pulled his lips into a self-conscious grimace as he looked at his sweat-stained clothing.

The truck driver broke into a loud guffaw. His hand came down on Paul's back between the shoulder blades in a sign of approval. The two men shook hands. "Thanks, again! And God bless you!" Paul said fervently, knowing the driver had risked his life, too.

"Where I come from, we help each other out, just like you folks do here in Indiana. I'm due back in Atlanta for another load right soon, so I better be moving on. Sure hope the young fella'll be all right. So long now." The trucker turned to leave.

"You both deserve a commendation!" declared the trooper. "Did you witness the accident, too, sir?" he asked the truck driver.

"No, sir," he replied. "I came along after the car was clean over there. This man here had pulled the driver out and was draggin' him along the grass. I figured he could use a hand. He's the guy you need to talk to, not me!" he said firmly. He waved farewell, strode rapidly to the cab, put on the Left Turn signal and pulled smoothly back into the stream of traffic.

The trooper knelt beside the young man, touching the side of his neck with the fingertips of one hand and watching his chest. "He's still alive, but he's bleeding pretty badly from the forehead. The paramedics are on the way."

"Good," said Paul, suddenly exhausted. The cool breeze had picked up, waves of chill swept over him, but he resisted trembling.

Flashing lights appeared on the overpass. A police car had stopped, and another trooper was ordering onlookers to return to their cars and move on. Reluctantly a dozen observers left the parapet and walked back to their vehicles. Paul looked up, surprised that people were there.

"The dispatcher called for paramedics because you reported the car was on fire." The trooper rose to his feet, staring at the heap of charred metal. The flames had died quickly. "It's lucky we had a soaking rain. If the grass had been dry..." He was frowning. "The dispatcher thought there'd be two burn cases, for sure."

The faint beat of rotor blades thrummed in the sky like the distant rumble of thunder. The rim of the sun peeked orange red from the horizon, casting the broad patches of gray cloud into deeper shadow and transforming trees into stark silhouettes.

The man on the ground stirred and moaned, lifting a knee beneath the army blanket. He called out a name that sounded like Elaine, mumbling it over and over.

"What happens to him?" Paul asked the trooper.

"He'll be taken to Methodist Hospital's trauma center, and his closest relative will be notified—if his ID shows next of kin. I'll also need a statement from you as to exactly what you saw happen, unless you want to ride to the hospital to be checked out yourself. In that event, we can get your statement later."

The beat of rotor blades was louder now. The giant dragonfly hovered over the interstate as the pilot assessed the situation—the charred heap about thirty yards to the west of the road, the body stretched on the ground, the two men standing beside it and the patrol car with lights flashing on the roof.

The helicopter moved to the side of the road, then descended slowly until it came to rest on the berm behind the police car. The rotor blade stilled. The side door yawned wide, and two uniformed medics jumped out, carrying a stretcher. They ran past Paul and the trooper and huddled over the young man, who had finally regained consciousness.

"No!" A quiet terror was in the strained voice. Again he called, "Elaine," as if pleading for her help. He tried to resist as the two medics lifted him onto the stretcher and strapped him down for safety's sake.

Paul went quickly to the young man's side. His face and T-shirt was stained with blood, and an angry swelling had risen on his forehead. The round face had a grayish cast, and glazed brown eyes looked around, stricken. The fear of a trapped animal that doesn't know how it got caught or what its fate will be burned in their depths.

Paul took the man's hand as it thrashed around in an attempt to break the straps that were binding him to the stretcher. He spoke slowly and calmly. "You were in an accident. Your car went out of control and off the road and crashed into a fence and trees. I got you out."

"Elaine . . . will be worried. Gotta . . . call her," the young man mumbled thickly.

"I'll do it for you. How do I reach her?" Paul reached into his inner jacket pocket for his notepad and pen. The pad was so damp, it would hardly take the ink. He leaned closer to hear.

The kid's head moved from side to side. "E. L. Malden. M-a-l-d-e-n." His voice was strained. "Kessler Boulevard. West Drive." His eyes closed as exhaustion overtook him.

Paul took in the location with some surprise. It was an affluent area. He released the younger man's hand and stepped back. The medics lifted the stretcher and hurried with it to the waiting helicopter. They shoved the stretcher inside, jumped in and closed the door. The rotor blades spun around, slowly at first, then faster and faster.

A strong whoosh of cool air buffeted Paul, but this time he didn't notice the draft. He was remembering the dazed face, the look of pain—and fear.

The dragonfly rose, paused, then changed direction and darted off, heading north.

Paul sat in the police car and recounted the accident as he had seen it. He hated to have to estimate the Buick's speed, but the trooper insisted. "Between seventy and eighty," Paul admitted, watching the trooper's set face. When he returned to the LeBaron, he reached for the city telephone directory he carried in the back. There was indeed a listing for E. L. Malden on Kessler Boulevard, West Drive. He dialed the number on his mobile phone.

The voice on the answering machine surprised him—it sounded silky and refined. Definitely too young to be the kid's mother. Too sophisticated to be his wife or girlfriend. A sister? A cousin? A probation officer? Whoever she was, Elaine was not at home.

Paul hung up the phone and thought again of the injured youth. What would the doctors have to do to him? He was clearly terrified already and surrounded by strangers. He decided to return to town and head for Methodist Hospital's emergency and trauma center. He would stay with the young man until this Elaine—whoever she was—arrived.

More questions, surprises and chilling moments than he could anticipate, lay in store for Paul Cooper as he headed back to Indianapolis on his simple errand of mercy.

CHAPTER TWO

At Elaine Malden's approach, automatic glass doors parted with a whisper. The doors, marked by a sign, Methodist Hospital Emergency Medicine and Trauma Center, were flanked by concrete block and opaque glass. As she walked in, she left behind a backdrop of velvet-black sky and the harsh glare of parking-lot lights.

She found a well-lit, compact reception and registration area. Three admission tables bearing computers stood in a line, an upholstered chair in front of each.

A young couple huddled together in two of the eight seats in the waiting area. The man's right hand and lower arm were wrapped in a makeshift bandage stained with blood. The woman held his left hand, as if to comfort him.

Elaine glanced at the clock on the wall over a large desk. It was 12:10 a.m. She lowered her gaze to her hastily donned attire to make sure her zipper was fastened and buttons were in the proper buttonholes. She had been close to a state of shock after turning on the answering machine to listen to the evening's calls. Dressed in nightgown and bathrobe, she had just stepped out of a warm shower and was ready for bed, quite unprepared for the resonant baritone voice that emanated from the machine's speaker.

"My name is Paul Cooper, Ms. Malden. I witnessed an auto accident on the interstate after six this evening. A white Buick sedan with a Save the Whales bumper sticker. The young male driver asked me to call you. He was asking for you. I'll stay with him at Methodist's emergency room until you arrive."

The man had spoken without haste or self-consciousness. His diction had been clear and self-assured, without a trace of a regional accent. Had the call come to her office, she would have assumed that Mr. Cooper was a successful executive, like the majority of her clients. Yet something about this pleasing masculine voice had touched her in a special way, leaving her confused. She didn't understand why.

The message that followed Mr. Cooper's had been transmitted by a woman's voice, in a tone both compassionate and controlled. "Please come to Methodist Hospital Emergency Room. Your brother Keith is here. He was involved in an auto accident this evening. He's conscious and asking for you...."

A woman in a white pantsuit emerged from the double doors at the rear of the reception room. She smiled pleasantly at Elaine, but spoke first to the couple seated in the chairs.

"Come on. The doctor can take care of that arm now." She smiled encouragingly at the young couple, who rose and followed her through the double doors. "I'll be with you in just a minute," she said to Elaine before she disappeared.

Elaine managed a fleeting smile. She touched the chiffon scarf around her hair again, aware that her fingers were trembling. She sank into one of the vacant chairs, gathering her leather shoulder bag into her arms. It didn't seem so long ago that she had held Keith in her lap in much the same way, she thought ruefully. The twelve-year gap in their ages had made her feel almost maternal toward her younger brother, especially since the death of their mother.

A vague sense of guilt began to steal over her. Was it something she'd said at dinner tonight? she wondered. Had Keith been upset when she left him at the restaurant this evening? He always put a heavy foot onto the accelerator when he was disturbed about something. What she wouldn't give now to wipe the tape of events clean, feeling her cheeks burn as she thought of the dinner they had shared at the Milano Inn only seven hours before....

She had glanced at her watch when she walked into the Milano. Ten after five. She was five minutes early. Keith had been already seated at a table covered with a red-and-white checkered cloth and he had looked deeply troubled. He had been looking down at the menu, but she'd sensed he was not truly seeing it. The expression on his face had puzzled her. Her brother had always been an optimist, shrugging off cares and worries with ease, never giving them a toehold. When he looked up and spotted her walking toward him, he'd given her his familiar grin, but she'd sensed it had taken an effort.

"Hi, Sis. How's it going in the T.D. penthouse?" That was how he usually referred to Commercial Bank's trust department, located on the top floor of the bank building.

"I took on three new clients today—the CEO of Brady Manufacturing, an orthopedist and a senior partner in one of Indy's best law firms," she had told him with pride.

"That's really something, Elaine. You've done okay. Mom would have been proud." Keith spoke quietly, looking a bit wistful.

"She'd be proud of you, too, hon. I don't know anyone else who's completed two novels at your age. I sure couldn't write a book." She smiled reassuringly, wondering if he had just received another rejection letter. "This is my treat tonight, by the way. I suggested we have dinner together, remember? I'm glad you let me know you're in town today."

Keith had seemed a bit distracted during the conversation, but at first she had paid little attention to the change in her brother's behavior. Then, over tossed green salad, warm bread sticks and chicken cacciatore, Keith's favorite dish, Elaine innocently asked a question she would later regret.

"How's the job going? How did you get the day off?" she inquired. "I was really surprised when you called me at work this morning and said you'd be in Indy today." She knew Keith had survived three months as an assistant manager in a pizza restaurant, and she felt encouraged. He was showing signs of accepting the fact that his writing had to be a hobby—at least for now—and that he needed regular employment to help support it. The interest he was drawing every three months on the trust account their grandparents had set up for each of them was not enough to meet his bills.

The look on her brother's face gave him away. She had steeled herself before the words were out of his mouth.

"I . . . got fired."

"Again? Why?" Keith was Mr. Personality—he got an offer for every job interview. The problem was keeping the job. Either he got bored and left when it got in the way of his writing, or his employer terminated him after the probationary period. "What happened this time?" she wanted to know.

"Being assistant manager at a pizza place wasn't right for me, Elaine. I need something with . . . more challenge." He was absently picking the green olives out of his salad and popping them into his mouth. The look of apprehension was on his face again. And there was something in his dark eyes that was new. Something secretive. He kept looking around to see if anyone was watching him. His nervousness was obvious.

Elaine felt a stab of frustration as she tried to understand his behavior. She couldn't help worrying about her baby brother, even if he stood three and a half inches taller than she. What kind of future was in store for him? Job-hopping was not her style. She had had only two employers since her graduation from Indiana University as a finance major fourteen years ago. The past twelve had been spent at Commercial Bank and Trust in Indianapolis.

"*Why* did they fire you?" she asked again, determined not to let him off the hook this time. She wanted answers.

"I . . . didn't show up for work for a week."

She gasped, and Keith held up his hand, as if warding off her disapproval. "I answered this classified ad in a national magazine. I got a call to come to Buffalo, New York, right away for an interview. What could I tell my boss? I knew he wouldn't give me any time off. So I drove to Buffalo, then I had to stay there four days, okay?" His gaze dropped defensively, and he reached for another bread stick. "When I showed up for work yesterday, he canned me."

"Buffalo?" she echoed, puzzled by the change that had come over Keith. Why was he considering employment out of the Indianapolis area? They hadn't been separated since their mother's death, except for the time Keith had spent on the I.U. campus at Bloomington. She wouldn't object to his moving to New York State, of course, if that was his choice. It was his obvious agitation that alarmed her. *Was the job a hazardous one?* she wondered.

"Just what is this job?" she asked. "What would make you want to leave Indy?"

At that point he became evasive, changing the subject and attempting jokes that fell flat. She had reacted with some irritation—she couldn't help it—and had left the restaurant frustrated and feeling resentful. Keith had always confided in her before....

Elaine thought about the events of the evening. Keith could be many things—bold, brash, naive, overconfident, and even a bit arrogant—but afraid? Elaine had never seen her younger brother afraid of anything or anyone.

Until seven hours ago.

The one fear that always tormented her seized her now. *Is he hiding out in Buffalo? Did he contact Keith? After twenty years? How did he find out we're living in Indiana? Was the story about the classified ad a lie? Did Keith say that so I wouldn't know he'd rushed off to Buffalo to see* him? *Oh, dear God! Keith was only two when it happened. Keith doesn't even remember him.*

The woman in the white pantsuit took her place behind the desk. "May I help you?" she asked pleasantly. Elaine rose from the seat and walked over to her.

"Someone from this hospital left a message on my answering machine about seven o'clock. My brother, Keith Malden, was brought here due to—" she inhaled quickly "—an accident on the interstate."

The woman consulted a sheet on the stand. "You're Elaine Malden, the patient's sister?" She gave her an encouraging smile. "Keith's been taken

care of and transferred to Five North. Room A5060.
Would you please stop by the admissions desk first?"

As ELAINE EMERGED from the elevator on the hospital's fifth floor, she found herself looking out the
window at the downtown Indianapolis skyline. The
Indiana National Bank tower stood out amidst a sea
of white lights. She automatically sought out the familiar outline of the nearby Commercial Bank and
Trust building where she worked.

The empty hallway was eerie in the nighttime silence. A soft glow emanated from a single row of
lights on the left side of the ceiling. She followed the
signs until she came to A5060. The door was open and
a dim light burned inside.

"Keith?" she asked in a subdued voice as she entered the room. A tan and white curtain was drawn
back, revealing an unoccupied bed by the window.
Vinyl chairs with high backs and long armrests stood
in a row against the wall. An old movie flickered on
the screen of the TV set nearest the door, the sound
turned down to a murmur.

"Over here, Elaine," Keith called from the bed
nearest her. His voice sounded odd, lacking its usual
exuberance. Elaine drew close to the foot of the bed.

Keith lay underneath a clean white sheet and light
blanket that were drawn up to his armpits, his knees
and feet mere lumps on the bed. He was hooked up
to a clear plastic bag of IV solution by a thin tube
stuck into his arm. A bandage was wrapped around

his forehead and fastened in the form of a cross. Tufts of chestnut-brown hair stuck ludicrously through the openings.

A man rose quickly from a chair beside the bed, startling her. His appearance, however, was oddly reassuring, despite his disheveled clothing. He was over six feet in height, Elaine estimated, about four inches taller than herself. He had an oval face and a well-shaped, narrow nose. Behind his glasses, his azure eyes had an astonishing clarity, the irises striking in hue. They were honest eyes, steady in their gaze without being intimidating. He had an aura of strength and dignity.

He was staring at Elaine as though he were seeing an apparition of some kind. Suddenly uncomfortable, she looked behind her to see if someone had followed her into the room. No one was there.

He's something of an apparition himself, thought Elaine defensively. His nicely tailored suit, obviously expensive, was rumpled and streaked with black, even though the man's face and hands were clean. The skin of his face betrayed a slight trace of pink, as though it had recently been thoroughly scrubbed. His dark blond hair was neatly combed. She liked the slight wave in it.

"You must be Mr. Cooper," she said, aware that she was being more formal than friendly. Personal appearance was important in her new position at the bank. She hesitated slightly before extending her hand—the man presented such jarring contradictions. "Thank you for leaving the message on my answering machine. I was out this evening and didn't return home until after eleven."

"You had a *date?*" Keith's weak voice sounded incredulous. "I thought you broke up with Claude a month ago."

Elaine walked to the side of the bed and grasped his hand with an affectionate pressure. "One of my clients gave me two tickets to the Indianapolis Symphony concert for this evening. I asked Jan, the department secretary, if she'd like to come along."

"I didn't think you were seeing anyone. You break up with all your boyfriends as soon as they get serious and start talking marriage. A woman can have both career and marriage...can't she, Paul?" He was talking with difficulty while gazing up at the bedraggled man standing beside the bed, who promptly looked up at the ceiling, obviously embarrassed at being put on the spot.

Elaine quickly looked back at her brother. "Never mind about me. How are *you,* hon? You look better than I expected, but you need your hair combed," she whispered softly, smiling and stroking the tufts of hair sticking up through the bandage. She was so relieved he was conscious and able to talk that she had to fight an urge to weep tears of joy.

"You'll have to take me just as I am...like it or lump it," Keith said wearily. "Including stitches. I have one big pain in my head, with lump to match." He touched the right side of his forehead gingerly.

"I'm lucky it wasn't worse, though. Paul's just been giving me the news about my car. It blew up."

"Oh, sure. With you in it, I suppose." Elaine was convinced her brother's keen imagination was once again getting the upper hand. He often dramatized events in the telling, and the result was usually one hell of a story. Often she envied his gift, but couldn't always sympathize with his love for a sensational tale with himself at the center. This was obviously one of those times. Elaine dealt with facts, not fiction.

She became aware of Paul Cooper's cool stare and felt her eyes lift to his almost against her will. She couldn't help but notice the square, stubborn jaw, emphasized when he compressed his strangely sensual lips into a straight line. His eyes were penetrating, but her first impression had been wrong—they weren't cold at all. They held all the warmth of twin flames. His resonant voice affected her as deeply as it had when she'd first heard it on the answering machine.

"I've never properly introduced myself, Ms. Malden. I'm Paul Cooper, publisher and editor of the *Hoosier Entrepreneur*."

Elaine gasped in surprise as she recognized the name of the monthly business magazine that had been in publication for the past year; the bank subscribed to it. She had read each issue with interest.

"My only connection with your brother is the fact his car passed me on the interstate as though he were on the Raceway Park track. Eighty miles an hour, would you say?''

Paul was staring pointedly at Keith, who slid farther under the sheet as if to hide.

''I was some distance behind Keith,'' Paul continued. ''I saw his car go out of control. I also saw it blow up. I reported my impressions to the state trooper, when I gave him my statement describing the accident. He asked me direct questions, Keith, including an estimation of your speed. I had to answer truthfully. Sorry.''

Keith's eyes had dimmed instantly at the mention of the police.

The reference had brought a knot of pain to Elaine's gut, too. As she glanced at Keith in silent communication, she realized they shared the same dread of something hidden. But the naked fear she saw in Keith's eyes undoubtedly exceeded her own apprehension. She recognized the look she had noted over dinner at the Milano Inn, almost eight hours ago.

She glanced quickly at Paul Cooper. If he'd noticed anything strange in their reactions, he didn't betray it as he informed Elaine briefly of the circumstances of her brother's accident.

''*That*'s from the fire?'' Elaine asked, pointing a slim finger at Paul's soot-streaked clothing. Her hand went to her mouth. ''Oh, dear God!'' Her stricken gaze returned to her brother, lying in the bed.

Suddenly she realized that Paul's eyes were assessing her. Their gaze was so penetrating that she experienced an irrational fear that he knew everything about her. Elaine swallowed hard and extended her hand to him in gratitude. His grip was warm and firm.

For once Elaine Malden felt at a loss for the proper words, so she spoke from her heart, simply and directly. "I—don't know how to thank you—for what you did for Keith! We will always be grateful!"

Paul's gaze softened, and he seemed to relax. "I did what seemed right under the circumstances. I was on the way home after work and... Now I guess I'd better be on my way home to Greenwood. I'll leave you two to catch up. It's been a pleasure meeting you, Ms. Malden." He looked at the bandaged youth and placed his hand on the corner of the bed. "Take care, Keith! I'll give you a call tomorrow."

As he started to leave, Elaine noted the signs of fatigue and strain on his face. "Did you have anything to eat tonight?" she asked. "If you were on your way home when the accident occurred..."

He looked uncomfortable. "No. I didn't take time to eat. Keith's been awake the whole time. I didn't want to leave him."

"I'll take a sandwich, Sis," Keith mumbled from the bed, sounding drowsy. His eyelids fluttered as if fighting against closing.

"That's your dinner coming down the tube," Elaine told him with a gentle smile as she lifted her eyes to the IV bag.

"The nurse gave him a shot for pain just before you arrived. I guess it's taking effect." Paul Cooper's voice was low. He was standing close to the side of the bed, gazing down at Keith compassionately.

He's good-looking, thought Elaine, studying him. Probably the intellectual type, although he had the lean, muscular body of a tennis player or a runner.

Elaine and Paul watched Keith's eyes slowly close. Then Paul patted Keith's shoulder in an awkward gesture of farewell. His hand was angular, with large knuckles and long fingers. The nails were neat, trimmed close, Elaine noticed.

Paul moved away from the bed, lightly touching Elaine's elbow. "I could use a cup of coffee to keep me awake before getting back on the interstate. How about you? Or would you prefer to stay here with him tonight?"

"There doesn't seem much I can do here, if he's going to sleep all night," Elaine said thoughtfully. "And I could use some coffee myself. I'd like to buy you something to eat—it's the least I can do."

There was nothing to be gained by remaining. Keith looked so relaxed, so oddly trusting after the night's events. Asleep, he reminded her of the youngster she had cared for when she was scarcely more than a child herself. She resisted the impulse to tuck him in before she left.

"I never argue with a liberated woman," Paul told her with a smile. "I accept your invitation to dinner...or is it breakfast? It's 12:55 a.m." He was staring at the wall clock. "I know an all-night restaurant that's not too far from here."

They moved into the empty hallway and waited for the elevator. The city lights cast a mosaic pattern all around them.

"Keith seems to be all right, but I wonder if I should look for his doctor just to make sure," Elaine said worriedly.

"I can tell you what the doctor in E.R. told me," said Paul. "They closed the gash in his forehead with sutures, but no blood transfusion was necessary and there were no burns. I got him out in the nick of time." He glanced self-consciously at the floor. "There may be internal injuries. He'll be here a day or two for additional tests. Keith may have a mild concussion—they'll be keeping an eye on him throughout the night—but there's no fracture. X ray ruled that out."

Elaine felt a rush of relief. She instinctively knew that Paul's account would be completely accurate. Paul took her arm as the elevator doors opened. They descended to the ground floor in comfortable silence. By the time they left the building and walked to the parking lot, it was past one in the morning. The sky was jet black, beaded with millions of blue stars; the breeze was cool and invigorating. Traffic along West 16th Street was light, Elaine noticed. A sense of relief was replacing the shock and dread she had experienced when she had parked her car almost an hour ago.

"I'll follow you over in my car," she suggested.

There were few cars in the Emergency parking lot at this hour. She went to hers, a dark blue Ford Escort, and watched him walk to an impressive silver Chrysler LeBaron, unlock the door and get in.

She followed his car up North Keystone Avenue. The restaurant was brightly lighted on the outside, and there were a dozen cars in the parking lot. They chose a booth in a corner with no one seated nearby. When the waitress appeared, they both ordered the omelette special with hash browns, whole wheat toast, coffee and lots of jelly. The waitress didn't even react to Paul's soiled suit. She smiled pleasantly, jotted down the order on a pad and left.

Paul leaned forward, forearms on the table. He was studying Elaine's face as if memorizing every feature. His manner was so intent she was puzzled. She forgot the state of his clothing, reacting only to the man inside—to his face, to his hands when they occasionally gestured to emphasize a point. She felt drawn to him. He was direct, to the point and clearly intelligent.

"What do you do for a living?" he asked in his compelling baritone voice. It was hauntingly familiar. Had she known him before? she wondered—in high school, perhaps. If so, how could she ever have forgotten him?

She swallowed and took a deep breath. "I work at Commercial Bank and Trust in the trust department. We keep an issue of your magazine on the reception room table. I read it as soon as it arrives each month. I especially like the column on banking news," she said. He was easy to talk to, a good listener. "You need an article about what a trust department can do for clients directly through trust funds. We handle portfolio investments for clients, too, to provide income for trust beneficiaries."

"Perhaps you'd like to write an article for us. On spec, of course," he added.

"Me? Oh, no," she protested. "I'm not the writer in the family. My brother is."

"What position do you hold in the trust department?" Paul Cooper asked.

"I was promoted to vice president six months ago."

He leaned back in surprise. "You're young for that position, especially in a trust department."

"And especially a woman, right?" she asked in a monotone, the feeling of warmth fading. "I'm thirty-four. I've been with Commercial Bank for twelve years. Before that, I worked as a stockbroker for two years. I have a degree in finance from I.U., and I completed my M.B.A. while I was working. I'm well qualified for my job, Mr. Cooper."

He blinked and looked down at the table. "I'm sorry. It's just that the only female bank VPs I've met were all in their fifties and sixties. That's all I meant. I have no doubt as to your qualifications . . . Elaine."

She noted the slight hesitation, the momentary flush of embarrassment. "You started to call me by someone else's name, didn't you?" she asked. "And you've been looking at me oddly ever since we met. Why?"

His composure cracked for a moment. He busied himself with stirring his coffee, even though he was drinking it black. "You...remind me of someone I...used to know," he answered in a low voice. The pleasant face had become set. Elaine sensed instantly what had caused the change.

"A former girlfriend—am I right?" she inquired. "What's her name?" She sipped her own coffee, peering at him over the rim of the cup.

It was obvious he didn't want to talk about it, but Elaine had a idea that he needed to, although she had no idea why she felt she understood this man so well. Refusing to let him off the hook, she gazed directly at him until his eyes lifted to meet hers.

What an amazing color of blue, she thought irrelevantly.

"Madeline. Madeline Pruett," he answered slowly.

"An Indiana girl?" Elaine prodded. She resented the woman already, whoever she was. She had obviously hurt Paul Cooper.

Paul leaned back against the padded backrest. "No. Madeline was the daughter of Americans who worked in Paris. She grew up there. She spoke three languages fluently and was the director of a private art museum in Washington, D.C. That's where I worked. We were engaged to be married...." His expression changed.

"When? What happened?" Elaine whispered. With a twinge of guilt, she thought of the proposals she had turned down over the past seven years. Paul's unhappiness made her aware of the anguish that could result.

"We had a good relationship. A close one. We didn't actually live together—her parents visited her often and she knew they wouldn't approve—but I never so much as looked at another woman for more than four years. I thought she felt the same way. I gave her an engagement ring, and we had a formal wedding planned—the invitations had even gone out—" He stopped.

The stubborn jaw set, and Elaine paused as the waitress appeared with their order. She set the plates down, refilled the empty coffee cups and departed.

"Who called it off? You, her or her parents?" Elaine asked, trying to sound casual.

"She did. She told me she couldn't get away from the museum for a honeymoon at the time. A new addition to the building had already been started."

"Oh, well..." Elaine waved her fork in the air.

"It was a lie. Three months later she married a big-name senator and moved into his Georgetown home." Paul sighed. "Later I heard rumors she had started seeing him after our engagement and never told me. I knew this man, too—I had interviewed him once. I just wanted to get away—we knew many of the same people. I quit my job, came back to Indianapolis—my hometown—and started my own publication. It was something I'd been dreaming of doing for a long time, anyway.

"When I first laid eyes on you tonight, Elaine . . ." He seemed to be struggling to find the words. "Well, you look very much like her—your hair, your height, your eyes, even your taste in clothes. It was a real shock."

"Well, I'm not like her, and I'm sorry if I acted like an ass when I met you back at the hospital. I was upset about Keith, and not just because of the accident. He acted so different this evening when we met for dinner."

"In what way?"

"Keith and I had a . . . *discussion* over dinner this evening. He had just walked out on his job to make a rush trip to Buffalo to answer an employment ad that had run in a national magazine. He was gone for a week for the interview, so of course he got fired from his current job. But he wouldn't tell me what the Buffalo job is about. He wouldn't tell me much of anything at dinner. He acted weird, too, as though he were afraid of something, yet he refused to share the problem with me.

"Paul, my brother is a superconfident person. I've never seen him scared of anything or anyone. Ever since college, he's been in and out of work. I told him at dinner he'd better learn how to hold a job and take

responsibility for his own life. I wasn't angry exactly—just frustrated.''

"How old is Keith?" Paul asked.

"Twenty-two.''

Paul looked surprised. "I'd guessed eighteen,
maybe nineteen.''

"He complains about looking so youthful. He told
me once he was thinking of growing a beard so he'd
look older. I don't think he'll ever do it. All the girls
love him just the way he is now!"

Paul's strong face relaxed into what she could only
describe as a male Mona Lisa smile. "That's a problem most men would like to have.''

Elaine smiled back at him. She felt a warm liking
for Paul Cooper. How could the Pruett woman have
treated him that way?

"Did you work for a magazine in Washington?"
Elaine asked between bites of buttered toast. She
wanted to find out more about the man. She was
hoping he would want to see her again. Soon.

"I was an investigative reporter on the staff of the
Wall Street Sentinel. I was based in Washington with
occasional assignments in Europe—Paris and Bonn
mostly. If you read the *Sentinel*—and most people in
the business and financial world do—you probably
read my exposé on—''

The toast in her mouth took on the flavor of saw-
dust. She managed to swallow it, and it hurt. "You're
that Paul Cooper?" Her words came out in a hoarse
voice. "I mean…I never imagined you were the man

who..." She stared at him in disbelief, the warm feeling inside her turning to icy shock.

The stubborn set of his jaw returned. "Apparently you...didn't care for the last series I did," he said smoothly.

"The insider-trading scandal, you mean?" she asked stiffly. "The one that resulted in a senate investigation and criminal proceedings? You really stirred up a hornet's nest with that one, didn't you? *Six men* went to prison, including two stockbrokers and a senator." She had to fight hard to hold back the tears that were stinging her eyes. She hadn't cried in years, except at her mother's funeral eight years ago. Why did he have to be *that* Paul Cooper?

"They broke the law and made personal fortunes doing it!" Paul protested.

"Those men had wives and children. Did you ever think once about what you were doing to *them* while you worked so diligently to send the men to jail?" she demanded.

"They should have thought of that before they broke the law. Their private lives are no personal concern of mine. My facts were accurate and objectively stated. I backed up every statement I made with documented fact. I'm not a tabloid journalist who builds stories out of rumor and hearsay. The *Sentinel* never had a single lawsuit for any article I wrote."

"And doing your job made you famous, with a good salary in the process, didn't it?" Elaine had lost her appetite, she just wanted to get as far away from the man across the table as she could. She slid to the end of the seat and stood up, hoping she appeared cool, that he couldn't detect the pounding of her heart.

"Look, Elaine, the only people who ever had anything to fear from me were the embezzlers, the cons, the frauds—the people with something to hide. I protected the public. That was my job, and I won three national press awards in the process—"

He stopped abruptly as she dug into her purse and slapped several bills onto the table—much more cash than the two meals were worth, but she didn't care. She just had to get out of there.

"I invited you, so I pay. Keith and I are grateful for what you did for him tonight. We really are!" She hoped her voice was steady.

"May I call you at the bank—to go out sometime?" he was asking.

"No! Don't bother." Elaine realized her sudden change of behavior wasn't making sense to Paul. His expression was incredulous, but she couldn't help the way she was acting. Fear was clutching at her insides, deepening to panic beneath the penetrating gaze that seemed to see right down into her soul, to see all that was hidden there.

The blood was pounding in her temples as she closed her handbag. This man had the power to destroy her, too. She could lose her position at the bank, all that she had fought so hard to win. If the bank officials ever found out... Her mind went blank. "It's late. I must be getting home,'' she mumbled as she headed for the door.

Paul leaned back against the seat, watching her disappear into the night, then took off his glasses and rubbed his eyes. He felt drained, totally exhausted, as he tried to sort out what had just happened.

She'd liked him, he knew she had, but she'd run like hell as soon as she'd connected him with the exposé in the *Sentinel*. She was hiding something, he was certain of that. She was running scared, but from what? It had a smell Paul didn't like. The woman was an officer in the trust department of a bank. She had only been a VP for six months. So how could she afford to live in the affluent area of Kessler Boulevard?

The sexy Ms. Malden was helping herself to client money. His instincts usually proved right when it came to crime and corruption, but damn it, this time he didn't want to be right!

He needed time to think. He raised his hand to get the attention of the waitress and smiled pleasantly when she approached. ''Could I have another refill on my coffee, please?''

CHAPTER THREE

THE DOOR to Paul's private office was closed. Ben Kellogg was in his usual position whenever issues of importance were being discussed—such as how to meet next month's staff payroll and where to find the money to pay the printer's bill: he was perched on the corner of Paul's long teak desk. His right hip firmly hugged the wood, while one foot swung in midair to punctuate his observations.

Ben's lined face was solemn. "You *really* think this woman you met last night is siphoning off money from clients' accounts into her own pocket with a little 'creative bookkeeping'? Bank procedure follows strict safeguards to prevent this kind of thing from happening, Paul."

Paul leaned back in his leather chair, pulled off his glasses and drew an arm across closed eyes. His back and shoulders ached from yesterday's activities, and he was lethargic from lack of sleep. He had been able to doze off only twice during the night and had encountered Elaine and Keith Malden in his troubled dreams. They had been running from him, as he pursued them, shouting something he no longer remembered. His alarm had interrupted the chase at 5:00

a.m. He had merely rolled over, only to awaken at seven, too late for his five-mile run through the quiet streets of Greenwood.

"What else *can* I think?" Paul slipped his glasses on again. Ben came into perfect focus. The older man's gray hair was thinning on top, and finely etched lines spread from the corners of his green eyes across his round face. Ben didn't have to wear glasses, even at fifty-eight. Paul envied him.

He realized he had been lucky the day Ben Kellogg had walked in the front door. Ben had retired once, from a Louisville paper. He and his wife Rita had chosen to relocate to Indianapolis to be close to their daughter, son-in-law and four grandchildren. Then the itch to work had resurfaced, and Ben had answered Paul's classified ad for a managing editor.

He had proved to be ideal for the job. Not only were his credentials excellent, but he was also tough and outspoken—qualities Paul respected. Ben could also be tactful, as he was proving now.

"You know people, Paul. You know your job. You're a reporter. I'm an editor. You're the one who's won the press awards, not me. It's just . . ." Ben was swinging his foot, a sure sign he was about to contradict his boss.

"Okay, Ben. Out with it." Paul took a long swallow of coffee from the mug on his desk. Mary made it the way he liked it—strong and hot.

"You've been wound up lately, tense as hell!" Ben crossed his arms in front of his chest.

"Sure I have. So have you, buddy. It isn't easy getting a magazine off the ground, building up circulation. I've got all my savings invested in this publication. If it flops, I start over again. I either go back to the *Sentinel* with my tail between my legs or apply to another newspaper for a staff job."

Ben laughed. The sound was a coarse guffaw.

"We're making it. We're making it fine. More subscribers are signing up every month, and newsstand sales are increasing all the time. This mag is all you've had on your mind since I've known you. A whole year. You need some interest in life outside of the job, Paul."

"I run every morning. Five miles."

"Then go for ten, maybe. Drain the tension out of your system. You've turned into a workaholic. Acting as sales director, art director and publisher—"

"To save paying out additional salaries."

"—you're preoccupied and tense—"

"So you can't stand me? You're ready to quit, is that it?" Paul buried his nose in the mug, eager for the caffeine. Today would be another full day. He had a feature article to write, two subjects to interview and appointments with potential advertisers. He felt like a time bomb, and he'd been more depressed than he cared to admit since his conversation with Elaine.

"Quit? Me? You *want* me to quit?" Ben looked hurt. "Have you got somebody to replace me— somebody who'll work for less money?"

Paul's head sank into his hands. *What the hell is the matter with me?* he wondered. *I'm driving everybody away.* "No, Ben. Of course I don't want you to quit. You're not just a top managing editor, you're a friend. I couldn't run this magazine without you. Never die on me. Promise!"

Relief flooded Ben's lined face. "Count on it!" He leaned forward. "Truth is, you need to find a good woman. You're still carrying a torch for Madeline Pruett. You're seeing her in every woman you meet. She's corroding your neurons. What's worse, she's made you doubt yourself, when the truth is..." Ben took a deep breath. "...she got a chance at a senator with lots of money and prestige, and that's what counts in a status-conscious town. That's what she really wanted out of marriage. That's the brass ring she grabbed when she got her chance."

"Who says?" Paul leaned back in his chair and glared at Ben.

Ben's back straightened, his eyelids fluttered to half mast. "A man of the world who's been around."

Paul grunted, grinning in spite of the way he felt. "Rita took you out of circulation thirty-four years ago. I'll wager you haven't looked at another woman since."

"I don't have to. The one I've got is almost more than one man can handle. Let that be a lesson to you." The beefy face broke into a grin—a grin that slowly faded. "Getting jilted does things to a man's self-confidence. Pick yourself a gal and go all out to win her. You've had more than a year to lick your wounds, tiger. Enough is enough.''

Paul sighed and leaned forward, both feet firmly on the floor where they belonged. "I need a shrink? Is that what you're saying?''

"Not necessarily. Just give the lady vice president a chance. You were attracted to her, admit it. So she rebuffed you. That makes her a prime candidate as an embezzler? What's happened to that famous objectivity?'' Ben leaned forward, dropping his voice to a conspiratorial level as he stared at Paul's solemn face. "What really happened, Paul? Did you make a pass at her and she got mad? Is that what's bothering you?''

"No!'' Paul glared at him. "I didn't make a pass—''

"Well, then, maybe she doesn't know you found her attractive,'' Ben declared. "Something obviously went wrong somewhere, but you don't need to jump to conclusions.''

Paul rose from his chair abruptly. "One thing I will never do is put you in charge of an advice to the lovelorn column!'' He walked to the window, shoved his hands into his pockets, looking down at East Market Street. The heavy rain had let up. There was no rainbow today.

"I think your male ego is getting in the way of your judgment, Paul.'' The kidding tone was gone. "I think you like the lady. A lot. Your feathers got ruffled when she walked out on you. History repeating itself?"

Paul turned and looked at Ben. The glance they exchanged was a long one. "The way she left last night, I doubt she wants to get to know me any better."

"The kid likes you, doesn't he?"

"Keith? Yes, we hit it off great. In some ways, he reminds me of myself when I was in college. So eager. Idealistic. Ready to believe in anything and anyone."

He had to admit, the years had taken their toll. *Have I become cynical?* Paul wondered as he stared down at the traffic. The rainbows had vanished for him, all right. He had almost lost all belief in the goodness of people. "What do you suggest I do, Ann Landers?" He turned and faced Ben, hands still in his trouser pockets.

The older man smiled. "Go visit the Save the Whales kid today. The sister will probably go to see him this evening, won't she? You've got a mutual bond in her brother. Use it. If you *want* to get to know her, that is. That's your decision. Just don't expect the lady to converse in French. We all have our limitations."

"Thanks, Ben." Paul walked over to him and grabbed his shoulder in a good-natured gesture. "In appreciation, I won't even charge you rent for parking on the corner of my desk."

Ben took the hint and slid off, eyeing the gleaming surface. "And I won't charge you $8.50 an hour for polishing it with the seat of my pants," he said gravely. He walked to the door, then halted and turned. The quiet murmur of Mary's voice on the telephone drifted down the hall.

"Flowers and candy never harmed a courting. Look what it won me. A wise man heeds expert counsel." Ben winked and disappeared.

BY SIX O'CLOCK the sun had emerged, and light was pouring through the glass walls of the main lobby of Methodist Hospital's A Building. Paul had come armed. He was gambling that Elaine would visit her brother after she left her office. Perhaps, in Keith's presence, Elaine's strange behavior in the wee hours of the morning might be reasonably explained. He held a box of French chocolates under one arm and an ivy in a ceramic planter in the other hand. The chocolates were for Elaine, the ivy planter for Keith.

Paul passed the information desk and made his way to the elevators. People smiled at him and he smiled in return. Indianapolis had become more cosmopolitan in the past twenty years, but its small-town friendliness remained. The thought left Paul with a good feeling as he stepped out of the elevator on the fifth floor.

He retraced the route he had taken with Elaine Malden only seventeen hours ago. He passed a desk laden with baskets of flowers, waiting to be taken to various rooms, turned left and headed toward another desk. No one sat there. He swung left again and was ready to go into A5060. The door was halfway open. He went toward it, about to give it a nudge with his foot, when he heard Elaine's muffled voice coming from inside the room. Just the sound of it stirred a strong reaction within him. He paused, not quite ready to face her again. Feeling a little guilty, he stopped, glanced down the hallway and saw it was clear. The corner prevented anyone from seeing him. He leaned his head closer to the crack in the door, but the voices were so low that he could hear almost nothing.

"No," Keith said resentfully. "I didn't blurt out anything. Why should I mention him, anyway?"

"I guess you wouldn't. You were only two at the time. You can't possibly remember him."

"I wish I could. At least *you* had a father until you were fourteen. I never had one at all. Jeff was a jerk. He never even talked to me, let alone throw a ball or take me to a ballgame. You don't know what it was like, being a guy and having Jeff for a stepfather—"

"Still, Cooper must have suspected *something,*" Elaine interrupted him. "Why would an investigative reporter with his reputation have followed you here, waited for me to show up?"

"'Cause he's a nice guy, that's why! When I came to, lying on the side of the highway, it was like he was standing guard over me, protecting me—"

"Like the hero in one of your novels."

"Yeah. The only time I've seen the inside of a hospital was when I broke my leg in my senior year in high school, during a game. I was terrified when I woke up, stretched out beside the interstate! The last thing I remembered was being in my car. These medics had hopped out of the 'copter and were strapping me onto the stretcher, I hurt all over, and there was blood all over my face and shirt. Then Paul talked to me, told me everything'd be all right, that he'd get in touch with you—"

"Beware of wolves in sheep's clothing. They're called reporters."

THAT PART PAUL HEARD loud and clear. He blinked and straightened and almost pushed the door open to walk in and have it out with her. He stopped himself, but just then a loud argument erupted from the room next door, making it impossible to hear the next part of their conversation.

Still blissfully unaware of Paul's presence outside, Keith continued. "I'm a journalism graduate, dear sister! I worked on the I.U. paper. What does that make me? A wolf, too? Or Dracula?"

"You didn't see fit to consult me for advice when you switched your major area of study from Phys Ed to English and Journalism," Elaine said in a soft voice.

"It was my decision, not yours. I wanted to learn how to write. And I did! You're getting paranoid,

Elaine. Paul Cooper doesn't suspect anything, and why would he care?''

"He's an investigative reporter! He can get a scoop to make me look like Frankenstein's daughter to my colleagues and clients. He'll probably write up all the gory details in a feature article for his magazine. Then just *watch* the circulation jump for that month. Money in his pocket, that's what I'll become!"

"I'm getting damned tired of hearing about that place where you work. For twelve years you've busted ass to do a good job there. Now you're running scared they might fire you for something somebody else did twenty years ago."

"He never got arrested, remember that! They never caught up with him. Is he really dead? Somehow I don't believe it! He may still be on the FBI's wanted list," she reminded her brother.

A painful pause followed. "Maybe he had reasons for what he did." Keith sounded as though he were trying to convince himself, Elaine reflected.

"There *are* no reasons to justify what he did! And don't put down my job at the bank—it means a lot to me!" she exclaimed, on the verge of tears.

The argument stopped in the room next door, but all Paul heard was a heavy silence, then, "I know you miss Mom, Sis. Jeff didn't give you much moral support either, did he? You didn't have it easy, taking me in to live with you after Mom died and Jeff remarried and moved out of state. You were always good to me, Elaine...I do appreciate it...." His voice trembled. "I've given you some rough times, too. I'm sorry...."

Paul heard a ragged sigh and sensed the agony in those simple words. He felt inexplicably moved by them.

"I would like to pay you back someday, Elaine, but I don't know how...."

Another silence. "When you win the Pulitzer Prize, invite me to sit in the audience. Then I can brag to everyone around me and say, 'That's my brother!'" Elaine said softly.

"I'll pay you back someday. Everything you've loaned me—"

"I don't want that, honey. I just want you to face up to one fact. For now your writing is still a hobby, and you need to support yourself with regular employment. Writing has to come second, not first. Until you make your first sale, until you get rolling with a publisher. Okay?" She spoke soothingly, as if to a child. Paul loved the sound of her voice.

A significant pause elapsed.

"This trip to Buffalo has something to do with another novel, doesn't it, Keith? You're into more research, aren't you?" Elaine asked, tension creeping into her voice.

Feeling for some reason this was important, Paul eased closer to the gap in the door, waiting for Keith's answer. It didn't come for many moments.

"This one will make it!" Keith said fiercely. "It's a bombshell topic no editor in his right mind would turn down!"

"Like the last one?" she asked gently. "*Twelve Hours until the End of the World,* with an antinuke hero? Or your story of the last white whale to survive the harpoon ships and oil-polluted seas? That one really got me crying at the end. I couldn't eat fish for a month. They are both significant social themes, hon, but no editor has snapped them up yet."

"I'm a failure. Is that what you're telling me?" The depression in the young man's voice triggered a memory, reminding Paul of early days on the *Sentinel,* when he'd wondered how long he'd be able to hang on to a staff position.

"No! Your novels are good. I'm no expert, of course, but I think you should keep writing. There's one thing I do know, though. Last night, driving down here, not knowing if you were seriously injured, I went through hell. We've been through a lot together, Keith. We're survivors. You do have writing talent, but maybe succeeding in fiction is some impossible dream. There's advertising or public relations . . . lots of ways to use your talents and still get paid for it."

He sighed heavily. "A regular, paying job. Maybe I should become an accountant like Claude. Is that what you're suggesting? If accountants are so great, why didn't you marry him? He was panting after you.

You don't have to look after me anymore, Elaine, and—''

"You had nothing to do with my decision. I...couldn't commit to Claude. I just couldn't!" The note of tragic finality in her voice piqued Paul's interest. "Be truthful, Keith—did your trip to Buffalo have anything to do with...*him?*" she asked. "Did he get in touch with you?"

"Hell, no. He's dead." Keith sounded incredulous.

Elaine's sigh of relief was audible, even from the hallway.

"Elaine, sometimes you worry me. You think that man is going to resurface in our lives after twenty years? Come on. He was declared dead. They never found his body, true...but even if he didn't drown, if he *were* alive, how would he know where to find us? Or what our new name is? Even if he did know, he doesn't care about...me...at all. Why would he bother to contact me?" Keith's voice had taken on a harsh quality. "I've got troubles enough of my own, and he has nothing to do with it."

"Troubles? Like what? I'm listening. Tell me it has nothing to do with this mysterious book. You're not writing about organized crime or something, are you?" Elaine's voice was stiff with fear.

"I can't tell you. It's better for you if you don't know. Elaine, I'm in trouble! Big trouble!" Keith seemed to be on the verge of tears. "You're the only one who can help me. Don't give me lectures now, please! My head hurts."

"What do you want me to do?" she asked, clearly subdued by what she was hearing.

"Go to the bungalow and get some things for me. Take 'em to your house. In case the police snoop around my place—"

"Why would the police do that? There's no reason—"

"I don't know what Paul told 'em about the accident. If you're right, and he's suspicious of us—"

"Now who's being paranoid?" she insisted. "Your car skidded out of control on a curve. Why—"

"Elaine, please!" Keith's anguished cry was followed by a moment of silence.

"Sure." She spoke more softly. "Write out a list. I'll go straight home from here and change clothes, then to the bungalow, okay? This evening, I promise. Here's a notebook and a pen."

Keith sighed. "It hurts to think. Just don't rush me."

Every instinct told Paul he'd stumbled on to something far more important than a mere automobile accident. Elaine and Keith were definitely in some kind of trouble. He also knew that he wanted to help—he just didn't know why. He straightened, neck aching, aware others were passing in the hallway. As a nurse approached, he dropped quickly to one knee, laying down the candy box and the planter, undid one shoelace and tied it again. The nurse walked past, and he busied himself with the other shoe. The ploy was working. No one seemed to be paying attention to him. He wished Keith would hurry.

"Is this the list?" he heard Elaine ask finally. Paul had tied and untied his shoelaces at least a dozen times. His fingers felt cramped, and he became aware that one of the nurses was looking at him suspiciously.

"Rifle? Ammunition and scope? Under the bed? What in hell is this?" Elaine seemed genuinely bewildered. "You don't even own a rifle."

"I do now." Keith's voice sounded strange, even to Paul.

"For what? You don't even believe in hunting. You told me so yourself. When did you learn to shoot a rifle?"

"The year I took R.O.T.C. in college. I dropped out after that. They kept telling me what to do, including how to make my bed!"

"Heaven forbid!" she said in a teasing way. "Photographs in a metal box *under the sofa?* Why under the sofa?" she asked.

"It's safer there. The flounce that goes to the floor hides anything underneath."

"January and February issues." She named a new men's adventure magazine. "Synopsis and first three chapters in locked desk drawer. What have you got here, Keith? A blueprint for murder?" she quipped with a hint of a chuckle.

"That's not funny!" Keith's voice rang hollow.

A warning prickle sped along the hairline at the back of Paul's neck.

Quickly he rose to his feet. Instinct told him that Elaine was about ready to leave, and he didn't want her to catch him eavesdropping. Instinct also told him that Keith would tell him no more than he had told his sister, but somehow he had to find out what was wrong. If Keith was in serious trouble now—for the commission of a felony, perhaps—he could drag his sister down with him as an accomplice. Paul had no doubt that Keith was involved in a plot that was destined to mean great harm to someone.

"So long, honey." Elaine's voice was closer now. "I'm glad that tube's out of your arm and you qualify for real food again. Don't give the nurses too much trouble. One of them told me you'll be home by Saturday, maybe sooner. It all depends on what kind of tests they plan to do.

"Just one question. This rifle hasn't been used in a holdup, has it? Fingerprints on the butt? All that good stuff?" She sounded apprehensive.

"No. It's brand-new. Unused, I think. Jeez, I hope! I don't know." Keith was obviously distressed.

At that moment Paul knew he had to follow Elaine to her brother's house and try to intercept her with the goods. He had to persuade her to let him help with Keith's trouble, whatever it was. The kid needed them.

"Mmm. Goodbye, hon. See you tomorrow. Don't worry."

Paul swept up the candy box and planter from the floor and looked around for a place to hide. He raced for the door leading to the glassed-in waiting room and from there saw Elaine leave Room A5060, her lovely face strained.

Instead of turning the corner and heading for the elevators, she strode swiftly past the waiting room and headed in the opposite direction. She disappeared.

Paul left the candy box and planter on the vacant hall desk and scanned the area. The nearest overhead sign pointed the way to Neurological Critical Care. There was no reason for her to go to that area. That left only the door marked Fire Exit to his left.

He opened the door cautiously and heard the heels of a woman's pumps beating in quick tempo below him. He understood. *She's upset. She needs physical activity to work the tension out of her system.* He was that way himself. As quickly as possible, he followed her down to the first floor.

He kept a safe distance behind her, thankful that Keith had slipped Elaine's address to him last night as he lay on the stretcher. Kessler Boulevard, West Drive. Paul still remembered the house number that he had looked up in the telephone directory. For some strange reason, everything about Elaine Malden seemed burned on his brain.

Evening was deepening to a purple-mauve dusk as he left the hospital through the Capital Avenue entrance.

ELAINE MALDEN'S HOUSE was one of the smallest homes in the fashionable residential area of northern Indianapolis. The asphalt driveway of the house in which the dark blue Ford Escort was parked had recently been renewed. The house was built in ranch style, of brick with wood trim painted white. The yard was not as large as those of the neighboring properties, but it was spring green and well kept. Flower beds had been prepared to receive annual plantings and the grass had recently been trimmed.

"How can she afford to live here?" Paul asked himself aloud as he waited, parked in the shadows down the street. Within him the answer echoed, cold, harsh and hollow.

Within fifteen minutes the object of his surveillance emerged, dressed in jeans, a short-sleeved blouse and canvas shoes, a flowered scarf tying back her shoulder-length chestnut hair. She carried a sweatshirt over her arm.

She didn't look once in his direction. As the Escort pulled onto the street, Paul's adrenaline started pumping. As he concentrated on the scarlet taillights of the car ahead, he felt as if he were back on the job again, working for the *Sentinel,* digging out the facts for a feature.

Paul made only one mistake during that unexpected drive to Brown County. He failed to tune in to a local radio station that gave evening weather reports. He listened to a Neil Diamond cassette tape instead.

It was a small error of judgment that would have significant consequences.

CHAPTER FOUR

IT WAS ALMOST NINE o'clock when Paul saw the Escort turn into a long graveled driveway in the woods of Brown County, sixty miles southwest of Indianapolis.

He pulled his car to a stop off the road, close to a dense clump of bushes, and quickly doused his headlights. When he heard a screen door slam shut at the end of the driveway, he got out, eased the car door closed and crept along the grassy verge.

A deep purple dusk filtered through the silhouette of the forest. Silence reigned, a hush so heavy that he trod lightly, afraid to make a sound. The air was heavy with moisture, fragrant with the musky odors of damp earth, the scents of fungi, mushrooms and rotting leaves. From the depths of the dark wood came the call of an owl. A hint of rain lingered in the air.

Paul advanced cautiously toward a small frame house in the center of a small, ragged yard surrounded by woods. The bushes were high and in need of trimming. The grass in the yard was ankle deep and smelled pleasantly of clover. Despite the impression of neglect, Paul felt drawn to the dwelling. A warm light poured from every window, giving him a feeling of welcome.

As he drew closer, he noticed one of the small boards on the floor of the covered porch was broken, waiting to ensnare a careless foot. But screens on the door and windows looked brand-new. Elaine's doing? he wondered.

Paul stole around the house in a crouching position, noting that there were two outside doors—the one that opened onto the front porch and another that served as an exit from the kitchen. The Escort was parked at the end of the driveway, in front of a garage. The overhead door was down.

He heard the sound of water running on the other side of the wall. Crouching below window level, Paul crept into the bushes. He planned to come out of hiding when Elaine left, carrying the items on Keith's mysterious list. He would confront her and insist that they talk about her brother's problem. Elaine was an intelligent woman; she would listen to reason, Paul kept assuring himself as he slowly rose to peer through the window.

What he saw amazed him. The woman was on her knees. The cotton blouse she had been wearing was hanging over a chair beside a round oak dining table at one end of the living room. She was clad in jeans and a black jersey halter. The canvas shoes sat side by side on the thin, worn carpet that covered the oak floor. The sweatshirt lay neatly folded on the dining table. Elaine Malden was barefoot as she scrubbed the linoleum on the kitchen floor that was stained gray with dirt.

She was facing away from him, offering him a provocative view of round hips with just the right fullness and lean, compact thighs. As white suds mushroomed on the floor, Elaine swung slowly around until she faced the window, her head down, hair still held back by the scarf. The energetic motion of her arm brought a soft rhythmic sway to the round, full breasts encased within the deep V-shaped pockets of the halter. The black jersey against the smoothness of her skin was a delicious contrast. The cups of the halter relaxed and gaped open.

Paul groaned softly and looked away, yet his eyes were drawn again to the beautiful woman inside the house. Her movements held a natural grace as she efficiently transformed the dirty kitchen. He was fascinated. He had never even seen his mother scrub a floor. He had grown up with a full-time, live-in housekeeper plus a once-a-week cleaning lady.

Elaine rose, emptied the soapy water into the kitchen sink and drew rinse water into the bucket. He heard the pump click on. His gaze fastened on the chestnut hair pulled back from her face. The gentle inward slope of her silky cheek was exposed along with the high cheekbones, the graceful nose, the pink, full lips created to be kissed.

Through the open windows, Paul heard her humming as she worked. He couldn't believe his ears. She didn't seem worried by Keith's concern about a po-

lice search of the house—or perhaps she was cleaning up in preparation for it, wanting everything to
look its best before the police entered. The thought
made him smile.

She lifted the plastic pail from the sink, leaned
forward, set it on the floor and resumed her kneeling
position. She wrung out a cloth and began to rinse the
floor by hand.

In the distance a bolt of lightning pierced the horizon, lighting a brilliant jagged path down the sky.
A roll of thunder broke. Paul looked up at the sky,
startled. *The list, Ms. Clean! Get to the list of items!*

Elaine finished the rinsing with swift, controlled
movements. She stood in the kitchen doorway, turned
her back to the window and moved into the living
room.

Paul moved around the covered porch to the other
window, raised it carefully and looked inside. He saw
a traditional sofa, covered with a faded print, soiled
clothes destined for the laundry piled on one end, and
a wicker chair painted blue, padded with thick cushions. Stacks of magazines and newspapers filled the
corners of the room. A mahogany desk stood below
the window. On the desk were an electric typewriter
and an answering machine, along with a scattering of
typed sheets with corrections made in red ink. A
portable TV sat on a table at an angle to the desk,
facing the sofa, with a VCR on the shelf below. A
stone fireplace occupied the end wall opposite the
kitchen. It was obvious that Keith lived alone.

Keith is well-read, thought Paul, eyeing the bookshelves that lined the comfortable room. *I wouldn't mind living in this place myself.* The forest solitude was wonderfully conducive to writing.

Elaine was gathering up the pile of soiled clothing, stuffing T-shirts, jeans and socks into a clean trash bag. She pulled out an old Hoover sweeper from a closet and vacuumed the worn rug. The high-pitched whine shattered the heavy, humid silence.

The roll of thunder came closer. *The gun, sweetheart, the gun! The carpet looks okay!* Paul pleaded silently.

At the repeated sound of thunder, she stopped and looked toward the window. Paul ducked into the bushes and waited, holding his breath as his heartbeat accelerated. He didn't think she'd spotted him. He heard the window roll downward, soon followed by a bang from the one in the kitchen.

Slowly he rose again to continue his surveillance. Elaine's deep devotion to Keith was obvious from the way she handled her brother's clothing and tried to brighten his environment. He sensed something almost maternal in her actions.

His moment of altruism was interrupted as a few large raindrops spattered upon his head and face, slowly at first, cooling and clean. Then the speed, intensity and volume rapidly increased. Within minutes the bushes, the ground and Paul were thoroughly drenched.

Another wool suit was about to be ruined. He resigned himself both to the loss and to the waiting. Into his mind flashed the memory of the housekeeper who had worked for his parents during his elementary school years. Scarecrow thin and strong as a mule, or so it had seemed to him, she had assessed Paul with alacrity. "Patient, stubborn, and one hell of a determined kid," or words to that effect. From the housekeeper's tone of voice the twelve-year-old Paul had been uncertain if the comment was intended as praise or condemnation. "Paul has staying power," his mother had answered in a dignified tone.

True to that assessment, half smiling at the thought, Paul stubbornly remained in the bushes, growing more and more chilled as the temperature dropped. He stole around the house and watched Elaine change the sheets and blanket on the bed in the room that seemed to be Keith's—the other bedroom looked unoccupied—while the rain streamed down steadily. She made first one side of the bed, then the other, with the precision of an army drill sergeant.

He watched her stuff the soiled bed linens into a separate trash bag, then she disappeared into a small room off the living room, a room that had no window. He decided it had to be the bathroom. *She'll probably clean that next,* he thought in gloom as the rain cascaded down his glasses and frigid nose. He walked around the house to the living-room window, as much for the sake of generating some warmth as to change his point of view.

Wistfully he eyed the dry porch. He could of course return to his car with its comfortable seats and warm heater. Even give up completely and go home to a warm shower. He decided to stay, his concern for the Maldens outweighing his growing discomfort.

What trouble had Keith gotten himself into? Paul genuinely liked the kid. After saving him from a hideous death, Paul felt he had a personal stake in Keith Malden. And he knew that catching his sister with the goods in hand would give him some bargaining power to dig out Keith's secret. Paul bit his lip thoughtfully, remembering Ben's sage comment. Keith was also a link to his sister, and Paul intended to use it for all it was worth to get closer to her.

Suddenly he realized Elaine Malden was no longer just a substitute for his ex-fiancée. The caring person he was watching was more woman by far than Madeline could ever have been. The realization came with an electric feeling, warming him. The chill became bearable.

Elaine emerged from the bathroom, a bedraggled toilet bowl brush in her hand. She walked into the kitchen and tossed it into the waste can. To Paul's relief, she went into the bedroom again, knelt and searched under the bed. He watched her blurred form—she looked mysterious, ethereal, almost an image from Wordsworth. She came back into the living room carrying a rifle. She moved with slow deliberation, sadness and concern expressed in her walk and in the manner in which she laid the firearm on the sofa.

Trying to wipe his glasses with a handkerchief that was dampened with rain, Paul suppressed a sneeze. His skin felt clammy and cold; his blood had turned to a sluggish, frigid stream within his veins.

Elaine turned from the sofa and headed for the desk under the window through which he was straining to see. A blinding flash of lightning was followed by sudden singing sound that seemed to explode against a nearby tree. She looked out the window, clearly startled by the sound, her eyes wide, her lips forming a soft, round O.

Through the blurred pane their gazes locked.

Elaine gasped, her eyes wide. She let out a scream that was quite audible through the closed window. She reached for the telephone on the desk and picked up the receiver to dial, jerking the draperies shut with her other hand.

Paul knew she was calling the county sheriff to report a prowler. While he was being arrested, she would be hiding that rifle under the bed. He'd never be able to convince the lawman he had a valid reason for being here. He could see himself landing in the county jail, soaked to the skin, and it would probably be morning before he could contact a lawyer.

He pounded fiercely on the window. "It's me! Paul Cooper! I'm here to talk to you about Keith! Let me in! Please!" A paroxysm of sneezes seized him, rendering him unable to speak.

ELAINE WAS ALREADY DIALING the county sheriff's office when the fierce pounding made her pause. She recognized Paul's voice immediately. Stunned, she put down the receiver and jerked open the drapes. Her heart was still beating a tattoo against her ribs as she stared at the blurred image on the other side. The man looked half-drowned. She heard a sneeze like an explosion. "I don't believe this!" she said to herself.

Curiosity got the better of her. She walked to the front door and unlocked it. "Well, whatever you're doing here, you'd better come in out of the rain!" she called, hands on her hips. She watched as he walked up and onto the porch, almost stepping into the gaping hole, unable to see it through his foggy glasses. Suddenly she realized that the temperature had dropped. The chill reminded her that she was wearing only a halter top. Quickly she pulled on her blouse and buttoned it up while he stood just inside the door, shivering, his teeth chattering.

"Close the door," she said, sighing. How had the man found the cottage? she wondered. Had her brother talked about this place, too, as he lay beside the interstate, waiting for the medical helicopter?

"Thank you," said Paul, obeying. "I'm dripping on your floor. Sorry." His voice had a nasal tone.

"So I noticed," she replied dryly, staring at his muddy wing-tip shoes on the carpet she had just vacuumed. "What in hell were you doing out there?" she demanded. "Do you know you could get yourself *shot* in these parts doing that Peeping Tom routine?

There are No Trespassing signs on all the properties."

"It's not what you think," he protested, leaning against the wall to take his shoes off.

"All right." She crossed her arms over her breasts. "I'll give you a chance. Explain why you're here."

For a moment, Paul was unable to answer. He was trembling, caught in the grip of a chill, and suddenly Elaine's maternal instincts took over. "Oh, get your clothes off!" she said curtly. "You can make your excuses later."

Blue eyes looked at her over steamed-up glasses. "I beg your pardon?" The man sounded hopeful.

"I'm not propositioning you. I just don't want to be responsible if you catch pneumonia. Go into the bathroom and towel off. Better still, go soak in a tub of warm water. I'll find something clean in Keith's bedroom for you to put on. He's forty pounds heavier than you, of course, but he's nearly as tall."

"Don't go to any trouble for me. A cup of hot coffee will be just fine." Paul drew a tortured breath.

The look Elaine gave him conveyed the intensity of feelings she was struggling to keep in check. He headed toward the bathroom—fast. "How did you find this place?" she called after him. He turned at the doorway to face her.

"I went to the hospital to visit Keith and I...realized you were in the room, too. You were talking. I couldn't help...overhearing...part of your

conversation. It sounded like he was in trouble, so..."
He shrugged. "So I followed you. I want to help."

Her mouth dropped open. "You *followed* me?
From Indianapolis? You *eavesdropped* on my private
conversation with my brother?"

Paul stepped into the bathroom and closed the
door. She heard the lock click on the inside.

"I don't believe this!" she muttered for the second
time that night. And now the man was protecting *his*
privacy in *her* bathroom. The irony almost made her
laugh aloud. Within seconds she heard the sounds of
water running into the tub and the hum of the pump
motor drawing up water from the well.

Caught in the grip of conflicting wonder and anger at Paul Cooper's actions, Elaine jerked open
every drawer in her brother's dresser. She frowned as
she opened the closet, where three suits hung in a neat
row. Four pairs of dress slacks and three pairs of
clean jeans were draped over hangers.

"I wonder how long he was out there, spying on
me? It's been pouring for half an hour, at least!" she
mused. He was unquestionably an unusual man—but
was that good or bad? Elaine sighed and picked up a
gray fleece warm-up suit that lay folded on the floor
of the closet. That should fit Paul. She had bought it
for Keith last Christmas, but he had complained it
was a size too small. She had never gotten around to
exchanging it.

She went back to the open drawers and removed a
clean pair of Jockey shorts, an undershirt and a pair

of white tube socks. As an afterthought, she took Keith's slippers from the closet, even though they probably wouldn't fit her unexpected guest.

She laid the items of clothing on Keith's bed while she listened to the sound of splashing water. She had to get the man thawed out and on his way home. Pronto. The errand that had brought her to the house this evening loomed large in her mind.

She went into the kitchen and heated some water to make a pot of coffee, then went to the closed bathroom door. "How do you like your coffee? Strong, weak or indifferent?" she called in a loud voice.

"Black. Any strength you like," came the muffled voice from within.

He's easy to please, she thought, shaking her head over his casual attitude. *And at least he's quit sneezing.* Then, to her own surprise, she found herself saying, "I didn't take time for dinner, so you probably didn't either, right?"

"If that's an invitation, I accept," came the cheerful reply. She heard a leisurely splash.

The man actually sounded as if he were enjoying himself! A mental image of Paul Cooper sitting nude, immersed in a tub of water, flitted through her mind. She touched her forehead with her fingertips and gave herself a mental shake.

"The only things in the house are sausage and eggs, Keith's favorite. And peanut butter and strawberry jam, of course." *This is crazy. Why am I doing this?*

"I *love* strawberry jam. Thank you." The voice sounded less nasal. "Eggs and sausages sound great!" She heard another splash. "You have great hot water! I'm thawing out. If I unlock the door, will you join me?" he asked playfully.

Elaine stiffened, blinked. Her face warmed suddenly. She hurried away from the door, not answering. This man was not as prim and proper as he appeared. His easy charm could be dangerous.

Did Ray Strothers charm Mother, too, to get her to talk? Elaine wondered, all the warmth draining from her as the hardness crept back into her heart. She clearly remembered the reporter on the staff of the newspaper in the small town in Ohio. He had misquoted her mother, choosing what served his purpose and ignoring the rest. As a result, a town's hatred had been ignited against her family. At fourteen, a freshman in high school, Elaine had been ill equipped to fight it. She had never been able to forgive Strothers for the misery he had brought. Like him, Paul Cooper was a reporter—the enemy—no matter how charming his manner or words.

And now history was threatening to repeat itself. Indianapolis was bigger, of course, and Cooper's exposé would not give rise to the same kind of threats Strothers's article had precipitated twenty years ago. No one was likely to torch her house with her inside. Not in Indianapolis. All she stood to lose this time was her job. Everything Elaine had worked so hard to earn over the past twelve years. The man paddling like a duck in the bathtub had the power to bring her life crashing down around her with a few well-chosen words in his magazine.

Damn Keith for having the accident! Why couldn't someone else have pulled him from the burning car? Why did it have to be an investigative reporter? Especially one with Paul Cooper's track record?

Her hand trembled as she measured ground coffee into the paper filter. A hard lump filled her throat. She blinked back hot tears, refusing them an outlet, took a deep breath and concentrated on her task. What had possessed her to offer this man a meal?

Elaine prepared an omelet and cooked the sausage links. By the time she heard the sound of water gurgling down the drain, the smell of fresh-perked coffee permeated the rooms.

Elaine heard the bathroom door open. "Clothes are on the bed" she called loudly. "Keep your wet clothes and muddy shoes on the bathroom floor! I haven't scrubbed it yet."

"Yes, ma'am!" Paul Cooper called back.

She saw a flash of nude skin move from the bathroom doorway into the bedroom. He hadn't even covered himself with a towel! She whirled to face the stove, her cheeks growing warm. Soon Paul Cooper appeared in Keith's heavyweight tracksuit.

The suit's not a bad fit at all, she thought, her gaze running over the man's neatly combed damp hair. The blue eyes behind the glasses were impossible for her to ignore—they were direct and honest and held her in their gaze. Feeling threatened and confused, Elaine looked away.

"Thank you for your kindness, Elaine. It was pretty miserable out there in that storm. I'm sorry that I frightened you." He looked embarrassed and glanced around the kitchen. "That coffee smells wonderful. In fact, everything smells wonderful," he told her appreciatively.

"Stop!" She held up her hand. It was becoming harder and harder to distrust the man, but she had to. It was the only protection she had against his kind— especially when her father had been on the FBI's wanted list. Was his name there still, after twenty years? Or had they accepted the charade of his death? Elaine hadn't. She couldn't. He was too smart to have died in such a foolish manner. She still loved the man. After all the damage he had done to her and her mother. If the bank officials found out about him... Everything in Elaine went still as death.

Paul Cooper was staring at her again, and for an instant she was afraid he could read her mind.

"Mind if I light a fire?" he asked. "There's cut wood on the porch."

"A fire?" she echoed, alarmed. Thoughts of the past moved closer, threatening to suffocate her.

"Aren't you cold?" Paul asked, breaking the spell. "The temperature's dropping outside. Do you have a furnace in this place?"

"The storage tank is out of oil. I guess Keith didn't think to reorder so late in the season." She smiled weakly. "I don't think we'll be here long enough to justify lighting a fire. It's ten-fifteen now. It's a long drive back to Indy, and it's a workday tomorrow. I'm not my own boss like you are," she said lightly.

Paul didn't return her smile. Instead, his face grew serious. "We have to talk," he said. "About Keith. He may be in trouble—over his head—and I'd like to help. Please let me."

Elaine's fingers fumbled with the wrapper on a stick of margarine; she almost dropped it before she could trap it safely on the butter dish. His gaze locked with hers. His eyes seemed to pull her toward him, and she felt herself growing warm and liquid inside. She took a deep breath. "Look, it's been a long day and I'm tired. And yes, I'm worried about my brother, too." Keith had a talent for trouble, yet he always meant well. "Oh, you may as well light the fire," she added, relenting. It looked as though it would be another late night. "Do you like French toast?" she asked.

"Love it!" Paul's face softened into a wonderful smile.

Elaine tried to ignore the sensations caused by his voice. She prepared the French toast, while Paul hauled in three logs and kindling from the porch and laid them in the fireplace. He seemed to know what he was doing, and flames were soon leaping high in the grate. The burning wood gave off a fragrant smell.

"The eggs will dry out if we don't eat soon." Elaine pulled the earthenware serving platter out of the warm oven, a mitt protecting her left hand. A mound of fluffy yellow lay in the center of the flowered plate, surrounded by a ring of golden sausage links.

"You're left-handed?" he asked quietly, watching her.

"What's unusual about that?" she countered defensively.

"Nothing. Nothing at all. It makes you special. Do you want me to pour the coffee?"

Elaine nodded, and they worked together. Paul poured the coffee and set the table. Somehow, this surprised Elaine. He behaved like most of her wealthy clients, people accustomed to the best money can buy, yet he was completely at ease in Keith's kitchen, helping her with their meal.

They ate at the round oaken table at one end of the living room, beside the crackling fire. They discussed their one topic of mutual interest—Keith. Paul proved a good listener, and he was soon successful in drawing Elaine out.

"My mother became ill when Keith was a freshman in high school. She died in his sophomore year. I had been working at the bank five years by then. She'd always worried about him—overprotected him, maybe. I . . . promised her I'd look after him. Jeff remarried in Keith's junior year—"

"Jeff?" Paul asked.

"Our... father." She cursed the slight hesitation, fearing it gave her away. Her stepfather's first name had just slipped out.

"You call your father by his first name?" Paul looked puzzled.

"Sure. Always. Don't you?" She felt a stab of fear in the pit of her stomach. How could she have been so careless?

"No. I call my father Dad. He called me Paul Andrew whenever he got mad and wanted to whale the daylights out of me. 'Course, he never did. My mother wouldn't let him." The grin that spread across the oval face indicated he was joking. "She's a very sweet Southern lady. But firm. They make a good team."

"Oh... well... our family has always been progressive. First names and all that..." She jumped up from the table and walked to the window, turning her back to him so he couldn't see her face while she sought to regain her composure. "How long can this storm last?"

Raindrops rattled against the windowpane like tiny marbles. Outside, the inky blackness was unrelieved by moon or streetlight. The woods loomed, suddenly sinister.

She dropped the curtain, acutely aware of Paul Cooper's presence. What was he *really* after? A conquest to satisfy his male ego or something more—a juicy story to run in his magazine, leaving *her* to pay the price?

CHAPTER FIVE

"TELL ME ABOUT KEITH. Does he smoke pot, drink to excess? Has he ever been in trouble with the police?" Paul asked all the questions Elaine had expected.

She didn't reply. She only sighed and played with her coffee cup and stared into the fire. It was impossible for her to trust a reporter after the painful experience with Ray Strothers.

"We're on the same side, Elaine! Why do you insist on putting a wall between us? If Keith *is* in trouble, you both need help. *Let* me help, if I can. I have all kinds of local and national contacts that might be of use."

Paul sounded sincere. But was he? Finally Elaine answered with a resigned sigh. "My brother doesn't do drugs. At least, I don't think so. I've never found anything suspicious around here. There's an occasional six-pack of beer in the fridge, but he's over twenty-one. He...does...have an arrest record."

Paul Cooper leaned back in his chair, his arms folded over his chest, his face impassive. "What charge?"

"Disorderly conduct. Resisting arrest. Keith was picked up during an antinuke demonstration, a rally for international disarmament. Some of the people he was with got out of hand. The police intervened."

"A peace rally that turned violent." He looked thoughtful. "A paradox, isn't it?"

"He was doing research for his first novel, which is based on an anti-nuclear-war theme. It was his first arrest. They were lenient with him," she hastened to add. "He was a college freshman, the youngest person in the group. And he did get the manuscript completed—I'll give him lots of credit for that. But . . ." She shrugged. ". . . no one would publish it. He didn't get discouraged, though. He got an idea for his second novel. He became friends with some university students who were connected with the Greenpeace movement. You may have noted the bumper sticker on his car."

Paul nodded. "Keith has a social conscience. I can't criticize him for that."

"In researching his second novel he went over to Japan the summer before his senior year on a demonstration against the whaling industry. A few tourists on the dock got out of hand, tempers flew...and a fight broke out.

"Keith played football in high school, but he's not the type to use his fists unless he has to, so I'm sure he didn't start the fracas. But he was at the front of the group—he's not one to hide in the rear of anything. He was one of the men arrested. Our embassy wasn't too happy. I had to make a quick trip to Japan on short notice. I was sure he'd end up in a Japanese criminal court. Luckily he didn't.''

"He completed *two* novels, you say, at the same time he earned a college degree? I'm impressed," Paul observed.

Elaine sensed that Paul was telling the truth. But maybe that was because she wanted to believe him. Maybe he was just a good liar. Nevertheless, she continued her story, wanting him to understand her brother better.

"Keith kept decent grades, too. *A*s in his major subjects, *B*s and *C*s in all the others." Her sisterly pride was obvious, even though she had been a bit testy when she'd discovered Keith had included journalism in his major at the end of his freshman year.

Paul was frowning. "Do you think his current trouble is related to research on another book?"

She sighed. "I know damn well it is! The synopsis—that's the outline of the plot, isn't it?—and the completed chapters are on the list of items to sneak out of the house in case the police arrive. The whole thing's stupid, though! The police aren't going to get a search warrant because of an auto accident. But I can't persuade my brother of that. He seems... anxious... for reasons I can't comprehend. In fact, he acted almost scared when we met for dinner shortly before the accident. And that's not at all like Keith!"

Paul's brow furrowed. He seemed lost in thought. "Let me see the list." Paul was holding out a hand. Large knuckles, long fingers, no calluses, she noted.

She resisted. "Keith and I have always been able to work things out for ourselves," she insisted stubbornly.

He leaned toward her. "Please, Elaine. I didn't risk my life to pull that guy out of a burning car, only to have him end up in jail for poor judgment or getting involved with the wrong crowd. I like Keith—he seems to be a decent guy, but he has an unfortunate tendency to get in over his head when it comes to research." His manner was intent. "I'm in this with you all the way, whether you like it or not. I don't want to see you get involved in this, either. Do you understand what I'm saying?" The blue eyes compelled her to look at him.

Thunder rattled. Rain beat a dancing patter on the shingled roof. She felt herself tremble and stiffened imperceptibly to counteract the effects of his disturbing, husky voice, his commanding, masculine presence. The hour was late, she was tired. She desperately wanted to escape the situation that confronted her, but knew she couldn't. She wanted to get away before she found herself confessing all about her father. She straightened in her chair. That much she could do.

"Trust me, Elaine!" Paul said softly in the voice that sent prickles running along her skin.

His gentle persistence was wearing her down. If Keith *was* into something in which the police might take an interest, she had to end the matter before the spotlight of attention was turned and their father's name was resurrected from the FBI's wanted list.

Silently she rose from the chair and went to her purse. She returned to the table, holding out the list in Keith's handwriting—and hoped she wasn't making a big mistake.

Paul took the paper and studied it for a few seconds. Then he moved to the sofa and dropped to his knees, searching for the metal box containing photographs, the first item on the list. "Do you want to check the magazines in the corners for the January and February issues? You know his filing system better than I do," he asked, looking up at her.

"There isn't any," she answered wearily. "He can't bear to throw anything away. He's afraid he'll need something as soon as he gets rid of it."

"A writer needs to keep reference materials at hand," said Paul automatically, his forehead brushing the carpet as his arm swept under the sofa.

Elaine rose, cleared the dishes from the table and carried them into the kitchen. She was surprised to hear Paul call out, "I'll help you with the kitchen cleanup after we gather these items together and make some sense out of what's going on. Leave the dishes in the sink, why don't you?" He stood up again as she returned to the living room, a thin metal container in his hands.

"That's too good an offer to turn down." Elaine moved to the nearest corner and started riffling through magazines, looking for the men's adventure magazine named on the list. It was not until she'd located the magazines that she realized that Paul had not spoken for quite some time. She looked up and saw that he was bent over the dining table, looking at several large black-and-white glossy photographs. He had a strange look on his face as Elaine approached him, triumphant, magazines in hand.

He glanced up and she felt suddenly wary. The man was...what? Angry? Suspicious? Despite his outward control, she sensed an underlying tension.

"What's your brother doing with photos of Garry Channing?" he asked. His eyes were narrowed, an icy glint in the dark pupils. There was a new toughness about him as he looked at her, his square jaw set.

"Garry Channing? Who's he?" she asked, perplexed.

"This man." He pointed to a man in one of the photos. A heavy ring made by a red marker completely encircled his body. "He's Garry Channing, I'm sure of it. I heard him speak at a convention of electrical engineers in California, one of my last assignments for the *Sentinel*. I interviewed him. I wrote more than exposés," he added pointedly.

"Channing patented a new feature to the polymer battery that can increase by tenfold the miles an E.V. can go before having to be recharged."

"E.V.?" she asked, puzzled.

"Electrical vehicles—cars and panel trucks for local deliveries. There's already a model scheduled for release. Commuters can travel back and forth to work in cars that don't need gasoline. Plug 'em in overnight for a recharge and they'll be ready to go the next morning. In fact, Channing's goal is to design and run an E.V. race car in the Indianapolis '500' one day. He told me so—off the record, of course."

"Keith wouldn't know such a man. Is Channing connected with the '500' race in some way?"

"Don't you read the Indy papers during May?" Paul sounded incredulous. "Besides owning an auto parts company, a plastics company and a company that manufactures regular batteries, he's also a race car owner and driver. He's never attempted to drive the Indy '500'—he told me it's out of his league, but he has a car in the '500' every year. He's a hell of a nice guy," Paul declared.

"My brother can't have any connection with this man." Elaine reached for the photos Paul was holding, glancing at them quickly. Each was marked in similar fashion, although the scenes were different. A red line outlined the same man in each print, setting him apart.

She studied the photos. One had been taken on a luxurious golf green. Four men, dressed very much alike in polo shirts and trousers, stood in a line as if for a press photo. Their manner, their posture, the expressions on their faces reminded Elaine of many of her affluent clients. All had lean, trim figures—not a beer belly among them—faces smiling with the self-confidence that was the hallmark of wealth and success.

Of the four men, only two attracted her attention. The man on the left had black hair streaked heavily with gray, a long, thin nose with flaring nostrils and lips that looked decidedly sensual. A raw sense of power emanated from him in the way he stood and in his confident—no, arrogant, she decided—expression. But it was the man on the right who was encircled in red. He lacked the blatant sensuality of the other man, but was no less attractive. His hair was lighter, and his genial face looked craggy and tanned, contrasting with his straight, white teeth. He radiated a dynamic quality so wholesome that Elaine could not help liking him immediately.

"A Californian?" she asked. The tan was a giveaway.

"Garry was born and grew up in Montana. His father owned a ranch there. He went to university in California and decided to remain there after he met his first wife, Marian."

Elaine studied the next photo. The setting was at poolside. The same man—once again circled in red—was seated at a patio table, the umbrella casting a shadow over one side of his face. He was wearing swimming trunks, and a towel was draped over his shoulders, framing the mass of curly hair on his chest. A woman sat in a chair beside him in a one-piece flowered swimsuit cut deep in the front, emphasizing a small but perfect bust.

"His daughter?" inquired Elaine.

Paul turned to the fire and stabbed at it with the poker.

"His second wife, Laura. She was a model in New York. Appeared on the cover of *Vogue*. She was there at the convention with him. They'd been married only a year at the time."

Elaine sensed that he wasn't telling all he knew, but he wasn't the type to indulge in idle gossip. "He divorced Marian, I presume?" she asked.

"Yes." He was staring into the fire, the poker still in his hand.

Elaine let the subject drop. The other photos featured full views of the same man, surrounded by others. He always looked pleasant, but the bright red circle drawn around his body reminded her of blood, making her feel uncomfortable.

"These are expensive prints, Paul. Why would Keith mark them up this way? It makes no sense. What do you make of this?" she asked, puzzled, suddenly aware of the rifle and scope and boxes of ammunition she had put onto the sofa just before she had noticed Paul outside the window.

"I don't know what to think—yet. Let's see those magazines!" Paul took them from her hands. He went through them swiftly, scanning each page quickly. Elaine realized he must be trained in speed-reading. He stopped abruptly at the classified ad section in the back of one issue. She could see that one of the ads was circled in black ink.

Paul's head lifted. His azure eyes flashed fire. "Read it!" He shoved the folded magazine across the table toward her. Reluctantly she did as she was bidden.

Recent vet. High-risk assignment. U.S. Short term. $20,000. 1/2 in adv. Need immed. Exc. opportunity.

The ad gave a post-office box number in Buffalo, New York.

Thunder crashed, rattling the house and sending a tremor through the wooden floor. Elaine looked up, puzzled. What kind of job was being offered? She didn't understand any of this.

Paul's face was grim. He leafed through the other issue of the magazine until he found the same ad, also encircled in black. He tapped it with a long index finger. "You've heard of contracts against someone, haven't you? Hit men? Killers for hire?"

It took a few seconds for Paul's meaning to register. When it did, her hackles rose. How *dare* he imply her brother could be party to such a monstrous deal?

"Keith's trip to Buffalo? Oh, no! Impossible! Keith's never been in the army. Just one year of R.O.T.C. at I.U., that's all. He hated it! He decided he wasn't cut out to be in the military. He couldn't

take being told what to do—and besides, he's a paci-
fist!''

Paul was staring at her, making her uncomfortable.

"This ad calls for a veteran," she persisted, seeing
that Paul was still unconvinced.

"Research!" he muttered, still looking stern.

She had a sudden, chilling thought and headed for
the desk where the synopsis and partial manuscript
were stored. Paul was a heartbeat ahead of her, and
they almost collided in their rush to discover the
truth. Elaine found the handful of typed papers first.
Paul held out his hand, and she reluctantly allowed
him to take them, still denying what she had begun to
fear he would find. "This is the most ridiculous thing
I've ever heard! Keith would never harm anyone!''

Ignoring her outburst, Paul was already studying
the papers. "The next thing on the list is a duffel bag
in the rear of the bedroom closet. Why don't you go
get it? I don't want to search his things," he said
without looking up.

Elaine pushed down the slight nausea of fear as she
went into Keith's bedroom and opened the closet
door. There was the duffel bag, all right—buried beneath a pup tent and stakes, a horseshoe set and
bowling shoes. She pulled it out, uncharacteristically
leaving his closet in disarray. "This is silly! This is
goddamn silly!" she muttered aloud, closing the door
firmly.

When she returned to the living room, Paul was slouched in a chair at the dining table, intent on Keith's typed pages. His long legs stuck straight out before him; the white tube socks outlined long, narrow feet. A rebellious cowlick marred the neatness of his dark blond hair, and Elaine quelled the mad impulse to reach out and smooth it down.

The wood crackled and popped in the fireplace as the rosy warmth radiated through the room. Thunder crashed again, the lights flickered, dimmed, went out for a second, then flashed bright again.

Paul looked up. Their eyes locked in a gaze so compelling that it sent a physical sensation coursing through her blood. His hand slowly rose from the table. An army dog tag was dangling from a chain he held in his fingers.

"Found it in the desk drawer. Along with this." His voice was flat as he handed her a folded document.

Elaine laid the duffel bag on the sofa. She looked at the metal tag. Keith's name was on it, also a serial number. She frowned. These items hadn't been written on the list. She unfolded the document, read it and gasped.

"Honorable discharge papers? This is crazy! Keith was at I.U. during those years." She felt as if she had entered the twilight zone. Her brother couldn't be in two places at once. Although she hadn't visited him regularly on campus at Bloomington, she had seen him several times each semester. "I don't understand this!" she said in confusion.

"False ID. A forged document. Not too hard to acquire if one knows the right—or rather, the *wrong*—people. Anything is available for a price, Elaine." His voice was still flat. He sounded fatigued, as if he'd come up hard against a brick wall he'd been hoping to avoid. "What's in the duffel bag?" he asked.

Elaine picked up the bag, feeling the outside. "Boxes of some kind. Shoes, no doubt." She reached inside and pulled out a box tied with heavy twine. She stood holding the box, afraid to open it. She felt the urge to flee, to escape this madness.

Paul was reading, his attention focused on the typewritten pages in front of him. It was the synopsis of Keith's new book. She studied his profile. *What an intelligent, attractive face,* she thought.

"You'd better open it!" His voice startled her as he looked up again. His face was stern, yet his voice was tinged with compassion.

Elaine slowly removed the lid. When she saw the contents, she nearly fainted. Inside were neatly arranged stacks of currency—ones, fives, tens, twenties, all bound with paper bands. Old bills. "I don't believe this!" she whispered.

Paul got up to look at the contents of the box. He fished inside the bag and withdrew another. He angrily broke the twine with his fingers and threw the lid onto the floor.

More money.

"Count it. I'll bet you'll find ten thousand dollars. Or close to it. It's a wonder he hasn't spent it yet." There was a sadness in his set expression.

"It's all there. In the synopsis. Your brother's doing research all right. Research in killer-for-hire ads. The novel ought to sell a million copies, especially after he guns down his victim." His laugh was brittle. "No wonder Keith's running scared the police might search this place. Conspiracy to commit murder is a felony. He can land in prison without even pulling the trigger."

Prison? A wave of cold fear surged through Elaine. Her brother's well-being wasn't the only thing at stake. Police were thorough. A police investigation could bring the family's past into the open. Right onto the front page of the *Indianapolis Star* for Commercial Bank officials to read. "But— when...?" She couldn't bring herself to say the horrible words. She reached out to place her hand on the back of a chair to steady herself.

Paul ran his fingers through his hair. There was sorrow in his eyes when he looked at her. Grief for her, for Keith, for Garry Channing, a man he liked and admired.

"There's no way of telling what the plan is. The synopsis isn't completed. The first three chapters just introduce the protagonist and the guy he hooks up with—not in Buffalo of course. Detroit. What's the difference?" He walked into the kitchen and poured himself more coffee. "It looks as if Keith is planning to plot this book around the actual events as they take place.''

The wheels of Elaine's mind started spinning. "I'll get Keith out of the country, to Canada or Mexico, until this whole thing blows over before any real harm is done,'' she said, clenching her fists.

"The hell you will!'' Paul exploded, staring at her.

So much for his wanting to help, she thought. I should have known better.

Paul went to the kitchen and pulled a grocery sack from the cupboard. He stuffed the incriminating boxes of money, typed pages, photos, dog tags and forged army document, magazines, scope and box of ammunition into the brown paper bag and set it on the desk.

Elaine watched him in mute despair. He walked toward her, holding folded sheets of paper toweling and bent over the rifle, wrapping the toweling carefully around the area next to the trigger, at the base of the shoulder rest. He lifted the gun off the sofa with more paper toweling.

"Where do you think you're going with that?'' she asked, jumping to her feet. Blood throbbed in her temples. She was going to get rid of this stuff one way or another, and Paul Cooper wasn't going to stop her.

"To the state police.'' His voice was firm but emotionless.

"You can't do that!'' she wailed. "They'll arrest him!''

"And you can't help the kid escape over the border to wipe the slate clean. Someone is out to snuff out Garry Channing. Can't you get that through your head? Keith is the only link we have to that—that—son of a bitch who ran the ad. We've got to get to the bottom of this while there's still time!"

"Keith hasn't done anything wrong...yet," she pleaded fervently. "I thought you liked him. Why are you assuming he's guilty before he has a chance to explain?"

"Keith's accepted the advance payment. That constitutes a bargain in legitimate as well as in criminal circles," Paul snapped. His azure eyes were blazing with a cold light. "I will not play Russian roulette with Garry Channing's life!"

For one terrible, silent moment they stared at each other. Then Paul strode to the kitchen table and grabbed up his billfold and car keys with his free hand. Still holding the rifle, he walked to the desk, threw his billfold into the grocery sack that held all the incriminating items on Keith's list. He went to the front door and jerked it open, unmindful of the wall of water streaming off the porch roof and falling against the black curtain of night.

Hot tears stung Elaine's eyes as she watched him. How quick this man was to condemn her brother! A prison term would destroy him, she was certain. And the truth would be out, costing her her job at the bank, negating all her hard work for the past twelve years. The bank officials would never give her a second chance—the omissions on her application for employment were the same as lies.

Fear released the tiger of anger within. She knew she had to stop this man any way she could. She leaped at Paul Cooper, surprising him as he returned to the desk for the grocery bag. With both hands she grabbed the rifle hard, jamming her thumb into the loop surrounding the trigger to get a better grip.

Thunder crashed again as lightning transformed the sky and the woods to the brightness of noon. Lights flickered, and then the house was plunged into darkness, except for the golden glow that came from the fireplace.

"What—in hell—are you doing?" Paul shouted as Elaine struggled to wrest the firearm from him. The end of the barrel swung crazily toward the ceiling, toward the floor, toward the window. Maternal protectiveness for her brother plus her own instinct for survival endowed Elaine with new strength. Paul's breath was coming in harsh pants as the muscles in his arms hardened, strained.

Suddenly their macabre dance was halted by an earsplitting explosion. The recoil sent paralyzing vibrations coursing up her stiffened arms as the windowpane shattered in a storm of tiny fragments. Elaine heard a quick expiration of breath and a grunt as Paul's body jerked against hers. Numb with terror, she released her grip on the weapon.

The smell of rain swept through the room in a draft of cold air from doorway and window.

Paul let the gun slip to the floor as his strong arms trapped hers and pulled her hard against him in a crushing grip. She was helpless as he held her tightly, his head lowered against hers.

Her heart raced against the solid wall of his chest. A pounding racked her temples, and dry gasps made her throat ache. Cool air washed over fevered flesh as they stood locked in each other's embrace, motionless.

Thunder echoed in the distance.

"The damned thing—was loaded. I—should have—checked—it first. Are you—okay?" Paul asked.

His warm breath fell against her cheek, a cheek that was damp with perspiration. She couldn't answer. Not only had she failed Keith, she had endangered Paul's life and her own.

"We could have shot ourselves in the foot, you know that?" he muttered thickly, lips pressed hard against the crown of her head. Then he chuckled. The sound was husky, deeply sensual. And all of a sudden he was no longer pinning her arms, leaving her helpless; his arms had moved to her upper torso, holding her body against his in a hungry embrace. The hard contours of his body made it plain that he was attracted to her, and she began to tremble uncontrollably, suddenly alive with sexual feelings she could not hide. He was showing no mercy, nuzzling her head as his hand moved down to her denim-clad rear, pressing her even closer.

She gasped, melting in his warmth, tingling in awareness of her own need. She thought of the bed in Keith's bedroom, with its crisp, clean sheets, and an idea began to form. If she offered herself to him, he might change his mind about going to the police. When his lips covered hers in a long, lingering kiss, she gave in to her own desire, pushing aside her fear. "Yes . . ." she whispered, anticipating what he would do next.

He didn't. Instead, he released her and stepped back. The look he gave her was touched with sadness—and regret. "That's quite a change, Elaine. You wouldn't be trying to buy me off, would you? I'm afraid I can't accept your offer, tempting as it is."

"How—how dare you say that?" Her cheeks were burning. She couldn't look at him. Her insides were on fire, betraying her resolve to best this man. She turned and walked to the fire, jabbing the flaming logs with the poker.

"More than one woman has tried to buy me off when I was on the trail of a story, but it's not something I expected of *you*," he said quietly, the huskiness of arousal fading from his voice. "I think we'd better get out of here," he said, once more in control.

Spots of angry color still stained Elaine's cheeks. The man had made a fool of her twice. He won't do it again, she vowed. "The things in that bag and that rifle belong to my brother. They are his legal property. You have no right to remove them from this house. If you try, I'll go to the police myself and press charges against *you*." It was a bluff, but it seemed to be working. She pressed further.

"You've made assumptions about Keith without even bothering to talk to him about your suspicions. You call that being a first-rate reporter? I don't! I'll take the things home with me. I'll take full responsibility for their safety. Come with me to the hospital on Saturday, when I take him home. I'll cook dinner for the three of us and you can question him to your heart's content. I won't interfere, I promise. I don't want an innocent man to die, either. I'm not quite the monster you assume me to be."

"How do I know you won't destroy the evidence before the police can see it?" he asked.

"You asked me to trust you, remember? Trust is a two-way street. If you want me to trust you, you'll have to trust me first." She spoke calmly, putting distance between them by her tone and manner.

The fire was dying, logs turning to ash. A tremor of chill swept through her. She walked to the open door, unaware of it until now. Raindrops clung to the tips of budding leaves, the smell of rich, wet earth, leaves decaying from winter and new clover hung in the air.

The storm had passed.

"I accept your terms." He, too, sounded distant. He looked down at his wristwatch; numbers glowed in the darkness. "It's ten till three. I have a staff meeting at nine. It's a long drive back to town for both of us." He sounded fatigued.

Elaine knew that she, too, was exhausted; far too tired to continue this battle of wills. "I'll put what's left of the coffee into vacuum bottles we can take with us. That might keep us awake until we get home." She found a flashlight.

Not a word passed between them as they made ready to leave. Without electricity there was no pump to draw water from the well. The dishes were left stacked in the sink. She looked at them, feeling emotionally depleted, drained. Unfinished business, like the rest of the evening's events.

She had been right in her suspicions. Paul Cooper had had an ulterior motive in following her here. Did he know about her father? That Elaine Malden was not her real name? He had lied when he said he wanted to help Keith, to help her, of that she was certain. He'd been all set to betray them until she'd tried her desperate bluff. Just as her own body had betrayed her. Now he was in a position to take away everything she had left.

CHAPTER SIX

ON SATURDAY MORNING Keith sat on the edge of the bed next to the doorway in Room A5060, his legs swinging nervously. The color television set mounted on the wall murmured, the sound wafting from the pillow speaker beside him. On the screen a father was showing his rapt ten-year-old son the proper way to cast a fly.

Keith's dark eyes were glued to the set, reflecting a quiet sadness. No father had ever taken *him* fishing. Jeff had always been too busy. Yet he didn't switch channels. He continued to watch, almost jealous of the boy on the screen, a boy who took for granted what Keith had never had.

Late-morning sun washed the inside ledge of the long window in white light. The occupant of the bed next to the window lay motionless, eyes closed, as Elaine and Paul entered the room.

Keith reacted instantly at the sight of Paul Cooper. He tensed, aware that the older man knew all about the research on the novel, the trouble he had gotten himself into. Elaine had informed Keith in a low voice during a visit yesterday, giving him sketchy details while keeping a wary eye on the sleeping patient in the other bed. By the time she was ready to leave, Keith had been ready to explode. The knot of fear still remained in his stomach. He felt Elaine had betrayed him.

"Hi! Hey, you're looking a lot better!" said Paul cheerfully. Too cheerfully.

Keith glowered at him. He'd managed to intimidate a lot of guys in the locker room that way. Paul retained his smile. It was plain that he didn't intimidate easily.

"Hi, Elaine," said Keith, pointedly ignoring the man who was meddling in his private business. Elaine was Keith's last chance, and he knew it. She was keeping the "evidence," as Cooper had called it, safely at her house.

Elaine laid a clean pair of jeans, Keith's favorite gold sport shirt and a plastic bag containing underwear and socks at the foot of the bed. "The doctor's signed a release order. We can go home now." She leaned close and gently ruffled Keith's hair, careful not to touch the bandaged area. She gave Keith a gentle smile.

"He's coming home with us?" asked Keith, thinking how pleasantly cool her fingertips were.

"Yes. We'll take home a pizza for lunch and then I'll cook dinner for the three of us. I'm going to make you guys an apple pie."

The mention of his favorite dessert failed to arouse his usual exuberant response.

"I like apple pie," said Paul, noting Keith's lack of enthusiasm.

Elaine looked up at the tall man with an appreciative smile.

Keith's eyes shifted warily from Elaine to Paul, from Paul to Elaine. There was something different about the two of them now, the way they looked at each other. Exactly what had happened that night in his house? Cooper must be a fast worker.

He doesn't look the type, Keith thought. "Can't I stay here longer?" he asked, dreading the grilling ahead of him. Elaine, always up-front, had warned him what to expect. She seemed to be preparing him for the worst.

The hell he'll get anything out of me! Keith vowed silently. *Cooper's nuts! He wants me to go to the police and tell 'em everything?* His head started throbbing and it was nothing to do with the accident. *Elaine's in big trouble if I do!* Brett Hawley had made it perfectly clear what he would do if Keith failed to carry out his part of the deal. If Channing didn't die, Elaine would. How could he tell his sister he had put her in such a spot?

Elaine touched his cheek gently, looking into his eyes, the way she always did when she knew he was hurting. "Get shaved," she suggested quietly. "Letting yourself go like this won't help a thing. We'll wait in the hallway while you dress."

Paul left the room, but Elaine stayed for a last word with Keith. Her encouraging smile was like a kiss.

"Paul says he wants to help us, but tell him...only what applies to this particular situation," she warned in a whisper. Her eyes communicated what her lips didn't dare. A shadow of worry lurked beneath her velvet-brown eyes.

Elaine left him alone, closing the door behind her, and Keith eased himself off the bed, every step to the bathroom jarring unpleasantly. *Yeah, everything'll be all right. Sure! Go to the police. Paul Cooper wants to put me away in state prison for five years. Hawley wants to kill my sister. Nothing to it!*

As he lathered his face and applied the safety razor to the two-day growth of bristle, he wondered if prisoners were allowed to use typewriters. Maybe he could finish the novel in jail.

THE SILVER LEBARON pulled into the semicircular driveway of Elaine's brick house on Kessler Boulevard. The inside of the car was fragrant with the smell of hot pizza. Keith carried both boxes as Elaine unlocked the dead bolt and they stepped into the house and onto an immaculate black slate floor.

"I'll take these into the kitchen," mumbled Keith as he wiggled his feet out of his athletic shoes, leaving them beside the front door.

Paul took the cue. He removed his leather shoes, leaving them beside Keith's. Elaine smiled her approval as she slipped out of her pumps and put on slippers. She handed Paul a pair of Keith's terry-cloth beach slip-ons.

"Is there another exit?" Paul asked Elaine.

She gave him a knowing look as she opened the louvered closet to their left. She took out a wooden hanger. "Do you want to give me your suit jacket? Keith will relate to you better if you're in shirtsleeves."

"Will he take off and head out of here?" Paul inquired in a whisper, jerking a thumb toward the kitchen doorway.

"I thought you agreed to trust me." She smiled, and in spite of himself, all Paul's objections melted. He watched her drape his jacket on the hanger, running her hand slowly over the lapel. "You have good taste in clothes," she said.

She waved her arm in a broad gesture. "Look around if you want. Make yourself at home. There's a half bath at the end of the hallway. Kitchen, dining room and family room are on the right. Bedrooms to the left, down the hall. Utility room at the end, next to the garage."

Keith appeared in the kitchen doorway. "Do you want to eat the pizza in here at the bar or in the family room?" he asked his sister.

Elaine suggested eating in the kitchen. While she put on coffee, Paul accepted her invitation to look around. He was curious. He wanted to find more clues about his mysterious lady whose smile and manner could be so inviting, even while she held him at arm's length.

He glanced into the living room. The walls were a very pale peach, lending warmth to the room. A rattan sofa, love seat and matching accent chair dominated the area complementing the ecru rug that lay on wall-to-wall carpeting. A glass-topped cocktail table sat in the center of the rug. Matching end tables bore ceramic lamps with fluted white shades. Chinese prints decorated the walls.

It was clearly a room for guests and conversation—there was a stereo but no television set. White pull-down shades covered the large window. It was a room decorated by a person of good taste.

He strolled down the hallway to the bedrooms. The wine and gray guest room was obviously occupied by Keith whenever he stayed with his sister. His clothes were in full view in the open closet.

Paul paused in the doorway to the master bedroom. Elaine's room. The color scheme was blue and yellow with earth-toned accents. The plain double bed was dressed with a flowered spread. Ceramic lamps stood on small round tables covered with identical cloths of earth tones. A large mirror took up one entire wall. An armchair for reading, with lamp and table beside it, occupied one corner. A colored photo of an attractive gray-haired woman sat on the oak dresser. It was the only picture in the room. Her mother, he guessed. The room felt warm, even sensual in its cheer, comfort and openness.

"Do you want to eat or not? We're waiting for you." Keith's irritable voice sailed down the hallway.

Paul cut the tour short and hurried to the kitchen, bracing himself for the ordeal to come. He hoped the meal would improve Keith's disposition. Paul was not looking forward to the hours ahead, when he would be cast in the role of inquisitor. The one thing that kept him going was the memory of the photo images of Garry Channing surrounded by blood-red circles. Paul was not about to let him die. His jaw stiffened at the thought.

In the sunny kitchen, fragrant with the odor of pepperoni, mozzarella, tomato sauce and oregano, Paul began his interrogation. He tried to make it sound innocent, but he had to deal with the doubts that were eating away at him. "This is a beautiful house. When did you move in?"

Elaine paused, thinking. "Four years ago this coming August. The widow who lived here moved to a nursing home."

"This is an expensive area. You must have been very frugal before you were made a vice president at Commercial Bank. I could never afford a place like this."

Elaine and Keith shared a secret glance.

"Keith and I were very lucky," Elaine answered at last. "Our mother's parents set up a trust fund for each of us in an Ohio bank. A principal of $50,000 was invested in both accounts to accumulate compound interest for eighteen years. The stipulation was that if we chose to attend college at that time, the interest payments twice a year would come directly to us to help pay our expenses. That way, college was assured for us and we could concentrate on our studies without having to take part-time jobs.

"If we chose *not* to attend college, we had to wait until the age of thirty before the interest checks started coming. I guess our grandparents figured we'd be married by then, with children of our own, and the money would come in handy." She fingered the half-eaten crust on her plate.

"After I got out of college, I put my interest checks into a money market fund and let it grow. Our mother left us her house—the one where Keith lives—and after I'd saved all my interest income for eight years I was able to put a decent down payment on this one—"

Keith interrupted his sister. "So we're not dope pushers, man, okay? I don't have to work at a stinking eight-to-five job if I don't want to. I got enough money coming in from the trust fund to pay most of my living expenses, even if I don't have a full-time job."

The younger man turned on the bar stool and looked pointedly at Elaine.

"You still need to work in a paying job, though. You spend more money than your interest check provides," she said patiently. "That's why your tires were in such bad shape. They needed replacing. Earning money, having a career of your own, is important for one's self-respect—"

"I have a career writing fiction," Keith interrupted again, looking defensive. "I just haven't sold anything yet. I'm doing valuable work already."

Paul saw his opening. "Yes, you are. You're a good writer, Keith," he said. "After reading the first three chapters of your new novel, I think you probably do have a future in fiction. Have you ever done nonfiction? Magazine articles?"

Keith's attention was snared. His eyes surveyed Paul's face as if assessing his sincerity. "You want me to do a piece for your magazine? I worked on the campus newspaper."

"Yes, I'd be interested. On spec, of course," Paul hastened to add. He wasn't going to commit himself to a fee by giving the kid an assignment. "A business topic that interests you would be a good way to start. Or I can suggest some topics we haven't covered in the past year. I always need profiles of local business people, something with an unusual slant. Three thousand words."

Once again brother and sister exchanged meaningful glances. Elaine looked confused, Keith, triumphant.

"I get my own byline?" Keith asked suspiciously.

"Of course. It's a policy of mine to give a writer the credit he or she deserves. I'll pay you five hundred dollars if I use it."

"*Okay.*" Keith felt the clouds lifting. An editor actually liked his work! "I'll work something up."

"Congratulations. You just won over my brother," Elaine commented in a low voice as she passed Paul on her way to the refrigerator. Keith had just left the kitchen to make a trip to the bathroom.

"I meant every word I said!" Paul protested, sensing her disbelief. "Your brother *does* write well."

"You're also softening him up to get his cooperation. I don't want Keith to get his hopes up, then take a fall."

Paul frowned, staring at the attractive woman as she rearranged the items on the refrigerator shelf after Keith had set them awry in his search for a cold can of beer. What did it take to win the confidence of this lady?

Still, he admitted to himself grudgingly, he was not altogether free of doubts about this sister-brother duo. Anyone who would agree to take money to kill another human being was definitely not high on Paul's "trust" list. Keith Malden and his sister came from the same genetic stock.

"Few people are fortunate enough to have grandparents establish trust funds for them that guarantee interest income," Paul said casually, careful to keep his tone light. "How did your grandfather make his money? Where in Ohio?" he asked, watching Elaine closely.

Paul noted an almost imperceptible gasp as her soft lips parted. There was a stricken look in her dark, velvet eyes, and her composed face paled.

"C-Columbus, actually. Boswell Tool and Die. Grandpa Walt was a pattern maker before he went into business for himself. He did very well. He died when I was in high school. Our grandmother lived five years after that."

Walter Boswell. Boswell Tool and Die. Columbus, Ohio. Died...sixteen to twenty years ago. Paul stamped the facts onto his memory until he could pull out his notebook and capture them on paper. He would check with Ohio agencies and banks in the hope that he could lay his doubts to rest once and for all. But if Elaine were siphoning off money from her clients' trust accounts and using it to maintain her comfortable life-style, she had to be stopped, regardless of how he felt about her. Despite her other sterling qualities—and she had many—she was violating the trust that bank and clients placed in her.

She was staring at him now. The gaze was electric; it fairly sizzled. "You don't believe me, do you? Since Keith has done something wrong, I must be just like him. I'm his sister."

The statement, more a declaration than question, so closely echoed his own thoughts, it made Paul acutely uncomfortable. The sadness in her expressive eyes made him feel like a heel for being suspicious. The silence hung heavy and awkward until Keith's return.

After both pizzas were only a memory and stomachs were ready to burst, Paul got down to business. Even though he liked Keith—he didn't want to think about what his feelings were for Elaine—if he had to act like a heel to save Garry Channing's life, he was ready to do so. First he asked Elaine to bring all the items on Keith's list from her hiding place into the family room, which adjoined the kitchen.

It was a shoes-off kind of room. A brick fireplace with slate hearth dominated one wall. Wood paneling with a light stain, a braided oval rug, a sleeper sofa with a hint of wear on the upholstered arms, a portable color television on a stand with a VCR beneath left no doubt that this was where Elaine spent most of her leisure time. The ambience was one of total comfort, one that Paul was trying hard to ignore. However, he did remove his tie and turn up his shirtsleeves.

Elaine spread all the items on the hearth. She looked apprehensive. "Go easy on him. He means well," she whispered, her eyes pleading. She even touched Paul's arm, as if in supplication. Paul yielded to impulse, took her hand and held it for precious moments while Keith watched.

"Are you making out with my sister?" Keith demanded after Elaine had left the room to start on the pie.

"No," answered Paul.

"'Cause if you are, she'll shipwreck you just like she did the others."

"Others? Shipwreck? How?" Paul asked, curious.

"They fall for her. Really hard. But she's not interested in marriage. All she cares about is that damned job. They call her up for dates—maybe she'll go out, maybe not. She couldn't care less. They go crazy. They want to get married to her. Can you believe that?" Obviously Keith couldn't. It was plain that he thoroughly enjoyed his bachelorhood.

"Why is Elaine so afraid of marriage? Is it because of a bad relationship, or was she always that way? Maybe your father was...you know...abusive with her.... Something like that. Did she ever confide anything of that nature to you?" Paul asked guardedly.

Keith stared at him, dark eyes wide. Then comprehension dawned. "Oh, heck, no! I don't think so.... You got a dirty mind, man, you know that?"

Paul gave an embarrassed grin. "Comes with the job. I can't help it." He sat down beside Keith on the sofa. They shared the beer, alternating swigs. "Tell me about Buffalo," he suggested, laying his arm along the back of the sofa behind Keith. He wished he had his tape recorder with him. He'd been afraid Keith would refuse to open up if he saw one, so he had left it at home. Well, he'd just have to count on his memory.

"You really like Elaine?" asked Keith, suddenly.

"Yes, I like her. Very much. The feeling doesn't seem to be mutual."

"You're a reporter."

"What the hell difference does that make?"

The distress on Keith's face was clear. The young man positively squirmed. One hand cradled his jaw, and he looked decidedly glum.

"What difference does it make what I do for a living?" Paul insisted. Keith was reinforcing Paul's opinion that Elaine had something she was hiding, that she was afraid of him.

Keith cleared his throat. "There was a guy—a reporter..." The distress in his face deepened to a look of pain. "...who...who..." He couldn't finish what he had started to say.

"I'm more than just a reporter, Keith. I like your sister. She's...special. Understand? I'm not going to take advantage of her, if that's what you and she are afraid of.

"I like you, too, Keith. You're a great guy with good potential as a writer. It's my opinion you got in deeper with this novel research than you intended, and now you don't know how to get out of it. Elaine is involved indirectly, too, through you. I'd like to help you both. Tell me about Buffalo and the people you met there. Tell me exactly what happened."

Keith leaned back against the sofa cushions, visibly relaxing for the first time since they had entered the house. He seemed relieved to be able to talk confidentially.

"Last year I saw a TV interview with someone who had almost been murdered by someone hired through a classified ad. I got to thinking. This should be a topic an editor would be interested in. A buddy of mine at I.U. has an older brother who served in Vietnam. A heck of a nice guy! He said he'd heard about hit contracts through the grapevine. Ads for mercenary soldiers willing to go fight in somebody's small war overseas. The ads are worded so ambiguously, it's hard to tell for sure what the job is. This guy told me what magazines I should check out. Then I spotted that ad you have in your hand."

Paul was holding the magazine, looking down at the Classified page with the ad circled in black ink.

"So I was lucky. I found a guy in Chicago who could get me fake ID and phony discharge papers. He charged me plenty, though. My bank account was nearly wiped out, and my interest check wasn't due for another three months. I had to use the money Elaine had loaned me for a set of new tires in order to pay the oil bill. I told her I lent the money to a friend. She wasn't too happy!

"Anyway, I answered the ad, and they told me to come to Buffalo immediately. So I walked out on my job. I knew they'd never give me the time off."

"You have the address? Where did you report?" asked Paul.

"Yeah, I remember it," Keith said. "A crummy, rundown apartment house. Probably won't do you any good. Nobody lived in the place. It was strictly a setup—no clothes in the closet, an empty refrigerator and kitchen cupboards.

"I met a big, beefy guy named Brett Hawley. Broken nose. Used to be a prizefighter. I sure wouldn't want to meet *him* at night in a dark alley. There were also two other guys—Jed and Lucky. They never told me their full names, although everyone knew mine. It was on my dog tags. They never showed me theirs." He sounded resentful.

"They checked your ID to make sure you were a vet?"

"You bet. The first night we sat up late, drank a few beers and swapped stories. Like a freshman college bull session, although I bet those guys never saw the inside of a campus classroom. Jed *bragged* about his dishonorable discharge from the marines. Like he'd really done something great!" Keith didn't seem impressed. To his credit, thought Paul.

"Actually, as guys they weren't too bad. We talked sports. And women." Keith grinned sheepishly.

Paul remained silent, his expression impassive. He didn't want to encourage Keith to digress. Keith appeared to take the hint.

"The next day Hawley drove us out to a farm. I tried to memorize the way, but he took too many damned turns. I couldn't tell you where the farm is. We did target practice at the back of a pasture. Cardboard figures shaped like a man. Tin cans on a stump. Then they started shooting birds. That's when I almost threw up. Crows, turkey vultures, mallards raining down all over the place."

"The two other applicants were good marksmen?"

"You bet. Jed, especially. He was the best! I...didn't do so well on the cardboard targets. I didn't bag a single bird, either."

Paul was puzzled. Why had Hawley given Keith the job? Why not Jed?

"We stayed at the farm two nights, did target shooting for two days, using rifles and semiautomatic pistols. Then Hawley took us back to the apartment. I was relieved my car hadn't been stolen or stripped. It was a rough neighborhood. I was glad to get out of there."

"When did you receive the money?" Paul wanted to know.

"Well, that's the funny thing. Hawley never indicated which one of us he liked best, if he was interviewing others or what. I drove back home, convinced Jed would get the job. Even Lucky scored better than I did. I figured I'd better forget all about the novel—it'd never get off the ground. I figured I'd struck out. But Hawley showed up at my front door about a week after I got back to Brown County. He told me I had the job. Me! I couldn't believe it! He said he had really liked me, that he could relate to me and wanted to give me a break." Keith grimaced as he noticed Paul's set face.

"So there's Hawley, standing in my living room, looking the place over good. He gave me everything you see here on the coffee table. When he handed me the cash—$10,000 in two shoe boxes—I didn't know what to say!"

"How about 'No, thanks, mister, take your job and stuff it!'" Paul suggested, glowering.

"I did. Well, not in those exact words. You wouldn't either if you were facing this guy in a room alone." Keith looked pained.

"You told him you'd changed your mind?" Paul was surprised.

"I—told him I didn't think I was—right—for the job." Keith stared gloomily out the window into the bright April sunshine. "He wouldn't let me off the hook." Keith's hands were clenched into fists.

"How could Hawley make you do something you didn't want to do?" Paul asked in a flat voice. Was this guy telling the truth or was he a good actor?

Keith swallowed hard. He was blinking as if trying to hold back tears. His thumb jerked toward the wall that separated the family room from the kitchen. They heard the sound of the radio playing soft rock. Paul could hear Elaine open and close a drawer; she was humming to the music. "You won't tell her?" Keith asked in a tight voice.

"Tell her what? No, I won't tell her," Paul added hastily.

"I had quite a few beers that first night in Buffalo. I was bragging about Elaine—what a good job she had, where she worked, even how much she made and about this house.... I should have had my head examined!" Keith looked tortured.

Paul was getting a funny feeling in his stomach. *Oh, God, no!* he thought, holding his breath. "Tell me," he said evenly, encouraging Keith to go on.

Keith couldn't look at Paul. He leaned forward and squeezed the empty aluminum beer can into a bow shape with his hands. "Hawley said—he'd—he'd—"

Paul waited, dreading what he knew would come next.

"—take it out on my sister if I reneged on our bargain, especially since I had half of the money in advance. But he wouldn't let me refuse the money, Paul! Even after I told him I had changed my mind and didn't want the job or the money." Keith's dark eyes were pleading for understanding.

"Take it out on your sister? Exactly what did he mean by that?" Paul's voice mirrored the tension in his body.

"He told me...I'd never see her again. That no one would ever see her again. That she'd end up on the bottom of White River." Keith whispered the words.

Paul's eyes closed. He slumped back against the sofa cushion and let out a hissing sigh. The kid was not only involved in a felony, he had put himself in the position of being his own sister's executioner if he failed to play along with the plotters.

"Hawley also warned me that if I went to the police, Elaine would suffer the consequences." Keith leaned forward, an intent look on his round face. "So you see why I can't let the police get involved in this."

"Elaine is in danger if you involve the police, and she's also in danger if you don't go through with the assassination. The only way she isn't involved is if you murder Garry Channing. That's quite a deal you got yourself into, isn't it?" Paul's voice was low but scathing.

As Keith bent his head, Paul saw the tears rush into his reddened eyes. The kid was mangling the empty beer can with his bare hands, probably wishing it were Hawley's neck.

"Elaine and I have to disappear. Get out of the country where Hawley can't find us. That's the only way out. If you really want to help us, that's the way you can."

"No! You're the only link to Hawley. You are the only one who can squelch this murder plot against Channing and save yourself and Elaine in the process."

"I don't know how." As Keith looked up, Paul noticed a tear roll down the younger man's face. His suffering was genuine, all right.

"Is Hawley the man who wants Garry Channing dead? Or is he the agent for someone else? Did he mention anyone by name?" he asked.

"Is Channing the guy with the ring around him in the photos? Elaine says you interviewed him once."

"Yes."

"Hawley never mentioned him by name. And he never mentioned working for anybody else, but I got the feeling he was just taking orders."

"When is the hit supposed to take place?" Paul would alert police and have them ready, standing by.

"I don't know." Keith looked miserable.

"What?" Paul asked, incredulous. With a sinking feeling, Paul realized that the mastermind behind this plot was no fool.

"Hawley didn't tell me. He just left the rifle and scope and told me to practice with it in the woods. To memorize the guy's face in the photos until I'd recognize him anywhere. I'm supposed to be at the Indianapolis Motor Speedway the first day of qualifications and keep my eyes open. Then Hawley said he'd get in touch with me."

"You don't take the rifle with you to the track on the first day of qualifications?"

Keith was staring at him. "Hell, no. How would I get into the track carrying a rifle?"

Paul felt weak at the prospect. And cheated. Even though Keith was the hit man, he was being apprised of very little. The less he knew, the less he could tell. Paul had very little to go on.

AFTER RETURNING to his apartment that night, Paul made a call to Mick Sturgis, a private investigator in Washington, D.C. he had worked with while digging out facts for his *Sentinel* exposé.

Mick was high priced but worth every dollar.

"Find out everything you can about Elaine Leah Malden and Keith Anthony Malden." Paul gave him the social security numbers he had obtained by going through Elaine's billfold and Keith's wallet. He also supplied him with birth dates, employment information and the names of the Indianapolis schools they had attended. Those they had talked about over dessert.

"Also check the grandparents. Walter Boswell owned Boswell Tool and Die in Columbus, Ohio. He and his wife are deceased. Their daughter, Elizabeth, married Jeffrey Malden, probably in Indianapolis sometime around the mid-1950s. I need this right away, Mick! Get me everything you can on these people." Paul tried to transmit his sense of urgency.

"I'll get right on it, Paul. Call you in a few days. Thanks for the assignment. So long."

Paul hung up with a strange feeling. There were risks in doing a background search on the woman with whom he was in danger of falling in love. What if Mick uncovered some secrets that were better left hidden?

What if there was a link between these secrets and Brett Hawley's hold over Keith? If so, it could cost either Garry Channing's life or Elaine's, depending upon Keith's actions.

Paul Cooper was not about to let either scenario become reality.

CHAPTER SEVEN

ELAINE WAS LOUNGING in a fleecy pink bathrobe while reading the *Indianapolis Sunday Star,* a cup of coffee on the table beside the family-room sofa. She curled her legs beneath her on the comfortable cushion, covering bare feet with the bottom of the robe. Not a sound came from the guest room down the hall where her brother was sleeping. It was ten o'clock and Keith, known to have the appetite of a bear, hadn't emerged from his cave for a hearty breakfast. Was he ill?

The telephone rang. Elaine sprang up to answer it before the sound awakened Keith.

"David made it! I found out Friday when his art teacher called us. Elaine, my son's on top of the world right now!"

Elaine recognized the excited voice of Jan, the trust department's secretary. She and Elaine had been friends for years. Listening to her now, Elaine had to remind herself that this was the same prim, restrained and efficient departmental assistant with whom she worked every day.

"Hi, Jan. David made *what?*"

"He's Best of Show winner in the '500' Festival of the Arts. You know, the art competition that the students of all the schools in Marion County enter in conjunction with the '500' race."

"Oh, yes, I remember. You told me about it."

"His portrait in pastels of his girlfriend, Marla, has been judged the best entry! David's walking on air!

"I just wish his father could have lived to see this day." Her voice was under control now, yet Elaine sensed the sadness in it for the husband who had died ten months ago. Elaine had been the only one in the department in whom Jan had confided her grief.

"Dave would have been proud. Tell David I'm proud of him!"

"The award presentations are this afternoon at the Children's Museum. We wondered...are you booked up this afternoon? Could you come? Your encouragement has meant so much to David. His artwork's given him a purpose since his dad died."

Elaine cleared her throat. The invitation was a total surprise. Paul had mentioned he might be dropping by this afternoon. "Would it be all right if I brought a...friend?" She heard herself almost stammer on the word. A reporter a *friend?* Yet a high-school senior like David might appreciate the presence of another male, especially in the absence of his father. "I'll have to check with him first, though."

"Sure!" Jan's voice brightened. "The high-school presentations are at three-thirty. Why don't we meet under the dinosaur in the courtyard at three-fifteen?"

"If I don't call you back by two-thirty, you'll know the arrangement's okay. Thanks, Jan, for inviting me to share David's big day. See you this afternoon."

"Bye now. Tell your friend he's welcome!" Jan said warmly.

Elaine paused, staring at the receiver still in her hand. She had called Paul Cooper a friend. A man she had met less than a week ago. A man who was the counterpart of Ray Strothers. Someone who held in his hands the power to wipe out all she had worked for these past twelve years.

She called Paul to extend the invitation, trying to sound cool and formal. To her surprise, he accepted.

THE SUN SHONE BRIGHTLY on the last Sunday in April as Elaine and Paul approached the man-made prehistoric creature that faced the entrance to one of the largest museums of its kind in the world.

The tawny monster towered on two rear legs, tiny front legs held close to its body. Elaine gazed in awe at the triangular head with big, pointed teeth gleaming in a malevolent leer. "We're a little early," she said, scanning the crowd. The front of the museum reflected the cheerful day—light blue, green and gold hues framed the massive expanse of glass. A gentle breeze blew. A human river was flowing in through the glass double doors.

Despite her outward calm, Elaine was feeling a bit nervous. This afternoon marked the first time she and Paul had had a formal date, the first time she would present him to one of her friends. She heard Jan's voice from below the stone steps, spotted familiar faces in the crowd and hurried down, Paul close behind her.

David, in his best sport coat and trousers, leather shoes shined to a gleam, opened his arms to embrace Elaine in an awkward gesture. Beside him stood the love of his life, long-haired Marla, dressed in soft pink.

"Mom told me she would help pay my way through art school," he said as he stepped back. His eyes were shining. He positively glowed. Elaine marveled at the transformation in the quiet young man. "I'll be taking a commercial art course starting in the fall. I may go into design later." The public recognition Dave was winning here today seemed to be directing his future.

Elaine introduced Paul to everyone, proud of his well-groomed appearance. He looked decidedly handsome in an understated navy-blue sport coat, striped dress shirt, tan slacks and maroon tie.

They joined the crowd that was quietly streaming through the four double doors and entered a huge lobby five stories high, bathed in natural light. They headed for the wide concrete ramp that wound its way up from the ground floor.

For a two-week period, more than three hundred display boards, some featuring two or three pieces of students' art, would be exhibited on the museum's walls, Jan explained as they headed toward the Lilly Theater.

"500" Festival volunteers seated behind folding tables were checking off lists of names and giving directions to the theater with smiles of welcome. The process of collecting, storing, cataloging, hanging and judging more than nine hundred entries was drawing to a close.

David departed to sit with a student group. Elaine, Paul, Jan and Marla spotted four seats together in the crowded theater and headed toward them. Paul reached for Elaine's arm as they walked down the carpeted steps. The gentle pressure of his hand sent an unwonted thrill rippling up her back. She saw Jan glance back at them with a look of approval. A hint of a smile crept over Jan's face as she moved along the row of cushioned seats.

She's getting the wrong idea. She thinks we're interested in each other, Elaine thought in dismay.

Despite her fears, Paul proved to be a pleasant companion. He was attentive to all three women, displaying a charm that Elaine found disconcerting. He was a good listener, too, speaking occasionally but clearly preferring to wait until Jan asked him direct questions about the magazine. He did not act bored or feign superiority, as Claude had done on various occasions when he had been the only man present.

The "500" Festival art moderator took his place behind the lectern and began to read off names. The presentation that had dramatically changed David's life was beginning.

The queen of the festival and her four princesses stood on the semicircular stage, attired in identical pink dresses, their silky hair crowned with rhinestone tiaras. This "royal family" was kept busy, alternately arranging entries on easels and presenting awards. Student-artists appeared onstage in groups of five, each dressed in his or her Sunday best, faces flushed with excitement. The art teachers and school principals also received awards and plaques.

Elaine gasped when she saw David's portrait of Marla displayed on one of the easels. The soft pastel tones created an ethereal image of her flowing hair and pensive face with its high cheekbones, soft lips opened as if to speak, blue eyes expressive.

That is love personified, Elaine thought, enthralled. She felt a burst of pride in David. The young man had professional ability, but it had taken this special event to bring that talent to the fore.

David beamed when he received the engraved plaque and a huge blue ribbon. His art teacher and school principal stood beside him, looking equally pleased.

Applause swept through the audience and people rose for a standing ovation. David's face flushed with emotion. Elaine knew it was the first public recognition he had received in a quiet life made difficult by the pain of his father's lingering illness.

"It's nice to see kids given a pat on the back for a change," said a woman sitting behind Elaine. "People are sure quick to complain and criticize when kids do something wrong, but we rarely hear much when they do things right! That portrait's good, isn't it?"

"Yes," answered her companion. "And I'm glad the teachers and principals get to shine a bit, too. They put in long hours for the pay they get. This exhibit's been the biggest thing all year for my granddaughter. She's in fourth grade. She didn't win nothin', but they hung her entry. Made the little punkin feel proud. Come on, I'll show it to you. She drew our kittens. In purple crayon. *That*'s creative." The woman giggled as she stepped into the aisle.

David rejoined them outside the auditorium. In a mood to celebrate, the five walked back inside and up the winding carpeted ramp to the fifth floor.

Suddenly Elaine's attention was captured by a familiar sound: the oompah rhythm of a calliope. Paul blinked and his head swung toward the music as his hand lightly grasped Elaine's elbow. "A carousel? Here?" He halted in surprise. They both stared.

Through the archway, hand-carved, turn-of-the-century wooden horses, gazelles and unicorns beckoned to a crowd of children.

"I haven't ridden on a carousel in years!" Elaine exclaimed wistfully as she watched the parade of carved figures slow to a halt.

"It's my treat," Jan declared, still visibly flushed with the excitement of the past hour. She walked to the ticket booth and bought five tickets for the final ride of the day. It was almost closing time.

To Elaine's surprise, Paul was willing. They all scrambled aboard. Elaine mounted a dappled gray mare with a flowing mane, large soulful brown eyes and prancing hooves, sitting sideways in the red wooden saddle.

Paul selected the unicorn beside her, the Peter Pan of the fanciful menagerie, its long legs spread wide in midleap.

Elaine looked around at the sound of a man's voice. "Oh, honey, I'm afraid there isn't room for us. All the animals are taken. We'll come back next Sunday, okay?" A father held his small daughter's hand as she stared wistfully up at the platform. Her disappointment was evident.

"Take this one," Paul offered, sliding off the unicorn.

"Thank you, but...are you sure you don't mind?" The man glanced at Elaine.

"I was saving the unicorn for you," Paul told the delighted child. She pulled on her father's hand, pleading with big dark eyes. He released her with a smile.

Paul lifted the youngster into the unicorn's saddle, and she wrapped her hands tightly around the pole that pierced its body and fixed it to the platform. Paul kept his hand on the child's back to steady her.

The calliope began to sing its raspy organ-grinder's tune. The wooden animals rose and fell and the carousel began its slow rotation. Paul stood motionless between Elaine and the child on the unicorn, one hand still on the youngster's back. As the carousel gathered speed, Elaine felt a warm, firm touch on her own back. Paul's touch.

Elaine's eyes closed and reality shifted focus. She was a child again, trusting in the gentle pressure of her father's hand to keep her safe. She was eight years old again, at a fair in Columbus, Ohio with her parents. Her father stood beside her, close enough for her to feel the warmth of his body, the love in his touch. The trusting child that was buried within Elaine resurfaced, and she suddenly felt buoyant, brimming with life. A long-dormant sense of well-being washed over her for one minute of enchantment.

The carousel began to slow. The calliope's song reached the final wheezing chorus. *Let me help you down,* she heard her father say, and reluctantly opened her eyes. The child within had vanished, like a genie into its bottle. The dappled gray she rode had halted at its highest position. The hand on her back was gone.

Elaine turned her head to watch Paul Cooper lift the child he didn't know from the unicorn's saddle. Gently he lowered her until the tiny feet, clad in white anklets and shiny patent leather shoes, touched the wooden platform. She scampered toward the edge and slid off into the arms of her smiling father, who nodded to Paul as he turned to leave, carrying his daughter in his arms.

For a moment Elaine envied that child.

Paul turned to Elaine. Without a word he opened his arms to her. He clasped her firmly by the waist and lifted her off the red saddle, their bodies brushing as she made the slow descent to the platform. For a moment they stood motionless in a half embrace, relaxed, dreamlike, Elaine's heart racing as she tried to sort out what had just taken place.

"The museum's closing." Paul's voice was husky. "When your eyes were closed, where were you?" he asked gently. His azure eyes held her in their gaze, melting her resistance as his hands spanned the sides of her ribs, his thumbs brushing the lower curve of her breasts.

She couldn't answer, afraid of revealing what she most needed to hide. She gave him what she hoped was a mysterious smile and headed down the ramp. Jan sent her a knowing look, making her want to scream. "I like him!" Jan whispered as she listened to David tell Paul about his project in chemistry class.

They said their farewells outside in the courtyard. Jan, David and Marla headed toward the parking lot. Elaine glanced up at the ankylosaurus as they walked past the place where they had met.

The malevolent full-toothed grin had turned into a mischievous dinosaur smile.

WEDNESDAY WAS ALMOST OVER, and Paul had still heard nothing from Mick Sturgis. That was not a good sign. He sensed that Mick had gotten into something deeper than he had anticipated.

Paul was also meeting renewed resistance from Elaine as they had dinner together at a nearby restaurant. She refused to turn over the evidence Paul needed to show the police. Furthermore, Keith was unwilling to discuss the matter with anyone official. As far as Paul could see, Elaine was making no effort to persuade her brother to change his mind.

It was not to save her own neck, Paul knew. Keith hadn't told her about Hawley's threat. He hadn't wanted to cause her any more pain, and Paul had agreed to keep silent—for now.

She looked beautiful tonight, he thought—composed and self-possessed in a dark business suit and snow-white blouse with a feminine bow. Her musky perfume assaulted his senses. However, her obstinacy remained intact.

"Talk to Mr. Channing first!" Elaine insisted. "After all, Mr. Channing is the one most involved in this situation, isn't he, Paul? Here you sit, the white knight determined to save the man, and he isn't even aware of the danger he's in. Confront him with it! Before you drag in the police. Maybe he'll decide to return to California right away. Then the Indy or state police won't even be involved. After all, it is *his* life in question."

She was too calm, too poised, and that disturbed Paul. He wondered if there was any possibility that she was in on the plot, too; he hoped not, with every fiber of his being. His attraction to her grew stronger each time he was with her, and he was all too aware of her nearness now.

Paul didn't answer her question, diverting his attention to the full coffee cup before him. Was the woman aware of the impact she had on him? he wondered resentfully. She seemed to invite him, yet when he approached, she always drew away.

"Or maybe there's been a threat made against Channing lately and he can put his finger on the person behind Brett Hawley. He could tell the California police." Elaine sounded detached, as if she were outlining some trust arrangement to a client instead of her brother's involvement in a plot against a man's life.

"I can't dispute your logic," Paul answered. But he would have preferred her cooperation in handing over the evidence, as she had agreed to do the night of the storm. Yes, so far, Elaine Malden held the winning hand in this deadly poker game.

"I'll call Channing as soon as he arrives in town. I have an idea where he might be staying," he told her curtly. The prospect of telling Channing about this mess was not a task he looked forward to.

THE NEXT MORNING, Paul called the Indianapolis Motor Speedway Motel, located next to the track on the west side of Indianapolis. Since Paul knew the manager there, he felt a discreet inquiry would not be out of line. He learned that Mr. and Mrs. Channing did have reservations there and would be arriving on Friday.

At five o'clock on Friday morning, Paul followed Ben's advice about banishing tension and ran ten miles instead of five. For at least the next hour he sat at his desk, physically drained, while Ben smirked.

At five-thirty the front door clicked shut behind Mary and the office was silent. With a cup of freshly brewed coffee to bolster his courage, Paul once again dialed the number of the Speedway Motel. "Have Garry and Mrs. Channing checked in yet?" he asked the desk clerk.

"Just a moment. Let me check." After a moment's pause, the clerk replied, "Yes. Mr. Channing is here. They arrived about an hour ago."

"Ring his room for me, please."

He heard the telltale pulsing buzz. Then a familiar male voice answered. It was warm yet vigorous, marked by a Western accent.

"Hello? This is Channing speaking."

"Paul Cooper here, Garry. The *Wall Street Sentinel,* remember? We haven't seen each other in a while. You let me interview you at a conference two years ago."

"Hey, Paul…you ole son of a gun! You in Indy for the race, too? Or are you covering it for the newspaper? I've got a good car this year. Also a new driver." He mentioned a name Paul recognized.

"Actually, I resigned from the newspaper more than a year ago. Some things went sour for me in

Washington A personal matter. But I grew up here in Indy, and I've got my own business magazine now.''

"You don't say! I knew you were too good to remain in anyone's corral for long—I suspected you'd break out for a place of your own. Glad to hear it!

"Laura and I just flew into Indy with a good friend of mine, Alex Rande, on his company jet." He chuckled. "I can't afford one of them things yet. Laura and I rode like royalty."

Paul had never met Alex Rande, the CEO of BMQ/OXO Corporation, a conglomerate, but knew he headed a half-dozen companies that were all under one corporate umbrella, some obtained through unfriendly takeovers. What Rande wanted, he took, and he had the reputation of being a master of intimidation.

Alex Rande also kept a very low profile, despite his wealth and power. He rarely granted interviews to business magazines and never to the popular ones. He had twice refused a request from the *Sentinel*. And despite a divorce three years ago, Rande also managed to keep his personal life out of the limelight. There had been no settlement fight, and his ex-wife had simply faded from sight.

It was rumored that Rande had been recommended for a cabinet post under the previous administration, but that he had refused, earning a reputation as something of a corporate mystery man.

Garry is running in high-powered circles, thought Paul.

"Let's get together for a drink in the next few days and catch up on things," Channing was suggesting, drawing him back to the reason for his call.

Paul took a deep breath. "I need to see you as soon as possible, Garry. I have to talk with you. Alone."

"Have you picked up on something concerning Todd?" Channing sounded tense.

"Nothing to do with your son. At least, I don't think so."

"How's your golf?" The relief in the older man's voice was noticeable.

"Tolerable," Paul answered, "but this is too serious a subject to work in between drives and putts, Garry. I need your undivided attention."

"They've got the sweetest course here at the motel. If you meet me in the lobby at six-thirty this evening, you and I'll go out in a golf cart, just the two of us. Will that be private enough for you? I'll put my clubs in the back to make it look good."

"Sounds great. Do me one favor. Please!"

"What, Paul?"

"Don't tell your wife you're meeting me. Don't tell Alex Rande. Don't tell anyone! It's important!"

"Jeez, Paul. That won't be easy. What's going on?"

DUSK WAS SETTLING around them as Garry Channing drove the white golf cart over the lush, manicured grass of the motel course. Clusters of golfers were gathered here and there, but a general feeling of stillness prevailed.

The soft hum of the golf cart's motor even drowned the traffic noise from nearby West 16th Street. As Paul told his story, the golf cart suddenly lurched to the left, narrowly missing one of the trees beside the fairway. His terse recitation of the murder plot had obviously caught Garry Channing by surprise. The entrepreneur brought the vehicle to a halt.

"Maybe this young fella is plain nuts. Maybe he made up the whole story and deserves to be put away."

Paul shook his head. "I've seen the magazines that ran the ads and the enlarged glossies of you and your wife. This man Brett Hawley—or someone else—circled you in each photo. Hawley never even mentioned you by name to Keith. Apparently it's meant to happen in some public place and they wanted Keith to be able to identify you easily. I've also seen the rifle and scope they want him to use and the cash advance—"

"How much money to 'ice' me?" Channing interrupted.

Paul found it difficult to go on. "Twenty thousand—ten thousand in advance, ten thousand upon . . . completion of services."

"That's all I'm worth?" asked Channing. He looked angry. "Cheap bastard! The patent I hold on my new concept for an improved polymer battery ought to be worth *millions* in royalties when it goes into production." Channing started up the golf cart again as he regained control of himself.

"Now that you know, what are your plans?" asked Paul.

The cart stopped. "Like what?"

"Like...getting the hell out of Indianapolis! To-night. You could make up some excuse and book a flight back to California right away." Paul stared at the expressionless tanned face behind the steering wheel.

"Turn tail and run? Is that what you're advising?" Channing asked with scorn. "And how will that change anything? Instead of going after me here, they'll go after me out there. Or in New York City on a business trip. Or Dallas. Or Phoenix. Running rarely solves anything, Paul. You gotta turn round and face 'em. Meet 'em head-on."

A long sigh escaped Paul. This was the answer he had expected. Garry Channing was not easily intimidated.

"Then do you mind if I call the police in on it?"

"Sure. The more the merrier," answered Channing. "I have to be trackside to supervise the new car when it's being tested, though. This time we've come up with a winner, Paul. I feel it in my gut."

He's more concerned about the car, thought Paul, amazed. "Who would benefit from wiping you out?" he asked abruptly. "Give that some long, hard thought while I make calls to set up a meeting with a committee of police. Be prepared for some personal questions, too."

"Like what?" The golf cart started up again, moving slowly.

"Like...did you require Laura to sign a prenuptial agreement before you married her? Does she inherit everything in the event of your death?"

The golf cart halted abruptly, almost unseating Paul. He grabbed hold of the frame in time to prevent himself from tumbling onto the grass.

"How dare you! I trust my wife completely. We think she's finally pregnant. We're going to have a child of our own. Did my ex-wife hire you to stir up trouble?"

"Then things between Marian and you are... strained?" At last Paul had a nibble on his hook. He planned to yank hard on the line.

"She hates my guts. I can't say I blame her. To ask Marian for a divorce after we'd been married twenty-three years because I'd fallen in love with a younger woman, well, it was hard on her. She got a good settlement, though. Half of everything, straight down the line. But...we both still live in L.A. It's not that big when we both move in the same social circles."

"And your son—did he side with his mother? Did you lose your son due to the divorce?"

"Todd is twenty-four now. All he has on his mind is women, Porsches and gambling in Las Vegas. He's in deep to loan sharks for gambling debts." Channing's sorrow was revealed on his open face. "He hit me up for money innumerable times. Never paid it back, of course. So I turned off the tap. He's still in my will, though. He's my own flesh and blood, after all."

"How much does he get?" Paul probed.

Channing flashed Paul a look of irritation. "You reporters never know when to quit, do you?"

"Everything you say to me is confidential, Garry. Off the record. Privileged communication. I'll be your link to the police. I just want to prepare you for the kind of questions they might ask."

"Todd will get three million dollars when I die."

Paul inhaled deeply. "Does his mother know this?"

"Sure. It was one of the terms of our divorce. She didn't want Todd done out of his inheritance." He steered the cart toward the fence, where its counterparts were sitting like a flock of white swans in repose.

"Look, Paul, I know where you're heading with these questions. I fired my comptroller in the auto parts company. He'd been dipping into the till and making the accounting records look good. An auditor caught it about six months ago, so I canned him—the comptroller, not the auditor. When a man's been working for me for sixteen years and I trust him, and he pulls shit like that, I lose pity for him. He'd probably like to see me drop in my tracks, too. I refused to give him a recommendation when a prospective employer called. I don't think he's been able to get a job.

So there are a few people who don't exactly wish me well. But leave Laura out of it."

The cart swung into formation beside the others. Channing hopped out and hefted his bag of clubs, slinging it over his shoulder.

They stared at each other. The tanned, lined face relaxed. Channing hit Paul's forearm lightly, in a good-natured way.

"I'll keep my mouth shut about all this. It'll be the first big secret I've kept from Laura. Won't be easy. I don't want to upset her if she really is pregnant this time. As for Alex—this is none of his business. Come into the Flag Room with me. I'll buy you a drink. Maybe Rick or Poncho or A.J. will drop in to catch up on the news. I'll introduce you around."

CHAPTER EIGHT

THE CALL FROM MICK STURGIS came Friday night after ten. Paul had been home about an hour after leaving Garry Channing in the Flag Room.

"Elizabeth and Jeffrey Malden did not apply for a marriage license around 1953-54, as you thought, Paul. It was in October 1971."

"What?"

"Jeffrey Malden is the stepfather, not the natural father. He must have adopted both of Elizabeth's children and had new birth certificates issued.

"The last name listed for Elizabeth on the marriage license application was Stamm. She also owned a car with an Ohio registration. It was in the names of Elizabeth and George Stamm.

"I tracked Elizabeth down to Marvella, Ohio, a town of about twelve thousand. It was a piece of cake from there on. Birth records on an Elaine Leah and a Keith Anthony—same birth dates you gave me—show a last name of Stamm. A marriage license was issued to George Stamm and Elizabeth Boswell in 1954. Elizabeth divorced George in Indianapolis in 1971. That's public record, too."

"Why did she divorce him?" Paul asked, feeling a tightness in his chest. Had Elaine been sexually abused as a child, after all?

"Desertion. He also committed a felony for which he was never arrested. They didn't catch him. Stamm robbed the Savings and Loan of two hundred thousand dollars. A good hunk of cash back in 1970."

Paul gasped. "Armed robbery?"

"Actually, Paul, it was an inside job. He didn't have a gun. George Stamm was assistant manager of Marvella's Savings and Loan. He knew everybody in town. Everybody liked and trusted him. He wasn't the kind one would expect to pull such a stunt. It shocked everybody. Left hard feelings."

"Give me the facts, Mick, not an editorial," Paul told him curtly. Mick was efficient in his work, but he wandered off track sometimes.

"In March 1970, on a Friday afternoon, Stamm walked out with money from the vault in two suitcases. The manager was on a two-week vacation, so Stamm had taken over for him. Stamm had access to the vault as a part of his job. He walked in with the suitcases that morning. He told fellow employees that he and the missus had had a tiff and she had ordered him out of the house, so he planned to check into a motel until she cooled off. Everyone bought the story, and no one wondered why he put the suitcases in his office instead of leaving them in his car. It was a busy day. Friday was payday at the two largest factories in town. People came in to cash checks. That was why there was so much cash in the vault.

"When Stamm left in his car for lunch, no one thought anything of it. But he never came back."

Paul sucked in his breath, making mental calculations. 1970. Elaine was fourteen at the time. Keith, two.

Paul was also making quick notes on the lined pad in his own style of shorthand. "Okay. Go on. Sorry if I was a bit short with you a minute ago."

"Yeah, Paul, you did sound upset. I figured there was a good reason," Mick responded carefully.

"Elizabeth, the wife, came under suspicion, of course. She denied her husband's story. Claimed there hadn't been a fight, that she hadn't kicked him out. She swore she didn't know the guy had planned the heist or where he was hiding out. The Marvella police chief was trying to charge her as an accomplice, but there was insufficient evidence. A police officer let me take a quick peek at the case file. The wife passed a polygraph test, but the newspaper articles failed to mention that little fact." Mick's tone bore more than a trace of sarcasm.

"Newspaper articles?" echoed Paul.

"Spread all over the front page of the town's only paper. *Ten days in a row.* I doubt the Kennedy assassination got that much space in this burg. The articles were written by a staff reporter named Ray Strothers. I dug them out from the paper's microfilm records. I'll send you copies. Very interesting, Paul.''

"Why?''

"Not the kind of stuff you write. Your stuff is *dry* by comparison—no offense intended! Strothers goes for melodrama, not facts, and passes it off as human interest, but it's more like a soap opera.''

A wave of irritation washed over Paul. Mick was no journalism critic. "Give me specifics, not generalities,'' he said tersely.

"I wish it were that easy, but Strothers produced more hearsay and rumor than fact. Most of the people he interviewed were just depositors blowing off steam about being ripped off. And what do you know...?''

Paul knew Mick loved a good story and was playing this to the hilt, but he wanted to hit him.

"Just get on with it!''

"It got Strothers promoted to managing editor of the paper two months later. He held the job for seventeen years—until his death three years ago. If he'd still been alive, I doubt the staff would have been as helpful as they were. One thing is certain, though. Community feeling sure got whipped up. It must have been *hell* for the mother and kids.''

"In what way, Mick?''

"I'll send you the stuff. Read it for yourself,'' Mick replied gruffly. "The wife and kids left for Indy in October 1970. A neighbor told me the wife landed a job there through an ad in the Columbus newspaper.

The police had nothing on which to hold her and they had to let her go.

"After Elizabeth's divorce was granted in Indianapolis and she'd married Jeffrey Malden, George Stamm's missing car was found in the Ohio River near Cincinnati, when a police diver was searching for the body of a drowned child. Stamm's body was never recovered. Nor the money. There was reasonable doubt he was still alive. Soon afterward, Jeffrey Malden in Indianapolis adopted Elizabeth's children, giving them his last name. The paperwork on this was completed in 1972.

"The Marvella police department thinks George Stamm got by with a fast one. They don't think he's dead, so I went to Detroit to see what else I could find out."

"How does Detroit figure into it?" asked Paul.

"Detroit's where George Stamm's aunt Bertha lives in a nursing home." Mick gave a throaty chuckle. "Boy, is Bertie something! Two FBI agents never got a word out of her as to her nephew's whereabouts. She played the deaf and dumb routine until they gave it up."

"Someone there in Marvella told you about Stamm's aunt?" Paul asked.

"Yeah. Someone she used to send Christmas cards to. I tracked her down to the nursing home. I heard she and the nephew were close at one time, so I figured she might know where he hid out—and if he was really dead."

Paul felt a tightening in his throat. There was something ironic in Mick's tone of voice. "He's alive?"

"You got it, Paul." Mick couldn't quite conceal his triumph in succeeding where the FBI had failed. "Alive and well in Seattle. The aunt said he's going under the name of Will Stinson. He married again fourteen years ago. Has two sons, twelve and eight. She gave me the address."

A hiss of astonishment escaped Paul's lips. Mick had certainly earned his fee.

"He's also crippled. Needs a wheelchair. He was in an accident a couple of years ago. Became a local hero. Saved a three-year-old kid who had run into the street after a ball. He jumped in front of a truck and pushed the kid out of the way in time. He got it in the legs."

"He can still stand trial for what he did," Paul declared grimly.

"The guy had a heart attack last year, Paul. The aunt's worried about him. The stress of a trial could finish him off. How would justice be served by that?"

"How does his family get by?" asked Paul.

"They have a business of their own. Shortly after he and his wife, Ada, got married, they bought a franchise. A fast-food restaurant. It's doing okay, according to the aunt."

"That's where the money went," Paul mused aloud. So what should he do with this information?

"Good job, Mick." It was more than Paul had bargained for. "Send me everything you've got. Plus a detailed written report. And your statement of services, of course, with a list of expenses. But tell me, Mick. I'm curious. How did you ever get the aunt to open up to you when FBI agents couldn't?"

Mick chuckled. "First of all, I'm not a cop. She sees me as another Jim Rockford—remember the TV series that featured James Garner? She told me she always watched it. Said I reminded her of Garner."

"You don't resemble him at all," Paul protested. Mick was short, wiry and wore glasses. "If you look like James Garner, then so do I!"

"Thanks, buddy! The dear little lady was real good for my ego, okay? But the real bond between us— you'll never believe this! We're both Cincinnati Reds fans. She's even got all the baseball cards. She let me have six spares to complete my collection. Now that's a lady with heart!"

ELAINE WAS GLAD she had showered and dressed early when she glimpsed the LeBaron pulling into the driveway on Saturday morning. Paul was ten minutes ahead of time.

Keith beat a hasty retreat to his room, closing the door. It was obvious he was reluctant to face the reporter again. When Elaine had told her brother that she was accompanying Paul to the opening day ceremonies at the speedway, Keith acted as though she had betrayed him. He had moped about the house, spilling his coffee and looking depressed.

"Don't worry. We're not bringing the police into this," she reassured him firmly. The look Keith gave her was one of disbelief.

"Why go? You don't even like this guy. Or do you?" The blunt question brought a warm flush to Elaine's cheeks.

I have to see Garry Channing. She couldn't put her thought into words. She didn't want to cause Keith any more pain or embarrassment. When the bell rang, she hurried to the front door and arranged her face in a careful smile.

The man on the threshold was dressed more casually than Elaine had seen him before, in chino trousers and a reddish-brown cashmere sweater with a round neckline from which peeked the collar of a blue shirt that intensified the blue of his deep-set eyes. Press credentials hung from the leather belt at his waist. His pleasant features seemed sharper in the harsh light of approaching noon.

Elaine wondered if he could see the appreciation in her eyes and looked away as she saw Paul begin his own assessment. She had taken pains with her appearance, pulling back her long chestnut hair with a flowered scarf, and coloring her lips a soft shade of coral. Her outfit consisted of a white long-sleeved sweater and full black jersey skirt.

But all he said was, "You'd better change shoes," letting his eyes linger on her stylish leather pumps. "I can't promise to-the-gate delivery service. Peak season at the track starts today. Be prepared to walk!''

Embarrassed, Elaine went to her bedroom and returned wearing walking shoes.

Paul gave her a smile of approval.

''Would lunch at a fast-food restaurant be all right? There isn't much time. We need to arrive at the track in time for me to get my camera set up before the mayor's opening speech,'' he told her. He sounded pleasant but distant, and seemed to be looking over her shoulder. Wondering where Keith was, no doubt. He looked disappointed.

''Fine with me.''

He raised one arm and touched the sleeve of her sweater with his thumb and index finger. ''That's attractive but maybe a bit too light for the first Saturday in May. It's cooler than it looks. Windy, too. Better take along a jacket.''

Elaine followed his advice and went to her bedroom for a sweater and beret. She knocked lightly on Keith's closed door. ''We're leaving now, hon,'' she said.

Keith didn't answer.

They exchanged few words on the trip to McDonald's. Paul's manner was withdrawn, his attractive features almost stern, yet they eased into a gentle smile and attention whenever Elaine spoke to him. He was equally quiet as they made their way to the track. He drove the LeBaron into the grassy parking area behind the Tower Terrace extension, and they headed for their seats.

Paul's press badge got them a choice spot next to the concrete wall that bounded the pit area, off-limits to the rest of the crowd. Elaine found herself close to a black-and-white checkered platform. "On race day the winning car sits there and gets lifted into the air," Paul told her. "The crowd goes crazy!" He was showing signs of "500" fever himself, Elaine noted.

The platform was already occupied by the mayor and "500" race officials, including the veteran race driver who would drive the pace car to lead the starting lineup. The festival queen and her court of four brightened the group, and grandstand seats on either side of the tower were packed with spectators. The mayor stood up and congratulated the weatherman on a sunny, if gusty, day.

Paul lifted his hand to wave at a man who returned his salute. Elaine craned her neck to see. She recognized the tanned, craggy face of the man in Keith's photographs. Beside him was the woman in the pool photo, wearing a chic cashmere suit with pumps to match. Her long hair was blowing in the cool breeze. Laura Channing was even more attractive in person, Elaine decided.

Elaine recognized a third face too. This man had black hair streaked heavily with gray, a long, thin nose with flaring nostrils, and lips with an arrogant tilt at the corners. He was dressed in California-casual style—a light-colored sport coat, turtleneck pullover and dark trousers. His hands were shoved into his pants pockets in an effort to keep warm.

"Who's the man standing next to Mrs. Channing?" she asked, pulling on Paul's arm to get his attention after a flurry of clicking shutters.

"Alex Rande, CEO of BMQ/OXO Corporation," Paul answered. "Garry introduced me to him in the Flag Room the night we met at the golf course."

"The conglomerate?" Elaine's eyebrows rose. She was impressed, wishing she could land *him* as a trust department client.

Paul nodded. Elaine returned her attention to the three people beside the platform. She noted that Alex Rande was standing next to Laura Channing, so close, in fact, that their arms seemed to be touching.

"Where's Mrs. Rande?" she inquired.

"How should I know?" Paul grunted. "He's divorced." He moved closer to click off several more shots.

Twenty-nine festival princesses lined the wall in front of the tower, forming a living ribbon of scarlet and white. The crowd packed into the seats on the grandstand took as active a part in the track's opening as the multitude of racing personnel, city dignitaries, track officials and members of the press in front of the pit wall. The air was electric as the speeches concluded, and anticipation escalated.

Paul took Elaine's arm and guided her over to the Channings and Rande. Elaine saw Garry Channing start when he heard her last name, but he quickly regained his composure. Had Paul mentioned Keith's name to him when they had discussed the plot? she wondered. His companions apparently hadn't noticed his momentary lapse, and exchanged cordial smiles.

"I suggest you import a new weatherman from Florida," said Rande in a deep voice that sent a thrill skittering up Elaine's spine. The man was dynamic. He emanated raw energy. She wondered about the reason for his divorce. Another woman, no doubt.

"Usually the first week in May is sunny and balmy here. This is *not* typical," Paul assured Rande as a cloud passed over the sun. "Why don't you all come with me into the press room in the tower? We'll warm up over coffee." He looked at Elaine and again took her arm.

So Elaine spent the next thirty minutes rubbing elbows with some of the greats of the racing world. It was a half hour she would never forget.

PAUL WANTED to drop off his equipment and rolls of film at his office. "Do you mind?" he asked Elaine.

What could she say? She needed a ride home.

Seeing the place that was so important to Paul was a revelation. It had a wood-paneled warmth that was neither stuffy nor pretentious; original watercolors lined the walls. "I bought them when I was on assignment in Paris," Paul told her when she praised them.

His desk was clear. Nothing in the suite of rooms was out of place, Elaine noted with approval. This office was his world—she knew it reflected him. Casual and relaxed on the surface, yet teeming with energy and drive underneath.

The walls of Paul's private office also bore numerous photographs. There were several of his parents—both smiling, attractive people—but most were of friends he had made on his trips to New York, Paris, Bonn and Rome. The remainder showed the magazine's staff, often with spouses and kids. They seemed like members of a large family, and she sensed that in a way they truly were.

A feeling of intimacy began to grow between them as he showed her through the remaining rooms. It was becoming clear to her that Paul Cooper was a caring human being.

"Want to see our caffeine-dispensing center?" Paul asked. "It's the command post of this disorganized operation."

She walked with him to the kitchenette lounge, which was located next to the small rest room and bore the sign Comfort Station. They talked over fresh coffee and nibbled at a pair of leftover doughnuts.

Golden rays of late-afternoon sun slipped through a half-drawn miniblind that covered the narrow window of the lounge. Elaine sensed Paul's tension as he abruptly lapsed into silence, sipping his coffee. Suddenly she was fourteen again, powerless to change the course of events, blamed by all who knew her for being the child of her father. Guilt was consuming her again as the silence lengthened, and she had to look away. Was it blame she was seeing on Paul's face, too?

"What's the matter, Paul? Are you thinking that I share Keith's responsibility for this mess involving your friend Channing? I'm sorry it happened. I would have done... *anything* to stop it. I must have failed Keith somehow, or he would never have—"

He looked up quickly, his eyes strikingly blue behind the dark frames of the glasses. He took her hand firmly.

"No, I don't blame you, Elaine! For anything! Anything, do you understand?" His tone was strange. His manner had been a bit unusual all day, Elaine reflected. At the track, Paul had acted protectively, as if shielding her from Channing's crowd. He looked down at the table. "If all this hadn't happened, we wouldn't be sitting together here now, would we? I have Keith to thank for this."

Elaine could feel the tension mounting between them. She was beginning to understand what she was feeling, and wasn't sure how to handle it. Escape had always worked for her before. Except for that one time, of course.... Then she hadn't been able to run fast enough, to scream loud enough, to fight....

Why do I have to be attracted to this man? She stood up in panic, pulled free from his hand and tried to distract herself by washing the cups and plates at the tiny sink and returning them to the cupboard shelf. Order. Everything in life depended on order.

Paul was watching her, she knew. "I was proud of you today. Proud you were with me." Again the haunting voice was sending shivers down her spine.

"I have to leave," she said in confusion. "I can take a cab home." She turned to pick up her shoulder bag and, from the corner of her eye, saw Paul rise from his chair.

Without warning he stepped close, drew her unexpectedly into his arms and kissed her firmly, yet it was a gentle kiss that asked nothing from her in return. Before she had time to react, his kiss deepened, lingered dangerously, then was briefly interrupted to allow her breath. As she gazed wonderingly into his eyes, Paul's arms surged around her once more, holding her close against his hard, masculine body. Very close.

Elaine couldn't help but respond. She found herself kissing him back, aware that her insides were churning, that her runaway heartbeat was pulsing in her ears, that her arms were around his waist. How had they gotten there? She felt dazed and confused.

His voice seemed to come from far away. "Let's have dinner at my place. I'll cook steaks and put some potatoes into the microwave. You can take charge of the salad. If you want to, that is." He looked at her closely as he released her and retreated a step. "My latest toy is an espresso/cappuccino machine. I'm dying to show it off. Want to help me figure out how to use it?'' His tone was persuasive; his compelling eyes were smiling.

On her tour of his world, Elaine had collected tiny fragments of this intriguing man and realized now that she wanted to discover more. She let out her breath slowly, struggling to conceal her lightheadedness, and raised a hand to her swollen lips.

"I don't think you need my help to figure out anything. But I would like to hear more about Ben and Mary and the rest of your staff. And Paris.''

"Is that a yes?'' Paul asked with a smile.

"Y-yes. I accept your dinner invitation. Thank you.'' Her words were marked by an aloofness she was far from feeling. Thank goodness he couldn't detect the rapid beating of her heart!

As soon as they entered Paul's apartment in the Saint Andrew's district, Paul told Elaine what he had to do.

With a sinking heart, Elaine assembled salad ingredients on a corner of the kitchen counter while Paul dialed the private number of a state police detective, James Dickerson, a man whose name was given to him by an official at the capitol.

She and Paul had argued throughout the drive from his office about calling in the police. Paul had been adamant, although he seemed saddened by what he had to do. He had informed Elaine of Channing's decision. Since the man refused to turn tail and run,

Elaine had acknowledged the seriousness of the situation.

Yes, Paul was right. Garry Channing had to be protected and the person behind the plot caught. After meeting the Channings this morning, Elaine could no longer view the situation in the abstract. Garry was all too real, and his life was in danger. She went through motions of tearing lettuce for the salad, while she listened with tears in her eyes. Tears for Keith. For herself. Would her brother be sent to jail? If so, his own decision was responsible for his downfall. Keith was following in their father's footsteps.

"Jim? Fred gave me your number. This is Paul Cooper, editor of the *Hoosier Entrepreneur*.... Good! I'm glad Fred briefed you on the matter. I talked with Garry Channing again on Wednesday evening. He's willing to meet with you whenever you say. He'd prefer the middle of next week. That's practice week at the track. Next Saturday is the first day of qualifications, as you know.... Yes, I'll bring the young man involved. His name is Keith Malden.... No, Jim, don't worry. Keith won't skip town."

Elaine felt his gaze fasten on her. The intensity of that look reminded her of her desperate threat to help Keith flee the country.

"Where would be best to hold the meeting? It should be a central location, someplace Channing can easily get to...."

At last Elaine saw something constructive she could contribute to help resolve this unholy mess. "Why not

Commercial Bank's VIP hospitality suite at the track?'' she volunteered. The suite looked out over the fourth turn and the entrance to the pits. The secluded area adjoined the grandstands inside the track boundaries, and would be convenient for Channing, who was staying at the motel next door.

Paul placed his hand over the mouthpiece. He looked pleased by her offer. ''Can you arrange it?''

''I'll give you the key. I'm supposed to be a hostess during the first day of qualifications,'' she said. ''I trust you and the police will take good care of the room.''

''How about Commercial Bank's VIP suite?'' Paul said into the phone. ''Call me, either at home or at the office, when you get everything set up.'' Paul recited both phone numbers. He looked up again, a guarded expression in his eyes. ''He wants your phone number and the address, because Keith is staying with you.''

Fear gripped Elaine's stomach. She had been afraid of police since she was fourteen. If the facts about her father came out now, she knew she would lose her job. She had failed to make full disclosure of a parent's criminal history at the time of her employment application. With such a background, what bank would trust her?

Elaine shrugged as though Paul's request meant nothing. ''Tell him.'' The nightmare was starting again. But if Paul suspected anything, he hadn't let on. Surely he would have mentioned it by now? She couldn't let her guard down, though. He was a very perceptive man. And he had won. At every turn, Paul Cooper had won. Now she was here. In his apartment. Why had she come?

I wanted to. Radish slices fell blood red from the knife to the chopping block as Elaine felt her face flush warm.

CHAPTER NINE

IN SPITE OF EVERYTHING, dinner was a success. They sat at the Danish-style table in the dining area near the kitchen. Since Elaine had without thinking slipped off her shoes at the front door, Paul had taken his shoes off, too. They had worked together in the compact white kitchen, creating their concept of the easy dream dinner.

The steaks had been done to perfection, medium rare, the potatoes were moist, the corn juicy, succulent and dripping with butter. Dessert consisted of chocolate fudge brownies Elaine had discovered in the cupboard and espresso coffee in tiny cups. It was the first time she had tasted the rich, concentrated brew. She decided she liked it.

Elaine gazed the length of the dimly lighted living room and out through the glass balcony doors. The lake below was a sparkling sheet of reddish orange, caught in the spell of the setting sun. She sat, relaxed and still, drained of all emotion since Paul had called the state police investigator.

The Gershwin and Sinatra selections he had chosen to play while they enjoyed dinner were over, but the silence between them was a comfortable one. There was no need for idle words.

Elaine was the one who broke the silence. "Thank you for taking me to the track today and introducing me to the Channings. I realize how selfish I've been. All I've been able to think about was Keith...myself, too..." she stammered, looking away from the compassionate blue eyes he'd fastened on her. "I never gave a thought to the intended victim. Garry seems like a wonderful man. Why would anyone want to see him dead? Who could want such a terrible thing?" She shivered, clasping her hands tightly in her lap.

Paul grunted. The stern look returned to his face. "I don't know—yet. Someone who doesn't see Garry as a fellow human being, obviously. Unfortunately, innocent victims of crimes are at the bottom of the legal totem pole these days. It's the criminals who get the media spotlight. We have our priorities reversed," he said.

"I'm trying to figure out how to tell Keith about next week's meeting with the police." Despite her efforts to remain calm, Elaine heard her voice tremble. "What if he refuses to cooperate?" She looked up at Paul's face in appeal.

"Talk him into it!" Paul's voice was calm, but Elaine could tell what lay beneath his outward composure. She was beginning to understand him. The muscle in his jaw was working, and he had thrust his hands into his pants pockets. "Keith has to take the responsibility for his own actions. He got himself into this situation and dragged *you* into it at the same time.''

Elaine felt a chill steal through her as she heard his challenge. ''Keith doesn't always listen to me. I was the one who wanted him to run away to hide in Canada, remember?'' A wry smile escaped her, but she knew there was no humor in it.

''Do you want *me* to talk to Keith when I take you home?''

''If you want to, it's all right with me.''

Elaine drank in the sight of him. He looked assertive, capable, confident. She really believed Paul Cooper could handle anyone, any situation, no matter how tough. Even her brother.

''I've enjoyed being with you today,'' she confessed, looking down at her hands again. ''I hate to leave,'' she murmured, an ache in her throat because the words were true.

Paul dropped to a crouch in front of her. He covered both of her hands with his and held on firmly. ''Then don't leave. Stay. Spend the night with me.''

She gasped and lifted her eyes to stare at him. The blue eyes challenged her, locking with hers, catching and holding her until she felt herself unable to break away. Their intensity almost made her panic. Then the sensation of the pressure of his lips on hers in his office returned in a memory so intense, she felt a stirring deep within her. But with that stirring came a residue of fear, a memory of another evening long ago. Once more she was fourteen, helpless and vulnerable, unable to defend herself against three older boys bent on revenge.

Elaine closed her eyes, trying to blot out the images. A chill stole over her and she tried to stop herself trembling. She pulled her gaze from Paul's and stared at her entrapped hands. As if he understood, he relaxed the pressure. Unlike them, he'd never force her. But then, Paul was unlike anyone else. Period.

Thank God! Her heart was racing, but not from fear, she realized in wonder.

"I'll clean up before we leave," she said, rising and feeling a bit unsteady on her legs.

"I can do that," Paul objected. "I do it for myself all the time. You're my guest."

"You fed me. You furnished the food. Let me do my part, okay?" Elaine stacked the earthenware dishes carefully and carried them into the kitchen, rinsing plates, cups and utensils under the stream of running water from the faucet.

"Load the dishwasher," Paul called from the living room. "No hand washing allowed in this place."

"No argument there!" she called back in a lighthearted tone.

A delightful swirl of violins and cellos stole softly into the kitchen as she loaded the dishwasher. "What is it?" Elaine asked, intrigued by the pleasurable sound.

"Ravel. Ballet music. *Ma mère l'Oye.*" The French words rolled comfortably off his tongue.

The sprightly prelude that followed added a note of gaiety. She risked a long look at him from the doorway of the kitchen. He stood outlined by the dark red skyline beyond the balcony doors. The sight brought a bittersweet ache.

Thoughts swirled around her like specters as the music penetrated her consciousness. The tempo had slowed, and her body responded to the languid rhythm. *The best years of my life are slipping away. Will I ever experience sexual love?* All she had to show for her life was a career, one that this man would be able to take away from her. A short article about her father in his magazine would do the trick.

"I'll call Keith now and tell him I'll be home soon." Elaine knew she had to try to hold her own against this man. "How long will the trip take if we start now? An hour?" she inquired, trying to force Paul's hand.

Paul just stood there, hands in his trouser pockets, looking at her with an unfathomable expression.

The dreamy music was affecting Elaine, filling her with unfamiliar sensations. Or was it Paul himself?

As if sensing her mood, Paul pulled his hands from his pockets and held them toward her. "Dance with me!"

"To that?" she gasped. The man must be crazy. "That's ballet music. I'd be all over your feet. I'm no Pavlova!"

He didn't move, but his serious expression melted into an open smile. "Don't underestimate yourself,"

he said in his husky baritone. "You *do* underestimate yourself, you know that? Stop being afraid of
me, Elaine. You're a woman of courage," he said
softly.

She knew that once again he was winning. And her
body was betraying her, flooding her with the tingling warmth of feelings she had suppressed until
now. Elaine knew she had met her Waterloo.

As if drawn by an irresistible force, she moved
across the room toward him.

He took her wrists and drew her arms gently
around his neck. "Just hold on. I'll do the work," he
said softly, a tender smile on his lips and a glow in the
blue depths of his eyes.

She laughed. It felt good to laugh. "You mean
you'll do the leading," she teased.

"Right." His smile broadened. Both his arms
slipped around her back. "Just relax. Don't think
about your feet. Move with my body. Concentrate on
my face." He gazed down at her as he began a slow
swaying, focusing on her eyes, her lips, her hair.
Elaine felt herself doing the same, blending with the
sensuous rhythm of the music, laughing self-
consciously at the pleasing movement. He began to
lead her in slow circles, almost as if he were waltzing.

The steps proved so natural that her body moved
as one with his. She was floating as the slow, yearning whispers of the strings grew dreamlike. The slim
buffer of space between them disappeared. Paul's
strong arms were slowly drawing her closer to his

body, and she could feel the muscles in his thighs and abdomen as their stockinged feet formed languorous patterns in the plush pile carpeting.

His warm breath was fanning her face, and she felt herself relaxing against him. Her arms tightened around his neck as her movements blended with his. His lips were so near, she yearned to make contact with them. She yielded to the impulse, lifting her head just enough to press her lips against his jaw.

The arms around her tightened perceptibly, and her breasts pressed upward against the pressure of his chest. Slow circles suddenly grew quicker. Elaine found herself clinging to him, her breath coming in shallow gasps. Her lips once again lightly brushed the side of his face.

She was light-headed from the repeated swirling movements; she felt almost drunk—drunk on Paul Cooper. The realization was just beginning to sink in. He was completely in control and she loved it.

All motion ceased as a fanfare sounded, a sparkling crackle of brass. Motionless, their bodies pressed together, snug in the warm haven of each other's arms, Elaine felt Paul's lips on hers, first gently, then, as her lips relaxed and parted, more firmly, and definitely more demandingly.

The music paused. As the haunting strains of *Rapsodie espagnole* began, the kiss deepened. Acutely aware of his muscular body, she yielded her mouth to the increasing insistence of his while the swaying resumed. He was lifting her slowly, his tongue prob-

ing the sweetness within her mouth, caressing, stroking, possessing.

A gypsy melody dimly penetrated her clouded
awareness—she was conscious only of Paul and the
desire building within him, within herself. Suddenly
he lifted his head, leaving Elaine gasping, craving
more. She couldn't restrain a tremor that matched the
erratic movement of the music, the pounding of the
tympani, the bohemian lilt. Her arms tightened
around his neck.

"Are you all right?" Paul whispered into her ear,
nuzzling the side of her face.

Elaine nodded, eyes closed, a smile on her lips.
"I'm dizzy," she confessed in a whisper. Her arms
remained around his neck. She felt enclosed in the
warm, safe bubble his arms and body created. The
past had ceased to be important, the future was no
longer of concern. The moment was now, the intensity of pleasure magnifying steadily.

The familiar strains of the *Boléro* began. It was
slow and sensuous, pleading, expressing Elaine's in-
nermost yearning. "Kiss me," she whispered, caught
in the spell of the music, of their ever-circling bodies. She expected him to stop. He didn't.

One arm across her back continued to brace her
firmly. The other arm rose and released the silver
barrette that imprisoned her hair, sending it tumbling to her shoulders. Then one hand grasped the
back of her head, cradling it, as he lowered his own
head to hers.

A pleasant flush of desire washed through her. They continued to move to the rhythm of the dance, fused together, each an extension of the other. His kiss was filling her, reaching deep, arousing primitive needs. She heard a soft moan and realized the sound was coming from her own throat. Her arms released their hold on Paul's neck in a desire to touch him. She was trusting him completely to keep her from falling. He stopped, suddenly motionless.

Her hands moved restlessly between his shoulder blades. Her fingers glided through his short silky hair. Again he lowered his mouth to her opened lips, his tongue capturing her mouth, taking possession with a sureness that made her want to yield.

He wants me. The knowledge seared with a blinding flash of light behind closed eyelids. It was cleansing, wiping away the stains of violation and pain.

As if he sensed her change in mood, Paul resumed the sensuous circling movement, while inside, Elaine was singing with the music. No words were needed. The beat pounded relentlessly, swelling steadily into a crescendo that left her gasping in joy and exhilaration.

The music stopped, but the throbbing of desire and need within her continued.

Slowly their lips parted. Both were shaken and breathless. Her head went on spinning. She nuzzled her cheek, her nose against his face. She drew a deep breath. The faint odor of his skin was exciting. His hand moved to the side of her face, and he kissed it tenderly—cheeks, chin, nose, eyelids.

"Elaine." It was a whisper, a plea.

She knew what he was asking. "Yes, Paul." She could barely speak.

In the space of a heartbeat, he swept her into his arms and carried her into the master bedroom. In those few breathless moments, Elaine realized that here was the man she loved.

He kept his eyes on her face as he discarded his clothing, and when he stood before her nude, she gasped in awe. His body was perfection; Michelangelo's *David*.

She wanted to tell him so but was too shy; instinct told her to communicate in other ways. She took his face into her hands, caressed his cheeks with her fingertips, kissed his closed eyelids.

The bedroom was cloaked in semidarkness, illumined only by the warm light from the living room. In that honey glow Paul helped her to undress, gently pulling the white sweater over her head, slipping the black jersey skirt down over her shapely legs, removing the white camisole, bra and panty hose. He pulled her against him and buried his face in her hair, running his long fingers through its silky strands.

Their bodies touched deliciously, his lips and tongue kissing and sampling all of her. Where Paul led, Elaine followed in a glorious rush of awakening. In Paul's exploration of her body, Elaine was rediscovering herself; her capacity to enjoy sensation and to trust a man. She was learning it was not fatal to be vulnerable, to open oneself to another human being.

When she was ready, Paul lowered her to the bed, stroking her legs and thighs with featherlike motions. She knew she had passed the point of no return. As if he sensed that birth-control pills were not part of her life-style, he reached for the bedside-table drawer and extracted a condom. Then he lay down beside her.

They made love in a pulsating silence. The *Boléro* still throbbed in her head like a ghost chorus as she thrilled to his hands, to his mouth, to the essence of his manhood. She brought him joy and received it in her turn. Paul's caring tenderness echoed her own newfound love.

Fear was gone at last, replaced by a floating serenity, a peace, a sensation that she was flowing into the air surrounding her. A sigh of contentment escaped her. Afterward, as they lay hand in hand, she knew that what she was experiencing was the mystical experience of love between a man and a woman.

The feeling lingered, blessing the rest of that moonlit night.

AT NINE-TWENTY on Wednesday morning, Keith arrived at the Indianapolis Motor Speedway with Paul.

The two-and-a-half-mile racing oval shone brightly in the morning sun. The wind was light, the sky clear, the temperature mild—a perfect day for practice.

If the circumstances had been different, Keith would have been ecstatic about the chance to view practice sessions of some of his favorite drivers from the vantage point of the air-conditioned comfort of the VIP suite. Not today. As he and Paul stepped into the small elevator, Paul was carrying a cardboard carton holding all the items taken from Keith's Brown County home. Cash, black-and-white glossies, magazines, the carbon copy of the letter he had sent in response to the ad, the synopsis and three chapters of his unfinished novel, the phony army dog tags and fake honorable discharge, the rifle, now disassembled to fit into a canvas bag, the ammo and scope.

What Keith feared most was the danger to his sister. The possibility of prison seemed remote; he couldn't visualize it. During the slow ascent of the elevator, he waited, sullen and silent.

The doors opened onto a concrete walkway with a row of closed doors bearing polished brass signs stretching into the distance. The well-known corporate names made little impression on him as he trailed behind Paul, a reluctant witness. Keith knew he was coming to the end of the line; soon there would be no turning back.

Paul stopped at a door bearing the legend Commercial Bank and Trust. Keith halted, too. Paul inserted the key in the lock and opened the door. He stood aside for his silent companion to enter first, eyeing him as though he didn't quite trust the younger man.

Visibly unwilling, Keith moved down a narrow hallway and stepped into a pleasant room bounded by glass panes that went from the ceiling down to a long bench covered with dark blue cushions. "Jeez!" he muttered. The thirty-by-thirty foot room was decorated with impeccable taste and quiet elegance. He walked to the wall of glass. A sliding door led to a sloping balcony containing rows of molded plastic chairs. The curve of the blacktop track lay beyond. The door was closed and locked. Keith tested it.

Paul turned on the wall unit to start the air conditioning. "Representatives from the state police, the Marion County sheriff's department and the Indianapolis police department will start arriving soon," he warned Keith.

Keith walked restlessly to the refrigerator, flung open the door and stood, torn between a can of cola and a frosty beer. His hand went toward the beer, then he glanced at Paul's stony face. He pulled out the soft drink instead.

"First impressions count. That's a better choice," said Paul in a tense voice. He leaned his elbows on the bar, looking elegant in a dark single-breasted suit, white shirt and tie. Keith glanced down at his pullover, jeans and sneakers with some misgiving. Not that he cared what Paul thought. His rancor had been building since Sunday morning, when Elaine had come waltzing in at ten in the morning with Paul behind her. For years Keith had been on the receiving end of Elaine's protection—now, for the first time, he wanted to do the same for her. He couldn't envision Elaine marrying a reporter who would find out about the skeleton in the family closet, the skeleton named George Stamm, so a relationship between the two of them made no sense.

Paul shifted uncomfortably under Keith's assessing stare. He headed for the coffee urn and filled it with ground coffee.

A knock sounded. Paul went to unlock the door. Keith heard a male voice, deep and rumbling, that hinted of a Western accent. He looked up, shocked. The man walking into the room could have stepped right out of the black-and-white photos. He was shaking Paul's hand in greeting.

"Luck was with us. The wife of one of the city councilmen took Laura on a tour of Claypool Courts and a local businessman took Alex out to see a vacant factory on Shadeland Avenue. He's talking up Indy real big to Alex—says it's a good place for a manufacturing facility. Neither knows I'm up here. I haven't mentioned a word to either of them about any of this."

Garry Channing turned to look at Keith, and the eyes of potential killer and victim met. Not a word was said. Keith noted the seriousness of the man's lined face, the pulsing of a muscle in his jaw. Slowly the tall man moved toward him.

Keith lowered his eyes, but caught the movement of a raised arm, a hand extended for a handshake. The older man waited for Keith to respond, and slowly he raised his eyes to meet a clear gray gaze that was without anger or blame. He shook Garry Channing's hand.

"You got courage, son. I've got a boy older than you. It takes guts to admit what you've gotten yourself into and to want to help me out this way by cooperating with the police. I thank you for your assistance."

Keith gasped. The words of forgiveness were more effective than a punch on the jaw. "Yes, sir," Keith whispered, unable to say more.

Knocks sounded with frequency from that point on as various plainclothes officers from the three agencies drifted in, one at a time, all in suits or sport jackets. Keith took refuge on the padded cushion of the banquette, his back to the window. He wondered if the men carried handguns, but detected no bulges in their clothing. He noted that Channing and he were the only men present in casual clothes. He began to feel a strange affinity to Garry Channing.

It was, however, an affinity that the other guests clearly didn't feel as they accepted Paul's offer of coffee, doughnuts and soft drinks. They treated Garry Channing with respect, but Keith was the recipient of hard looks and stony silence. He had already confessed; the evidence, including the two shoe boxes containing ten thousand dollars in cash, lay spread on the table in their midst.

The synopsis and sample chapters remained untouched. In their minds the budding novel clearly had little importance. They seemed to assume that desire for the money had been Keith's sole motivation and that Paul had found out the plot in time and dragged the truth from him.

Keith told them all he had told Paul about writing a letter to answer the classified ad and Hawley's telephone call telling him where to go.

"Have you got that conversation on tape?" one asked.

"Hell, no. I don't have any recording equipment. Isn't taping telephone calls illegal?" Keith inquired.

Someone in the group snickered.

Keith had to retell his story several times so that the detectives could see if the details varied in any way, if he was embellishing or withholding information.

"So you and two guys who only have nicknames went with Hawley to a farm whose location you don't know to hang out there for two days, buddylike, and go target shooting with rifles and handguns and drink beer, eat hot dogs and talk women. Is that right?" Dickerson wanted to know.

"Yes. That's what I said, isn't it?" Keith replied sullenly. Despite the detective's no-nonsense attitude, Keith couldn't help liking Dickerson and planned to model the policeman in his novel on him.

"You were the *least effective* marksman there?"

Keith shrugged. "I shot the cardboard targets in the foot. Didn't hit a single duck when they flew overhead. The other guys were good, though."

"But *you* got the job." Dickerson looked puzzled. "Why?"

"Let's take a squint at that ammo. Maybe it's got a homing device like some of the torpedos did in World War II," said one of the sheriff's deputies with a casual drawl.

Smiles flickered over set faces. Then silence fell. Keith felt all eyes on him. He hated the feeling. Even winning a Pulitzer Prize wasn't worth all this hassle.

Keith shrugged. "I do well in an interview situation. I always get the job I apply for. People like me." His glance scanned the solemn faces surrounding him. "Or they used to. Hawley and I hit it off okay."

"And a week later he shows up on your doorstep, without warning, with all this stuff." Dickerson's hand swept over the items spread on the table. "No other instructions but to be at the track on the first day of qualifications, to sit in the terrace grandstand and watch for Mr. Channing to show up in the pits with his car. To watch him and study him until you'd know him anywhere in a crowd. Is that it? That Hawley would be in touch with you close to the time to give you final instructions?" Dickerson was verifying Keith's written statement.

Keith nodded.

"How? By phone? Mail? Another drop-in visit?"

"I don't know."

"Is that drug money in that box, mister? Are you dealing?" exploded the voice of one of the men from the city police department. "I don't believe a word of this cock-and-bull story! His sister found the cash and he made it all up, using his novel as an excuse. Possession of the magazines don't mean anything. Or the photos. He could have got them anywhere. We're wasting our time here. Find out who's supplying him with the white stuff."

"No! That's not it. You gotta believe me!" Keith cried.

"Why?"

"Because my sister's *dead* if I don't go through with killing Channing!" Panic-stricken, Keith turned to Paul for confirmation. Paul closed his eyes, his oval face pale. The silence was heavy.

"Hawley threatened to get her if you backed out on the deal?" asked Dickerson in a tone of compassion that surprised Keith.

Keith blinked hard, fighting the lump in his throat. He fought to keep the tears from his eyes. All he could do was nod.

He heard a softly muttered oath from one of the men present. "I believe him," Dickerson told the others.

Keith felt the impulse to hug the man. He watched Paul's eyelids slowly open. The expression on his face was strange.

"There's something different about that rifle," said Paul. "I've seen rifles before, but this one..."

Everyone crowded around it. One of the men assembled it, part by part. Even Channing looked on, fascinated at the sight of the instrument intended for his destruction.

"Israeli make, do you think?" muttered one.

"I doubt it. Designed for terrorist activity, I would guess. More plastic than metal to escape detection in airport luggage scanners. Highly sophisticated design, yet simple," said another turning over the assembled weapon in his hands. "You did check this for fingerprints first, didn't you, Jim?" he asked.

"Yep. We found only the kid's here, Paul's and the sister's. Not even a latent print we can use. This Hawley's smart and this weapon's brand-new. He must have worn gloves when he handled it."

"Let's see the ammo," said another.

The group huddled around the table. "A nine-millimeter P cartridge. But this is no Uzi—the Uzi's made with sheet-metal stampings." The detective sounded puzzled.

"This is the weapon you used for target practice at the farm outside Buffalo?" Dickerson asked Keith.

"Yes. It's light. Handles well. You'd be surprised. Hawley told me to go into the woods behind my house and practice. I told you—he thinks he's giving me a break by giving me the assignment. He likes me."

Garry Channing was questioned next. They were leading questions—about his current wife and her possible boyfriends, about his ex-wife Marian, about his son Todd, who had connections to organized crime through the loan sharks, about Todd's three-million-dollar inheritance, and finally about the comptroller Channing had fired and refused to recommend to potential employers.

"Did you ask your current wife to sign a prenuptial agreement?" Dickerson wanted to know. His manner was polite and tactful, his tone soothing, his eyes alert.

Garry Channing glared at him hotly. "Hell, no! Why should I? She loves me."

The other men cast careful glances at each other.

Channing got up, plainly irritated. He strode to the sliding glass door leading to the balcony, unlocked it and opened the door, letting himself out. He pulled a stopwatch out of his pocket.

"The guy's a sitting duck out there. He makes me nervous," complained one of the policemen, watching as the solitary figure looked down at the track. With the door open, they could all hear the rumble and zoom of cars speeding around the turn and down the straightaway.

"He's upset. Give him a minute to cool off. I'll bring him in," said Paul. He walked out and joined Garry at the parapet, standing beside him in companionable silence. A red-and-black car screamed around the turn, one of several doing practice runs.

"That's one of the Penske cars," Channing told Paul as he stared at the red-and-black car come around the fourth turn a second time. He clicked the button on top of the stopwatch. "Two hundred twenty-five miles per hour. That's what we have to beat." His lips pulled into a worried line.

Two other cars passed in quick succession.

"You're making the guys inside nervous, Garry. You make a good target standing up here—" Paul didn't have a chance to finish as he noticed another car approach the fourth turn at high speed. The squeal of huge tires as they lost traction made Paul and Channing grab the rail and look straight down.

The car brushed the concrete wall, describing a circle. Both side wheels hit the wall with a thunk as the vehicle rubbed the wall below them. The wheels popped off, bouncing high into the air, and Paul and Garry Channing retreated quickly. As the wheels descended, one spun in place and fell to its side, while the other rolled down the track.

The sound of the crash brought everyone onto the balcony at a run. They stood next to the rail, peering down, silent. The driver looked almost lost in the cockpit opening, an orange-red helmet gleaming in the blazing sunlight.

"The yellow flag is out to warn the other drivers," said Channing.

The cars remaining on the track slowed as they came around the turn, holding position as airplanes do in drill maneuvers, and a fire truck approached, followed by an ambulance.

Still no one spoke. All eyes were on the red-orange helmet. Only when the medics helped the driver out of the car and he stood upright, apparently dazed, did the tension break. They watched the driver in his one-piece fire-retardant suit climb shakily into the ambulance. The fire truck sped off, its services not needed, and the ambulance followed.

Within a minute, the deep rumble of the mammoth hornets, the steady progression of cars at practice speeds of two hundred fifteen, to two hundred twenty-five miles an hour around the oval track resumed.

"The green flag is out. All systems go," Channing announced.

It was a moment and a phrase that Keith would remember.

CHAPTER TEN

THE FIRST DAY of qualifications was warm and clear. The Saturday crowd of more than 200,000 spectators, armed with portable coolers, was streaming into the Indianapolis Motor Speedway in a party mood and filled with high expectations as Paul, Keith and Jim Dickerson met in the grass-covered parking area behind Tower Terrace. Rows of vehicles stretched before them as far as the eye could see.

They stood beside a white 1982 Buick sedan in much better condition than the one Keith had wrecked. Dickerson, looking casual in jeans and a loose-fitting Indiana University sweatshirt, handed Keith the keys to the vehicle on loan to him for the Channing job. Everything was ready for Brett Hawley to return and for Keith to make the trip to the location of his assignment.

"A tracking device has been attached. It sends out a signal that enables one of our unmarked cars to follow you. Do you have an answering machine at home?" Dickerson asked. "In case Hawley tries to get in touch with you?"

Keith gulped, nodding. He was understanding for the first time what it might be like to be an undercover operative. He stared down at the keys in his hand. "At my place and at my sister's. Are you planning to put a listening device on the lines?"

There was no response. The detective's face was impassive. Keith felt his despondency deepen as the prospect of prison loomed larger. Was the detective wearing a transmitter to record their conversation? Keith had no way of knowing that, either. "The only instruction I've had from Hawley so far is what I told you." Keith clutched the car keys hard in his fist.

"Be careful. You know what's at stake if Hawley finds out we're in on this! He may carry through with that threat against your sister," Dickerson warned. He looked at Paul, squinting in the bright morning sun, his brow wrinkling. Paul looked as unhappy as Keith felt.

"You don't have to tell me that. I know," Keith answered curtly. The guilt for dragging Elaine into this by bragging about his sister, the vice president, roiled in his gut. He didn't want to eat. He'd been sleeping a lot lately—sleep was the only escape available to him.

"Good luck, Keith! Be careful with the car, okay?" Dickerson threw a warning look at the younger man as he walked away to meld with the crowd heading for the steel-framed glass tower.

"Are you okay?" Paul asked, concern on his face. He was touching Keith's shoulder, and the reassuring gesture was what the younger man needed now more than ever.

"You take care of my sister," he blurted out.

Paul's face was grim. "You'd better believe I will. She's a very special person."

"She's a dedicated career woman, Paul. I don't think she'd buy the kids and housewife routine—just so you know. She's dated lots but none of the guys last very long. She dumps them. Of course, you're different from the ones I met—"

Paul turned. "Yes. She hates the way I make my living." His lips pulled into an ironic smile. A sigh escaped him. "Why did Elaine major in finance in college? Why did she choose to go into banking? Do you know?"

"I think she wanted to prove she was better than—" Keith suddenly caught himself. This was more than an idle question, he decided. The guy had a reason for wanting to know. *Does he suspect anything about our father after all? Is he trying to pump me?* He felt a moment of panic. Paul's steady gaze was disconcerting.

"That she's smarter, with more integrity than...some people," Keith stammered. "That she can be trusted...with other people's money...in a job where males have the edge. To prove herself, maybe. You know how women are," he added hastily, spreading his hands in a plea for male understanding.

To prove she was better than their father, Keith longed to say. He had a sudden yearning to confide all to Paul in the hope that he would understand and appreciate her for what she was. But Elaine would hold it against him forever if he did, he knew. *I'm the one who got his genes. Look at who's headed for prison,* he thought morosely, tossing the car keys into the air and catching them as they fell.

"You okay, buddy?" Paul asked again.

"Sure. I'm fine," Keith answered curtly. "We better split up now, in case Hawley's in the crowd. Too many people here already know you're a friend of Channing's. I don't want to blow my cover." He smiled. There *was* some excitement in working as a police operative. The novel was stirring to life in him once again, with himself as the hero, of course. If only he knew where the story would end. Behind prison bars, no doubt. The knot in his stomach tightened.

Keith watched Paul head in the opposite direction, picked up the small cooler in which Elaine had packed his lunch, and trudged toward the glass- and steel-framed tower, which rose like a monolith against the pale blue sky.

Seats were filling fast. Keith found a seat in the Tower Terrace extension that afforded a good view of the pit area as well as the yard of original brick that constituted the Start/Finish line and had earned the speedway the nickname Brickyard.

Keith was soon surrounded by others, all armed with coolers containing lunch and soft drinks or beer. He sat alone, half fearing he might see someone he knew and be asked to join the group. Small talk was beyond him right now as he followed Hawley's curt instructions. One soft drink and two peanut butter and strawberry jam sandwiches later, Keith saw Garry Channing emerge from Gasoline Alley, the garage area where the race cars were housed. He was dressed in black trousers and white zip-up jacket with red trim, aviator-style sunglasses covering much of the tanned, weathered face. His dark blond hair blowing in the wind, he was seated on a small flatbed tractor, which towed a black-and-white race car with red trim.

The driver sat inside the cockpit of the car; the chief mechanic rode near its nose, perched next to the wide rolling tire as he talked to the driver and held his white helmet. Other crew members rode on the flatbed truck with Channing—and two other people whose faces Keith recognized from the photographs: Channing's curvaceous young wife and the dark-haired member of the golf foursome.

The procession slowly made its way north in the two-lane blacktop pit artery, followed by other tow vehicles with their loads. The walkway beyond the concrete protective wall that bordered the pit area filled rapidly with a steadily moving crowd—press teams, men and women wearing headphones, cameramen and -women with video-cameras balanced on their shoulders, and still photographers with cameras around their necks. There were also mechanics dressed in the racing teams' colors; uniformed policemen and -women, always in pairs, truncheons and guns hanging from their hips; track officials; radio and TV announcers on their way to the tower. The eyes, ears and heart of the Indianapolis Motor Speedway were open to the world.

Al Unser, Jr. walked along the pits ahead of his car, his cap pulled down securely against the wind. A cheer broke out from the army of spectators crowded on the wooden seats; many leaped to their feet while the veteran driver smiled and waved greetings. Other drivers did the same as they passed, all men whose faces were familiar: Rick Mears, Mario Andretti, and a tall man from Brazil of regal bearing, Emerson Fittipaldi. Keith recognized Teo Fabi of Italy, Tero Palmroth from Finland, Belgium's Didier Theys, Raul Boesel of Brazil, Bernard Jourdain from Mexico City. Keith had seen their photos and brief bios featured in the sports pages of the *Indianapolis Star*.

Keith felt his depression lift in the vibrant warmth of the human spectacle passing before him. His third sandwich sank to his thigh, half-eaten, as he observed and drank in the colors, the sounds, the mounting excitement. He sat surrounded by young couples in love, holding hands, arms wrapped around each other, by couples with children, by the young, the old and everyone in between.

He scanned the sea of faces. Brett Hawley was not there.

Relieved, Keith directed his attention to the group of three standing side by side along the pit wall— Garry Channing, Laura Channing, and the unknown man from the golf foursome. His black hair was streaked heavily with gray, cut businessman conservatively, yet with a hint of fullness and definite sideburns. His long, thin nose with flaring nostrils and moderately full lips hinted at a sensuality even Keith could recognize. A raw sense of power and authority radiated from the man. It was in his bearing, in the way he stood. His sophistication made Garry Channing look like a transplanted cowboy.

The man stood very close to Laura Channing, their bodies almost touching. She wasn't edging away, Keith noticed. They talked comfortably inside the retaining wall, leaning against it, while Channing, preoccupied, stood with stopwatch in hand, clocking the four laps of each competing driver, oblivious of his companions.

Keith's attention was drawn to the track by announcer Tom Carnegie's deep, vigorous voice. "Emerson Fittipaldi from Brazil, ladies and gentlemen, car #20. He just got the green flag. He's taking the run...both wheels below the line in turn two...high exit off two...now in turn three...high off four, exit on main straightaway."

With a loud, heavy roaring sound, the sound of engine power, the car hurtled past the bleachers where Keith was sitting to conclude the first of the four qualification laps. "221.948 miles per hour," announced Carnegie. The green flag waved again from the wooden tower at the Start/Finish line. Soon the car flashed past again. The third time, Keith noted, a white flag fluttered. One lap left. Then the checkered flag fell. "222.475 miles per hour average!" Carnegie's jubilant voice rang through the loudspeakers. Fittipaldi's computerized image in amber flashed onto huge report boards visible from seats on both sides of the track, followed by the speeds of each of the four laps plus the average speed of all four.

Channing's driver started out with the green flag but, after three laps with speeds of two hundred fifteen miles an hour, the crew apparently decided that wasn't fast enough. The yellow flag waved and the car moved into the pits parallel to the track instead of crossing the Start line for the fourth time. Obviously, Channing had decided to wait for another qualifying attempt at a higher speed and a better position in the lineup.

He looked crushed. Keith removed his sunglasses so he could see the man's face better. Channing's wife placed her arm around her husband's shoulders as if to comfort him.

The man beside her stepped back and turned, looking up into the bank of green wooden benches in the Tower Terrace extension. His eyes locked with Keith's. Keith felt the impact like a fist to the stomach. Something in the man's expression altered before he looked away and turned to speak to the chief mechanic.

Keith glanced down, checking his clothing to see if something was amiss to draw such attention from a stranger, but saw nothing about himself or around him that was out of the ordinary.

At six o'clock he began the weary trudge back to his loaned car. Why had Hawley insisted he be here today? Nothing had come of it, and all he had done was get a good look at Channing in sunglasses and racing colors.

The yellow flag was waving over Keith, for sure. Everything seemed on hold for him, too. He felt as if he were being sent back to the pits to wait longer, just like Channing's car, which had failed to qualify.

But after all, there was still another weekend and another Sunday to fill the field of thirty-three competing racing machines.

ON THURSDAY a Federal Express package arrived from Washington, D.C. in the hands of a uniformed deliveryman. Mary accepted it and brought it immediately to Paul's office. The package bore Mick Sturgis's return address. The statement for services, which included the list of expenses plus a higher per diem rate than Mick had charged two years ago, almost knocked the breath from Paul.

"Hold all my calls. I'll return them later," he told Mary curtly as he disappeared into the kitchenette for a mug of hot coffee. When he returned to his office, he closed the door, thus giving a signal to the rest of the staff to leave him alone.

Mick had done his job well. He had earned every cent of his bill, Paul decided as he stared at the copies of newspaper articles and the long typed report. Paul noted that Mick had listed all his sources—

names, addresses, agency names and addresses, business telephone numbers.

He began to read.

PAUL SAT IN NUMBED SILENCE. He slipped off his glasses and held his head in his hands, elbows on the office desk.

It was the closest he had come to tears since his grandmother's funeral. He had been twelve at the time. Gradually he became aware that the telephones had stopped ringing, that there were no voices beyond the paneled partitions.

Everyone had gone home, leaving him undisturbed. The hands holding his head parted to reveal streaks of a red-gold sunset peeking through the half-opened miniblind. His desk lamp was burning, casting a harsh light upon the evidence of what had been done to Elaine Stamm's family by an ambitious small-town reporter who coveted a top position on the newspaper where he worked. To win it, Strothers had made himself a hero.

Paul ran his fingers through his hair. "No wonder she hated me when I told her what I did for a living," he said aloud. Restoring the glasses to his face, he realized that he felt ill. "This guy should have been a novelist."

Paul had read each article over and over. Facts were few, but the emotional appeal was strong and dramatic. Strothers had hammered away day after day from the front page, stressing George Stamm's treachery in betraying his fellow citizens by the theft of their savings. The articles clearly implicated George's wife as a willing accomplice and implied that their daughter couldn't be trusted even as a baby-sitter, since a child in her care had been injured while climbing a tree in a public park.

Strothers had worked up the entire community in a series of inflammatory articles that had made him both judge and jury of Stamm's deed—and managing editor of the paper. Paul's lip drew into a thin line as he picked up one of the later articles.

The piece on the torching of the Stamm home, attributed to arson by persons unknown, hadn't been written by Strothers. The article bore a woman's byline, Paul noted. It was also a story devoid of any evidence of emotion, in contrast to Strothers's pieces, composed mostly of interviews with indignant victims of the theft and savings and loan employees afraid of being implicated for negligence.

It was the two inches of column space buried on the back page, in the police reports, that was the worst of all—a report of a gang rape by three high school males, all unnamed because they were juveniles. The crime had taken place on high school property, the fourteen-year-old girl having been dragged to a shed one evening as she tried to enter the main building to attend a play rehearsal. Mick's note identified the victim—Elaine Stamm.

She had been innocent, hurt beyond measure by adults consumed by greed and ignorance, and she was in grave danger now from Hawley, a danger from which Paul wanted to save her.

He paced the floor and finally came to a decision. He hoped it was the right one. He doused the lights, locked the office and headed for the airport.

THEY SAT in Elaine's cheery kitchen at a butcher-block table large enough to seat four. The clock on the wall showed the time: nine-twenty. The blackness of night was visible around the edges of the mini-blind at the kitchen window. Elaine was wearing her pink bathrobe, the belt pulled tight at her waist. Paul's call from the airport had caught her warm and damp from the shower.

"You worked late, then went straight to the airport? Have you eaten? I'll make you a sandwich." She rose from the chair and headed toward the re-frigerator.

"I stopped for a sandwich on the way." Paul touched his waist above the belt buckle. "I'm fine, thanks."

His suit jacket and tie hung on the back of the kitchen chair on which he sat. He had forgotten to take his shoes off at the front door, but Elaine had said not a word. Keith had started the shoe-removal custom as a joke, after she had scolded him once for wearing muddy sneakers indoors. Elaine decided the joke had gone far enough.

"I'll accept a cup of coffee though," he added.

"You're planning a business trip now, Paul? How long will you be gone? The '500' Festival Mini-Marathon and the Queen's Ball are next Friday, only a week from tomorrow. I made out an application for tickets to the ball through the bank. Oh, be sure to have a tuxedo reserved, too. It's a black-tie affair. The food is delicious, I hear."

She opened the refrigerator door, pulled out a gallon of skim milk and poured a glass, setting it in front of him.

"Pretty pale for coffee," he commented, staring at the glass.

"You drink too much coffee. You're training for a *race,* remember. What kind of training diet are you on? Think of your heart. I am."

He lifted his eyes. The twinkling of humor she expected to see in them was missing. His whole attitude was subdued. He had said hardly a word since walking in the door. "What's wrong, Paul?" Elaine returned to the kitchen chair she had just left.

He raised the glass of milk, eyeing it critically, took a token sip, then set it down again. "I hate milk," he told her.

She leaned over to kiss his lips, but he didn't joke, pull her into his lap or tease her as she was expecting. "Is it Ben? Is Ben sick?"

"No."

"Has something gone wrong with Keith? Dickerson hasn't called you, has he?" she asked in alarm. Elaine hadn't talked with her brother in five days, not since the first day of qualifications. After the track's closing, Keith had come home in a white Buick, telling her the car had been loaned to him by a friend, and had packed his clothing. He had left for his own home, kissing her and telling her not to worry. That had been easier said than done.

Paul grasped her hands. "Steady, hon." He rose from the chair. "I haven't heard a word from Jim Dickerson since I saw him Saturday at the track." He sighed, the troubled look still on his face as he walked to the kitchen counter and drew himself a glass of water. Hands clasped in her lap, Elaine waited patiently for him to open up. For moments he stood with his back to her, hands braced on the countertop. Finally he turned.

"I know about your father, George Stamm. I know everything you were either unwilling or afraid to tell me. I hired a private investigator I used to work with in Washington. He sent me copies of Strothers's newspaper articles in the Marvella paper."

Elaine went quite still. She wasn't aware of breathing. It had finally come. Paul knew and had turned against her. Like all the others, this man was judging her by what her father had done. The kind of character she herself possessed made little difference.

"Did Keith let it slip?" she asked. "Is that why you checked up on my family?" She was hardly able to speak, stunned that her own brother would betray them this way.

Paul took a deep breath, his nostrils flaring. He was staring into the stainless-steel sink. "No. Don't blame Keith. I didn't suspect anything like that. The P.I. informed me after he checked your mother out."

"Then why did you hire an investigator if you weren't suspicious?" Her voice trembled as she lifted her eyes. For once, he was the one who evaded her gaze.

"First I had Mick check out if your story about the trust fund set up by your grandparents is true. Then I wanted to go deeper to see if Brett Hawley had any connection with you or Keith in the past."

Reluctantly he looked at her, and Elaine felt the quiet warmth of anger steal upward within her. "What, exactly, did you expect to learn? That there was no trust fund, that I was taking money from the bank?"

Now he was staring down at the tile floor. "I had to be sure. I thought you are smart enough to pull it off despite the bank's safeguards. Forgive me."

Each word was a blow. Unexpected. It was a nightmare come to life, the thing she had been dreading most since that night in the restaurant on North Keystone Avenue. Strangely, it was also a great relief. The lying, the hiding, the pretense was finally over. It hadn't been easy lying to the man with whom she had fallen in love. She had known Paul Cooper only four weeks, yet in some ways she'd felt as if she had known him for a lifetime. Now, suddenly, she was seeing a stranger before her.

"You assumed I am dishonest."

"You were withholding the truth from me, Elaine. I could feel it."

"I *evaded*. I just . . . didn't tell everything. Do *you* always tell everything? You didn't hesitate to go behind my back and hire a P.I. to dig into the garbage of my past! Why didn't you tell me about *that?* What did you intend to *do* with the muck you expected to find?" she asked intensely.

He stood silently, facing her, still unable to meet her eyes. He looked sallow, ill. He made no attempt to defend himself.

To Elaine, his failure to respond could mean only one thing. "What a great feature for your magazine, Paul," she said softly, putting steel into her tone.

"No!" He looked up sharply.

"'Indy's youngest female bank vice president turns out to be daughter of a savings and loan thief who was never brought to justice. Watch out, folks, she's taking from your piggy banks.' I can see it now. What a lead for a story!"

"Elaine, stop this!" Paul protested.

"All the men licking their wounds because women have beat them out for promotions will hail you as their savior. What a great thing this story will be for your magazine's circulation! Get the hell out of my house, Paul!"

She clenched her fists while hot tears forced their way into her eyes. This time she didn't try to hold them back. The treachery of the man who had set out to win her confidence—and her love—while trying to get the goods on her behind her back was more than she could bear. "My father's dead, damn it! Why can't you let him rest in peace?" She didn't recognize her own voice. It sounded strained and shrill.

Paul was coming toward her across the kitchen. She whirled about, hurting more than she had since the nightmare in the school shed. She felt him touch her. His hands were on her forearms. She tried to shrug them off. He persisted, holding on.

"Your father's alive, honey. Mick found him through Aunt Bertha. She's been corresponding with him for years. He's living under an assumed name in Seattle, Washington. He's married again. You have two young stepbrothers and a stepmother."

The room seemed to be swaying. Elaine grabbed the edge of the table for support. She felt Paul slowly turning her about, holding her under the arms.

"Alive? In Seattle?" she gasped.

The old Paul was with her now, the Paul she had been reckless enough to love. His voice was warm, his manner caring. "He's . . . been crippled by an accident. He's also had a heart attack recently. Aunt Bertha's worried about him."

Elaine felt a sudden chill all over her body; the room was starting to spin. In all the fantasies she had had through the years, fantasies in which she punished her father in sad, genteel ways, never had she wished such things upon him.

Paul embraced her. The warmth of his arms was surrounding her again. "There's still time to see him. Make your peace with him. Talk to him about what happened that day. Tell him you love him. You still do. I can see it in your eyes."

"I can't go to him!" she whispered, starting to tremble.

"It's the only way you'll ever be free, darling. Free to live your life fully, to marry, to have children of your own. The way it is now, you're tied to him forever through your resentment of him and what he did. You'll never be free from him until you face him and forgive him. Now is the time to do that. Before it's too late."

Angrily, she broke away. That beautiful something between them had suddenly cooled. He was demanding the one thing Elaine could never give.

Silently Paul reached into the inner pocket of his jacket. He laid a long envelope on the counter. "This is a round-trip ticket to Seattle. The flight leaves Saturday afternoon. That gives you time to tell Jan some emergency has come up and arrange to take your vacation in Seattle. The return portion is for two weeks from Saturday."

He waited for her answer. She was unable to give one. She simply stood there, her arms shielding her chest.

"You wanted my help, Elaine. Well, this is all I can do. I can't force you, I can't lead you by the hand.

You have to grow up. You have to face your own father and have a meaningful conversation about what he did and why he did it. Yes, it'll take a lot of courage.''

She turned her back on him, laid her forehead against the coolness of the refrigerator, aware of its gentle hum. Long moments passed, during which hot tears slid down her cheeks. She heard Paul's soft steps as he left the kitchen, heard the front door close and the lock click into place. Gasping for breath she turned back, hating the loneliness, dreading the silence.

Her father had married again. She had a stepmother. What was the woman like? Did she even know about her husband's other children?

He's alive. Suddenly that was more important than anything else. Elaine wiped her eyes with paper toweling and walked slowly to the counter. On top of the envelope containing the airline tickets was a small sheet of notebook paper, the kind Paul always carried in his pocket. On the paper he had written the names Will and Ada Stinson, an address and a telephone number. That was all. No personal message. If she followed Paul's advice, she would be away from Indianapolis until after the ''500'' race was over.

She looked up, dazed. Would she ever see Paul again? She doubted it. He knew everything. The shame she had borne for twenty years burned within her.

Her glance strayed to the kitchen table. What she saw took a moment to sink in. The glass at his place was empty. Before Paul left, he had drunk the milk.

CHAPTER ELEVEN

ON SUNDAY Paul was busy at work in the office located in his apartment when the telephone rang. He had left the answering machine off, hoping Elaine might call, fearing she wouldn't.

"Elaine's missing!" Keith's anguished voice came onto the line instead.

The hairs on Paul's forearms seemed to prickle. "What do you mean?" he asked, gripping the mouthpiece of the receiver.

"I was in Columbus, visiting a friend for a while yesterday. When I got home, Elaine had left this message on the answering machine. She said she was flying to Seattle and she was calling from the airport," declared Keith, sounding agitated.

Paul leaned back and allowed himself to breathe deeply. His plea had borne fruit. Elaine had decided to follow his advice and confront her father. She would be far away from Hawley and the monster who was paying him. Tears of relief welled into his closed eyes.

"Paul, you there?" Keith demanded.

"Yes, I'm here," Paul answered, trying to sound calm. "Exactly what did Elaine tell you?"

"She said she had business in Seattle and would be gone for a while."

"It's something to do with the bank, then." Paul was afraid to tell Keith that George Stamm was alive. The kid had enough pressure on him already; that knowledge could bring him to the breaking point.

"No, it doesn't! I just called Jan at home. She told me Elaine took vacation leave on very short notice. Elaine told her boss that an emergency had come up concerning a relative in Seattle and that she had to attend to it."

Paul felt his throat tighten. "So she went out of town voluntarily. She's okay. What's worrying you?"

"We don't have any relatives on the West Coast at all!" Keith protested. "Maybe she could lie to Jan, but why would she lie to me? Something's wrong!" A long silence elapsed. "Do *you* know anything about this, Paul?"

"It's your sister's private business. When she's ready, she'll come home."

"Damn it, buddy, you do know something! What's going on?"

Paul was aware that the telephone line could be tapped by the police, who were expecting Brett Hawley to call. He wanted to keep them out of the matter of the missing George Stamm and the fortune to which he had helped himself twenty years ago. He also dreaded confessing to Keith that he had hired a P.I. to check on him and Elaine.

"It has nothing to do with the trouble you're in now, Keith. Maybe she just needed to get away for a while. Don't crowd her and don't worry. She'll be back," Paul reassured him. "She'll be okay." As Paul replaced the receiver, he felt a sense of relief. Also a deeper respect for Elaine. The lady had courage as well as beauty and intelligence.

It would be very easy to fall for a woman like that.

AT EIGHT ON MONDAY MORNING, Seattle time, Elaine dialed the number on the sheet Paul had given her. A pleasant female voice answered. "Hello. Stinson residence."

Elaine almost put down the receiver when she heard her stepmother's voice, but forced herself to go on. "Hello. My name is Elaine. Elaine . . . Stamm." She hadn't uttered the name in eighteen years. It didn't come naturally. What if this woman knew nothing about her husband's past?

She heard a gasp, then a long silence. "Elaine? Will's told me about you! Are you alone? Does anybody else know he's here?" The woman sounded fearful.

"I'm alone. The police are not a part of this. Don't worry. Aunt Bertha finally shook loose with your name and address. She said . . . _he_ was in pretty bad shape." She could not bring herself to use the word "father."

"He's—had some medical problems. He's a man of courage. I know he wants to see you, Elaine. He's talked so much about you and Keith. How old is Keith now?''

''Twenty-two.''

''Then you must be...thirty-four. My word! Will's missed out on all those precious years. Did Aunt Bertie tell you we have two sons of our own? Mike is twelve and Jordan is eight.'' The woman's voice was soft and much younger-sounding than Elaine had expected.

''Keith always wanted a brother,'' Elaine observed in a monotone. *And a father.* The thought echoed in her mind, reverberating with almost a physical sensation.

''Why don't you come to the house to spend some time with us, dear?'' Ada urged. ''Are you at the airport now?''

''No, in a motel. I arrived early yesterday. I...needed to rest first and have time to think,'' Elaine told her.

''I understand, but we do have an extra bedroom here. Not as luxurious as some motel rooms, but it's clean. There's a window overlooking the street. You'd be welcome to stay. Motel rooms are so expensive. Do you have a job? Or are you looking for one? Is that why you're here?''

''I'm employed,'' Elaine replied stiffly.

''Doing what? Secretarial? A teacher? A nurse?''

Everything in Elaine went still. ''I've been in banking for the past thirteen years. I'm a vice president in the trust department of Commercial Bank and Trust in Indianapolis.''

There was a long silence. Elaine felt satisfaction at having made her point. She had succeeded in the very industry in which her father had failed and tarnished his name beyond all repair.

''Please don't hurt him!'' The woman's voice sounded distant now.

''What?''

''Don't hurt Will! He's been hurt enough. Do you really want to see him or just poke holes in him? The doctors won't make a guess about how long the dear man has to live. He had a bad heart attack six months ago. I won't see him upset, you understand?''

This time the silence was at Elaine's end. When she spoke, the words slipped out, amazing her. ''I came here to see him. To talk to him. I've...missed him.''

''He's missed you and Keith. He's talked about you to me so many times. Aunt Bertha lost touch with your mother after your mother remarried. A line or two on a holiday greeting card doesn't fill in many of the blanks, especially when children are growing up.'' An accusing note was in her voice now.

''Mother and Aunt Bertha weren't close. They never had much in common except for...Will.'' Elaine felt she should show her father the courtesy of referring to him by the name his wife used.

''Well, it will be nice to see you at last. Will you come to lunch?''

"Y-yes. I'd be . . . glad to, but I've never been to Seattle before, so you'll have to tell me how to get there."

"First tell me where you are." Ada proceeded to give her directions and Elaine wrote them down. "I'm sorry your mother passed on," Ada added.

"I am, too."

"I'm looking forward to meeting you, Elaine. I've always wanted a daughter. Please, bring your suitcase and plan to stay with us for a while."

IT WAS ALMOST NOON before Elaine pulled up in front of the house at the address Paul had left her. The house was of 1920s vintage and recently painted. Lace curtains and pull-down, off-white shades hung at the windows.

Mother hated lace curtains, thought Elaine. She glanced at the suitcase in the back seat. She had decided to rent a car instead of taking a taxi because she wanted mobility, freedom to leave at a minute's notice. She'd put the suitcase just inside the front door. She doubted she would stay the night. She was apprehensive, not of the stranger who now called himself Will Stinson, not of Ada, but of herself. Of her own memories, her own unmet expectations and resentment.

Yes, Paul was right. I've been filled with resentment for years. Paul's a wise man. But he deceived me, too. The anger still burned, reducing to ashes many of the good feelings she had so recently experienced for him.

She looked up and down the street at the other homes in the older, middle-class neighborhood. Some were weather-beaten, in need of paint, others were in good repair. Yards were very small but well kept, the grass dense and green. Paper cups and candy wrappers littered the curb.

"What did he *do* with the money?" she whispered aloud. *And what am I doing here now?* Suddenly drained of energy, she was tempted to start the engine and drive away. Let her father live out his life in peace with this new woman. All desire for revenge went down the drain like so much dirty water as Elaine stared at the modest Stinson home, her heart beating fast.

She noticed one of the lace curtains part and lift, then drop back into place. The front door opened wide. It was too late. A petite woman stood in the doorway, waiting. She looked serene and dignified in a pale green cotton shirtdress and tan canvas shoes. Dark blond hair was drawn up neatly into a ponytail. She stood motionless, her quiet gaze fixed on Elaine in the car.

Is she afraid, too? Afraid of me? I can't drive away now and hurt her, thought Elaine.

She got out of the car and walked toward the house, carrying her suitcase. As she climbed the steps to the porch, she noted the older woman's heart-shaped face, green eyes, a clear complexion free of makeup.

Ada Stinson held out her hands. "Aunt Bertie never let on what a pretty lady you've grown into."

"I haven't seen Great-aunt Bertha in years."

"That's a pity, dear. Ties of blood and kin are too important to neglect." Ada stepped close and embraced Elaine. To Elaine's surprise, she returned the embrace. The response seemed natural.

"Let's go inside. Will got himself into a real state when he found out you were coming." Ada stepped back, a shadow of worry veiling the green eyes. "Are you certain you haven't told the police where he is?"

"No. Do you think I would turn in my own father?" Elaine asked stiffly.

Ada smiled gently and looked relieved. "He's always regretted what he did. He's turned to the Lord God since then. Thank you for giving him a chance." She moved aside so that Elaine could be the first to enter.

They stood in an entranceway that resembled a bower of flowers, with roses on textured paper climbing the walls. A small table stood below an antique mirror on the right and wooden pegs projected from the wall for coats and hats. A stairway to the upper floor rose to the left. The aroma of chicken simmering on the stove, the doughy smell of egg noodles and the scent of warm homemade bread filled the hallway.

"I've almost forgotten what he looks like," Elaine whispered to Ada, freezing at the doorway. "Everything burned when the house caught fire two months after he left town—all the snapshot albums, the clothes. We were asleep, but the dog's barking woke us. We barely got out in time. Everything of his was gone. It was like he'd never existed."

"What a terrible thing for you!" Ada touched Elaine's face with her soft hand. "We have to walk away from the bad things sometimes. We have to lay them in the hands of the Lord God and trust He'll take care of them. And us."

No one had ever talked to Elaine in this manner. She set her suitcase down in the hallway before following Ada into the living room. The room was cool yet filled with sunlight. The lace curtains at the window were gossamer white, the upholstered furniture worn but comfortable in appearance, the mahogany furniture tidy and gleaming. Elaine detected the faint odor of lemon oil, the same polish she used at home.

A man sat in a wheelchair, his back to them. The television set was on, tuned to a football game, its volume control turned low. The man's short hair was the same chestnut color as Keith's and her own. With a shock she saw that the brown was heavily threaded with silver.

Ada walked up to him, bent and laid her arms across the broad shoulders. She pressed her lips against the man's silvered temple. "She's here, hon. Your daughter's come to see you."

The man didn't move. Or speak. Ada stood erect and clasped both hands nervously in front of her. "I've got things to attend to in the kitchen. Lunch will be ready soon." She gave Elaine an encouraging smile and a mist filled her green eyes, then turned and walked through the dining room and into the fragrant kitchen.

Who are you? The words beat in Elaine's head as she stared at the back of the stationary chair, at the figure rising above the back of the seat. *Who the hell are you to keep your back turned to me?*

Her throat was dry. It ached with dryness. Her eyes felt dry, too. She forced herself to speak. "Dad?"

A hand rose to a box on the side of the chair. There was a humming sound and it turned. Elaine caught her breath. Her father's face was thin, almost gaunt. His whole body looked too thin for the shirt and trousers he wore, the legs of the trousers neatly folded at the knees. Large dark eyes were looking up at her pleadingly, although his lips spread in a smile.

"Thanks for coming, Baby." The resonant baritone seemed so familiar that she found herself trembling as he uttered the pet name she hadn't heard in twenty years. In quality, in timbre, the voice sounded similar to Paul Cooper's. She blinked in astonishment. "I'm sorry you have to see me this way," he was saying. "You've turned into a beautiful woman."

They stared at each other, motionless, each drinking in the sight of the other as though the thirst of years was about to be slaked. Then her father's arms slowly opened.

The hardness Elaine had nourished with such care over the years, reinforced by her mother's bitterness, began to soften. Resentment faded, leaving her weak and dazed. She dropped to her knees and put her arms around his neck, hugging him as she had done many times as a child.

"Sorry I can't take you in my lap. You'd fall through," he joked, his voice turning hoarse.

She leaned back on her heels, looking up at him. "Why? Why did you do it? Just walk out and never call us? Never write us? When the police called Mom in Indianapolis after she'd married Jeff to tell her the car had been found in the river—"

"You thought I was dead."

"Yes."

"That's what I wanted everybody to think so the search for me would be called off," he explained as Elaine released her grip around his neck. He gazed down at the floor with a set face, as he allowed memory to open up those painful days for him. "The day I walked out of the Savings and Loan, I drove to a vacant farm property across the county line that was up for probate sale. I hid the car under hay in the barn and stayed there a week, scrounging for food—eggs from a henhouse I visited at night, bread put out for birds. One night I even ate dog food. I don't know where the hell the dog was. I cooled off by then, realized what an idiot I'd been and wanted to drive back to Marvella and explain it all. But when I read that Strothers guy's articles every day—"

"You read them?" she asked, incredulous.

"I heard the rural delivery car along the dirt road at six that first evening, so I sneaked out and got the Marvella paper from the box down the road. I realized after reading the crap that guy put out that I didn't dare go back. The townspeople would hang me from the nearest tree if I did. When I left that day, I burned my bridges behind me."

"Why did you do it? I thought it was to run off with *her*...."

"You—knew about her?" he asked, a look of pain on his face.

"Half the people in town knew about her! You met her in the bar downtown, didn't you? She hung out there. Kids talk in school. Did she put you up to it? When she got out of town fast, was she going to meet you?"

"I never saw her again after the day I walked out of the savings and loan. I swear it, Elaine. I didn't take the money in order to run away with another woman. I admit, I did slip—a time or two—but it wasn't love. It was something else."

"You could have talked it over with me—or Mom," she protested.

"You? You were a kid of fourteen. No, it was my problem. Your mom and I had kinda forgotten *how* to talk to each other. It always ended up in arguments we didn't want you kids to know about." He shrugged.

"Then why did you do the crazy thing you did? Tell me, Dad. Tell me now so I can understand. I want to understand so it won't drive me crazy anymore."

Elaine heard the sound of an eggbeater whirring softly in the kitchen.

"Ada tells me you're a vice president in the trust department of a bank. How old are you, girl?"

"Thirty-four. The promotion came six months ago."

"I don't think you *can* understand."

She got to her feet, suddenly angry. "That's a cop-out! Maybe you didn't even have a reason. Maybe you just wanted to see if you could get away with it." She was disappointed. She had expected more than this, a fight or a tearful apology. Something cathartic.

"Maybe you're right, Baby. You see, you're a success. You've won promotions. How many years you been at that bank?"

"Thirteen."

"I was at the Savings and Loan *sixteen* years. Never promoted to manager. Always good, old, faithful George. Let George Do It was the sign that hung around my neck. And they did. I did the manager's job most of the time at half the salary. The customers all liked me. I knew everybody in town by their first names. I *was* savings and loan—" he gestured toward his chest with his thumb "—yet no one

ever praised me for a good job. Just a word of praise,
just the step up the ladder I deserved, that's all it
would have taken. Won't pay the mortgage, for sure,
but it keeps a man's spirit alive. Makes him think well
of himself. If you lose that, there's not much left.

"I tried to tell your mother how I felt, how I
wanted to quit. Job opportunities in Marvella were
limited if I didn't want to work at one of the two factories in town. I could have been a clerk selling shoes
or an agent with the insurance agency on a commission basis only. That wouldn't have paid the bills.
And your mother didn't want to work—lots of wives
and mothers stayed home then. That was all right
with me. But I wanted to move to Columbus. I was
sure I could find a job there. Your mom would have
nothing to do with the idea! She had her house just
the way she wanted it, she belonged to her clubs, sang
in the local chorus. Her life was set. I was just in the
way. If I was unhappy in my job, that was too bad.

"Then they moved in another manager over me.
For the third time. The guy was the nephew of the
president of the company and a *slob* in his security
measures. With an outside entrance nearby, everyone on the staff had access to the vault. My recommendations to beef up security were ignored. When I
complained about him to the head office in Cincinnati, my wrist got slapped in a memo. Nobody, but
nobody, had the privilege of criticizing the boss's
nephew. After I complained about him, he gave me a
poor review. I never got the raise I was entitled to.

Just a warning to keep my mouth shut and never go over his head again.''

Elaine gasped. She remembered how silent and glum her father had been shortly before the terrible day he had run away. She recalled the argument he'd had with her mother when they'd thought she was asleep. Her mother had let fly bitter words about a woman he had been seeing, about his absences from home in the evening.

"I wanted to show top management in Cincinnati how easy it would be for anyone to walk off with the contents of the vault. The new manager didn't seem to care and wouldn't pay any attention to my recommendations, so I set out to prove my point. And I did! I planned to come back a couple of days later or send the money back by messenger—I don't remember now exactly what did go through my mind. I was upset, not thinking straight. I was mad at the company. I was mad at my boss. I was mad at your mother for not putting me first in her life. Every time I needed to talk with her, she was always fussing with your baby brother.''

He pressed the remote control, clicking off the TV. "When I read the articles by Strothers in the Marvella paper, I knew people would never believe me. He had me sounding like Jack the Ripper! I was scared to go back and tell 'em, 'Hey, I'm sorry, here's your money!'

"In sixteen years on the job, I hadn't taken so much as a paper clip home, but I knew I'd go to jail, anyway. If a posse of townspeople didn't hang me first." He winced. "So I stole a plate off an abandoned car and drove by night to Cincinnati. I parked the suitcases in the storage lockers at the bus station, then drove to the river and pushed the car in during a rainstorm. The water was running high, so the car went down like a rock. I hitched a ride back to Cincy, got a burr haircut, nicked up my face like I'd been in a fight and took off on the bus with two suitcases and a knapsack for a change of clothes.

"Eventually I wrote to Aunt Bertha, using the name Will Stinson. When she told me about Elizabeth getting the divorce, then the police diver finding the car in the Ohio, I knew I was legally free. There was doubt I was still alive, and you kids and your mother were better off without me.

"I worked my way up to Seattle. That's when I met Ada. I was about at the end of my rope. First time I laid eyes on that dear woman, everything changed. I told her everything. We talked and talked. She didn't judge me. She let me know I still amounted to something." He folded his hands in his lap, staring down at them. He seemed to be waiting for a flood of recriminations from Elaine.

"That's it? That's a *stupid* reason to commit robbery. To show someone? To get even for being passed over in promotion? For not getting a raise?

"You know why I went into banking? You want to know?" Elaine put her hands on her hips. "To prove I was better than my father. I'm responsible to widows and children, to the mentally incompetent, to the sick, to the survivors. I administer their trust funds, I write out the checks that keep people going." She knew she was hurting him—she could see it in his eyes—yet she couldn't stop herself. The dam had burst.

"Lunch is on the table." Ada stood in the doorway, her tone stern, hands thrust into her apron pockets. The disapproval in her face told Elaine that she had been listening.

Ada had prepared a feast. Elaine felt ashamed. Her father was withdrawn, had trouble eating.

"Look, I'm sorry," she told him after the empty dessert plates had been cleared away.

"That's all right, Baby. I had it coming to me."

He lay down after the meal. Ada helped him into bed upstairs while Elaine busied herself cleaning up. The boys came home and Elaine met her stepbrothers. They accepted her with a calm curiosity that amazed her.

Before the evening meal Ada asked Elaine to accompany her to the attic. Elaine was almost afraid, but accompanied her up the stairs. Reaching the top, the older woman opened a closet door. She dragged out two small leather suitcases that Elaine recognized instantly. They were scarred and battered. Ada unfastened the clasps and threw up the lids. Elaine gasped. The suitcases were filled with cash, neatly banded with paper.

"You think Will was greedy? You think he took what didn't belong to him in order to live a life of ease? He made his way cross-country, working at odd jobs, driving an old car with these locked in the trunk. The money we paid down to get the franchise on the restaurant came from my folks. The restaurant furnishes our living. I took over managing it after Will's accident. I took today off.

"It takes a special man to hold this sum of cash and not feel it's his own to spend. A terrible temptation, and he didn't yield to it. You bear his genes all right, missy. You can be proud of it!"

Ada closed the lids, fastened the clasps. "For years we've been talking about how to get this money back. It would do no good to send him to jail now. He'd only die there alone, without anyone who loves him to hold his hand." She replaced both suitcases in the closet and shut the door.

"He was a foolish man, yes. He did a foolish thing. He acted spiteful and hasty, and he fell into sin, but he's made his peace with the Lord. He did his penance when he saved that child and lost his legs for it. If there's any love in you at all, girl, you'll show respect. You'll help your dad now when he needs it most."

"How?" Elaine could barely speak, shaken by the discovery that things were not entirely as she had assumed them to be.

Ada took her arm. "Help us find a way to get this money back to Marvella, wipe the slate clean before Will has to move on to our Maker."

THE HAMMERING BEAT of the electric typewriter faltered, then ceased. A blue-gray dawn filtered through the living room drapes. The silence was thick and heavy.

Keith stood and yawned, bleary-eyed with lack of sleep. He pulled open the drapes and peered out at the tranquil woods. Narrow shafts of yellow sunlight slanted between the trees. A haze wafted upward from the thick tangle of green. A million dewdrops shone with the brilliance of diamonds.

He stared at the desk calendar open on his desk. It was only six days until the "500" race. Elaine had been gone for nine days. The word Tuesday spread across the top of both pages.

Where was Elaine? What could have called her to Seattle for such a long time? Keith had telephoned her home on Saturday and Sunday and again last night. Only the warm voice on the answering machine had greeted him.

The feeling that Paul Cooper knew more about this than he would admit was gnawing away at him. He pulled the paper out of the typewriter cylinder, staring at it. Writer's block was horrible, like a well gone dry or a refrigerator that was empty when hunger hit.

Looking at the half-empty page, Keith finally admitted the source of his block. He had inadvertently put Elaine's life in danger because of his own dreams of success. What would his success be worth if he lost her in the process? He crumpled up the sheet of paper and tossed it into the wastebasket along with the others that were all he had to show for his night's work.

He shuffled into the kitchen on slipper-clad feet and found a mug among the rinsed and neatly stacked dishes that awaited washing. He cleaned the mug under the kitchen faucet and heated water for a cup of instant coffee.

After drinking the coffee, he lay on the sofa and tried to nap, but the peaceful oblivion of sleep refused to come. He felt apprehensive. Hawley would have to make his move soon. He would expect him to line up Garry Channing in the sights of the scope and pull the trigger. If Keith refused, Elaine would be the victim instead. For the first time in years, Keith wanted to cry. He rose from the sofa and paced the floor, hitting his open hand with the fist of the other.

The thrum of a V-8 engine and the sound of tires crunching on the driveway gravel startled him. He turned to the window and looked out. The glistening sheet of dew diamonds had vanished, the gentle golden light from the sun grown harsh. He expected to see Jim Dickerson get out of the tan car that had pulled in behind the Buick. He saw Brett Hawley emerge from the car instead.

"Oh, God!" Keith breathed, his gut twisting into a knot. The words were as much a prayer as an exclamation. He heard heavy footsteps on the porch, then a loud knock on the locked door. With a sinking feeling, he went to open it.

"You got a new car," the ex-prizefighter greeted him.

"An '82. New to me," answered Keith, stepping aside for the man to enter.

"Guess you spent some of the advance money. Why not? A man needs wheels," said Hawley, stepping into the living room and looking around. "Glad you changed your mind about carrying out this assignment." He looked around the room and stared into the kitchen. "Talked to your sister lately?"

A spasm shot through Keith's body. "No. Haven't had a chance. She stays busy."

"You didn't know she's out of town?" Hawley asked. He turned to face Keith, and the cold intensity of his gaze made Keith's scalp tingle unpleasantly.

The younger man blinked and rubbed his head. "No. My sister doesn't tell me everything. I don't tell her everything. What's the big deal? She's probably out of town on business. She'll be back soon."

"She's clear out in Seattle for two weeks. Something to do with a relative. What relative's out there?" asked Hawley.

Keith froze. His heart was pounding so loudly, he feared Hawley could hear it. *How in hell did he find out so much? From Jan?* "None that I know of. She must've used that as an excuse. Probably went to spend some time with an old boyfriend. Or a friend from college. How the hell should I know?'' He made his voice gruff and stared belligerently at Hawley.

The tactic worked. Hawley looked away first. ''I hope you're telling me the truth, kid.'' Hawley let out a slow sigh. ''We're leaving now. Throw some stuff in a bag—clothes, razor, whatever. Bring the rifle, scope and ammo. You're going to earn the rest of your pay.''

Their eyes met. Hawley's were flat, expressionless. Keith knew he could expect no compassion, no pity from this man.

''Sure.'' Keith's empty stomach wrenched in alarm. ''Do you want to eat something first?''

''There's a small kitchen where we're going. You can fix something after we get there. Hurry it up!''

Keith did as he was told, fearing not to. Luckily the police had returned the rifle and ammo the week before. ''Don't practice with this. Take it with you for the actual shoot,'' Dickerson had warned him at the time. The detective had not explained why.

As they left the house, Keith headed toward the white car, which held the tracking device.

''No, we'll go in mine,'' Hawley insisted.

Keith stared at the other man, fear threatening to overwhelm him. Nothing was going as planned. He climbed into the tan Dodge, realizing it was not the same car he had described to Dickerson. There would be no way to trace him now.

They backed out of the driveway rapidly, tires spitting gravel. As they sped off, Keith kept glancing into the rearview mirror for a sign of an unmarked car following them. There was no vehicle in sight.

"What's the matter?" Hawley asked suspiciously, looking into the mirror himself.

"Nothing. Just checking to make sure we're not being tailed," Keith mumbled.

"Nobody's gonna follow us if you kept your mouth shut," spat Hawley. There was a definite threat in his tone.

"I kept my mouth shut! Get off my back!" Keith retorted with a boldness he didn't feel. He stared out the window with a sinking feeling. Where was the car assigned to follow him? He was being kidnapped, and that was definitely *not* part of his plot.

CHAPTER TWELVE

SKIN STILL GLOWING from the shower after his shortened morning training run, a terry-cloth robe wrapped around him, Paul sat at the table at the end of his living room, staring down at the full breakfast plate before him. It was Thursday.

For several days he had been loading on complex carbohydrates—spaghetti, pasta, breads, oatmeal, potatoes—to improve his performance during the thirteen-mile "500" Festival Mini-Marathon tomorrow morning. It was a day he had been looking forward to for the past six months. Now he had no appetite and felt edgy. He had been waiting to hear from Elaine in Seattle. No call had come, either here or at his office.

Why doesn't she let me know she's all right? Paul asked himself, irritated, as he glanced at the wall clock. Ten after seven. He had to get dressed soon.

Elaine Malden had changed many things for Paul in the few weeks he had known her.

He felt vulnerable, and the feeling was not a comfortable one. He remembered their argument in Elaine's kitchen just a week ago—she had been standing with her forehead against the refrigerator door, her eyes closed, shutting him out. She had looked so proud, so angry, so alone....

The telephone rang. He sat erect, a feeling of joy sweeping through him, and made it to the telephone before the third ring.

It was not Elaine wishing him good luck for tomorrow.

"Paul, this is Jim." Paul suppressed a keen disappointment as he heard Dickerson's voice. "Has Keith Malden been in touch with you?" The detective sounded worried.

"No. I haven't called him, either. I assumed he would leave a message on my answering machine if necessary. He hasn't. What's up, Jim?"

"He's gone."

"Gone? But the tracking device—"

"The car's in the driveway, all right. With the lack of activity, our man decided to check on the kid. Signs of a hasty packing job or else a search—and no sign of the rifle, scope or ammo. Thought Keith might have been in touch with you."

"No! You guys are the ones doing surveillance on him."

"No sign anyone took off through the woods, Paul. We checked that out with a dog. Looks like Hawley came and got him. We did get a pretty good tire imprint at the side of the driveway where a car got off into soft ground." Jim sounded uncomfortable. "The sister's gone, too. All I get is a canned voice on tape. Her secretary said she'd gone out of town on vacation but she refused to tell me where. I didn't identify myself. Thought I'd touch base with you first."

"How did Hawley slip past your man?" Paul wanted to know.

He had to divert Jim's attention from Elaine, and wasn't about to tell Jim her whereabouts if he could help it. Elaine would hate him if he led them to her father.

"The man we assigned is allergic to yellow-jacket stings. He didn't know it, and we didn't know it. It wasn't on his medical record. He had his car parked off the road right over a damned yellow-jacket nest. The warm weather the past few days must have gotten things stirred up. They got up into the car through the opened window and buzzed him, he swatted around, and before he knew it, the suckers were all over him."

"That can be fatal. Is he all right?"

"He radioed for help, pretty sick, but he didn't black out. He wasn't too alert, he admits. He was in pretty bad shape by the time an ambulance reached him and got him to the county hospital. In all the confusion, there was a lapse of time before another man was assigned to take over, but that was the only break in surveillance."

"When did he get stung?"

"Tuesday morning about eight o'clock. Surveillance was in operation again by ten. Nobody has been to that house since."

"So Keith left between eight and ten Tuesday morning," Paul mused. "I don't think he ran out on us, Jim. Hawley came for him and Keith was unable to call us to leave word."

"Is the sister in trouble?" A sigh sounded at the other end of the line. "I hate cases like this. Trying to prevent trouble is always harder than the mop-up job afterward. I just wish Channing had headed back to California two weeks ago so the guys out there could deal with it. Now it looks as if we've got to worry about the sister, too. Do you think Hawley has her?"

"I wouldn't jump to conclusions, Jim. In fact, I encouraged her to take her vacation now. To get her out of town until the race is over."

"Did you tell her her life may be in danger?"

"No. Keith was adamant about that. He didn't want her to know." Paul wondered now if he had done the right thing in deferring to Keith's wishes.

"She *should* know." Jim confirmed Paul's own misgivings. "She could be walking right into a hostage situation." He paused. "Tell me immediately if you hear anything from the kid."

"You bet I will, Jim!"

"Thanks, Paul. Oh, you're running in the Mini-Marathon tomorrow, aren't you?"

"Yes."

"Good luck. A couple of our guys in the department are running, too. They're in real good shape." Jim sounded envious.

"Thanks," Paul responded glumly.

The line went dead.

FOR THE REST OF THE DAY, every time the office telephone rang Paul rushed to answer it, hoping to hear Elaine's voice, or Keith's. The disappointment was like a wet blanket, heavy and chill.

Even Ben noticed the change in his manner. "Got nerves before the big event?" He thrust his gray-thatched head into the doorway of Paul's office, as if to invite confidential talk. Paul waved him away and hunched over the sheets of layouts for the next issue, unable to concentrate.

It was a little after two when Mary buzzed. "Mr. Channing's on the line, Paul."

Garry's familiar voice came booming through the receiver. "I've got tickets to the mechanics recognition party—fried chicken, roasted corn, the works. Why don't you and your lady take a break and come out to the speedway to eat with Laura, Alex and me and my crew? The party's open to the public."

"You sound cheerful, Garry." Paul found Channing's debonair attitude to the murder plot against him almost unbelievable. Either the guy knew how to play it cool or he didn't believe he was in much danger.

"Our car passed all the carburetion tests today with flying colors! My driver pushed her to the limit, and held it. Kinda crowded out there on the oval today, Paul!" He chuckled, a hearty deep-throated sound. "No oil leaks. Water pump held up fine. Electrical system purring like a kitten. I'm ready to celebrate. Thought of you." He hesitated. "You *do* eat the day before the Mini-Marathon, don't you?"

Paul had to laugh. "You put gas in your race car before you sent it out on the practice runs today, didn't you?"

"Car won't run without it."

"Neither do I. The job I'm doing now is driving me nuts. I'd be glad to get away from it for a while. What time should I be there?"

"Five o'clock. Come to Gasoline Alley. Boy, has there ever been a crowd today! It looks like race day. We're not sitting in pole position in the starting lineup come Sunday, Paul, but this car is a sweetheart. I think we got a good chance of crossing the Finish line first this time!"

As Paul hung up, he marveled. All the man could think about was his car. Could it be that what Paul and the police officers had interpreted as courage was simply a reluctance to believe there was any threat at all? A denial of reality?

He stared at the phone in his hand, shaken.

AT EXACTLY FIVE O'CLOCK, Paul was at one of the gates in the fence surrounding Gasoline Alley. His press badge, prominently displayed on the front pocket of his sport jacket, got him past the vigilant guard.

Three long concrete-block buildings stretched ahead of him. The area was teeming with people—crew members, race drivers and their families.

Paul located Garry's garage, its overhead door rolled up and out of the way. Garry stood lean and tall in brown leather jacket and Levi's beside a car whose colors repeated those of the large black-and-white floor tiles in the twenty-four- by twenty-four-foot area his parts distributorship had been assigned.

Garry was talking to his head mechanic, and no one had noticed Paul's arrival yet. The scene was one of orderly confusion. Wide tires were stacked against the back wall; a cardboard carton of cans of motor oil stood near the middle of the floor, next to the car. Boxes of tools, lines, hoses, chains, pulleys and other equipment lay strewn about the floor.

Laura Channing sat perched on a high stool against a wall, out of the way, her full skirt draped over shapely legs, a cotton pullover outlining rounded breasts, her graceful feet in leather sandals. Alex Rande stood beside Garry, while a team of mechanics surrounded the car. With a shock Paul recognized the face of one of the undercover policemen who had attended the meeting in the hospitality suite. No doubt hired by Channing as an extra crewman to help out for the busy two-week period, he was dressed in a mechanic's coverall. The glances of the two men locked for an instant, then Paul looked away. He felt relieved. The security net for Garry Channing was in place.

Alex Rande, in gray and blue sport shirt, gray slacks and black leather jacket, had an air of authority. He was peering down at the engine, joining in the conversation with the head mechanic, who crouched on his heels, pointing at the water pump with an index finger.

Paul saw Rande's hand grip his friend's shoulder reassuringly. The two men grinned at each other like the old friends they were. "I'd be willing to lay some good money down on the line that this baby finishes in the top three places on Sunday, Garry."

"Not legal in this state, Alex. I'll let you take Laura and me to dinner instead."

"Hell, I'll take the whole damn crew to dinner! Best spot Indianapolis has to offer!" said Alex. All the crew members looked up and grinned.

"Paul! Where's Elaine?" Laura had caught sight of him.

"Sorry. She's out of town on business. She sends her apologies." It was one of those white lies.

The head mechanic lifted his head, sniffed the air. "Hey, that's fried chicken I'm smelling. Let's lock up and go eat!"

Channing, Laura, Paul, Rande and the driver took off first, leaving the crew to lock up and trail after them. They headed for the red- and white-striped circus tent, the setting for the mechanics recognition party, and joined the long food line. Race fans stood elbow to elbow with international drivers and crew members who wore their colors proudly. The festival queen and princesses stood in line with everyone else.

All had come for the food and the ceremony to honor mechanics and crews at 6:00 p.m. A band was playing and everyone was smiling and laughing, the prerace tensions eased. Racing fans spoke to the famous and got a smile, a nod, a friendly reply, sometimes even a handshake.

"Democracy in action. I love Indianapolis and the '500'!" Paul heard the voice of Alex Rande behind him. Rande was gazing at the queen, who was dressed in casual clothes, looking like the college junior she was. Laura was engrossed in conversation with her husband, eyes on his face, held securely within his arm. Paul felt a stab of shame for the doubts he'd been having about her. She hardly seemed the type to be masterminding the death of her husband. But someone was. The same person who was responsible for Keith Malden's disappearance.

Over a paper plate heaped with fried chicken, steamed ears of corn and hush puppies, with the rumble of cheerful voices surrounding him, Paul experienced both an inner quiet and a sense of solitude.

He missed Elaine. For the first time he was realizing that her absence left an empty space within himself.

ON FRIDAY MORNING Paul parked the LeBaron in the reserved section he leased each month in an indoor parking garage. His breakfast had been light—only yogurt and half a bagel.

He left the garage dressed in running shorts, a cotton undershirt and running shoes. At eight o'clock a crowd was already assembling on Monument Circle—runners; the 74th army band from Fort Benjamin Harrison; festival volunteers; relatives and friends of the runners who had come to see them off at the sound of the nine o'clock starting gun.

Paul joined others he recognized who were busy doing warm-up exercises. None of the magazine staff was there—at his request. Paul had given them the day off so they wouldn't have to fight the crowd and traffic. Ben had volunteered to be at the speedway Finish line at ten-thirty to take Paul downtown to pick up his car.

The army band began to play in front of Christ Church Cathedral, the sound pouring through loudspeakers. The queen and princesses, wearing red and white, held huge bouquets of colored balloons in their hands. The mayor stood waiting to make his introductory remarks as a clergyman sat with the Bible in his lap, ready to speak the opening prayer into the microphone.

Paul did his warm-up stretches and walked over to talk with other runners. Each of them now wore bold, black entry numbers. The sky was blue and clear, and the sun shone down upon the sidewalks and street packed with human bodies. Nine thousand runners had assembled in the small area, and tension was mounting. The spectators also filled the temporary bleachers set up along North Meridian Street so people could watch the memorial parade the next day.

"All runners please move behind the Start line," a clear male voice called over the loudspeakers. A long orange ribbon stretched from one side of the street to the other. In orderly fashion, the nine thousand entrants obeyed, Paul among them.

First there were opening remarks by the dignitaries, then the prayer, and finally the instructions to the runners. "Fourteen water stations are along the thirteen-mile route for your use. Medical personnel are stationed around the course, if needed. If you feel ill or need help, please don't attempt to finish. We urge you to drink plenty of water along the way!"

Paul lined up shoulder to shoulder with runners of all ages. The army band broke into a sprightly tune with an infectious rhythm. Led by a police motorcycle unit, the contestants in wheelchairs started first, muscular arms and hands driving the wheels of their conveyances as sunlight was reflected in dancing beams from the whirling spokes. Excitement was mounting.

The green flag fell. The orange ribbon dropped, and the mass of bodies began to move to the beat of the band music, a beat that seemed to carry Paul along. The butterflies of tension vanished and only the excitement remained as he hit an easy warming stride past the crowded bleachers. There was a spirit of exhilaration in the bobbing ocean of runners all moving at the same speed. The energy generated by the band music pulsated beneath the pavement, streaming upward through his feet and legs. He was possessed by it, borne along, elbows thrust away from his body, arms and legs pumping, hands in a curl, shoes slapping the pavement.

Trees and buildings glided past, and he focused on breathing and on that invisible center deep within himself. His entire being settled into a state of calm as breath and muscle, joint and tendon pulled together in unison, expanded, contracted, were released, and the solid ribbon of street rolled away beneath his pounding feet. A year of daily training and good nutrition had brought Paul's body to peak performance.

He was riding the wind. He was free.

THE SUN BEAT DOWN without mercy.

The ocean wave of runners had thinned to a trickling stream.

Reaching a steep hill after about eight and a half miles, Paul began to fall back. He began a duel with a male runner whose face seemed strangely familiar. They ran beside each other as they headed south on Cold Springs road to 16th Street. Paul leaned hard into the turn and took a two-second lead at the ten-mile mark.

Humid heat had turned West 16th into a test of endurance. A carpet of paper cups crushed by pounding feet lay spread before him. Every fifteen or twenty minutes he slowed, pausing long enough to pick up a paper cupful of water, sipping four to six ounces each time. Sweat streamed down his body. His thin garments were soaked as searing heat enveloped him, cascading from above and welling up from the pavement.

The festival volunteers who manned the long tables holding the containers of water called out words of encouragement and praise. Neighborhood residents lined the streets, applauding and cheering. There were no strangers along the race route. Only friends.

His mind numbed by the punishing heat, Paul watched the familiar-looking man, his body moving with perfect ease, slowly pass him.

The stands of the motor speedway loomed into view. As he made it through the gate of the speedway, the attendant called out, "You're home! Finish line ahead! Good job!" The man was beaming.

Paul was running on the asphalt oval track now, the same track over which Channing's Lola-Cosworth had sped the day before, pushed to its limits. Suddenly Paul knew how it had felt. He rounded the fourth turn, passed under the empty seats of the hospitality suites, and stumbled on toward the Brickyard, his legs propelled only by willpower. He heard the announcer's voice pour from the overhead speakers.

"Ladies and Gentlemen, Evan Bayh, governor of the state of Indiana, has just crossed the Finish line, completing the 13.1-mile course in 1.46."

Evan Bayh. The governor of Indiana. No wonder he'd looked familiar.

Paul almost tripped. He slowed to a painful walk and headed toward a lane on the left, handing the volunteer his ID ticket. He longed to collapse but was too stubborn to do it. He even resisted the impulse to sit on the concrete pit wall.

"Go get yourself sprayed down. Canned drinks and cookies are ahead. Go help yourself. Good job!" a volunteer told him.

Paul headed toward the spray, feeling the pleasant shock of cool water on his burning body. When he emerged, the terrible sensation of crushing heat was passing, aided by a cool breeze. He stumbled on, still numb below the knees, hoping Ben had remembered his promise to be at the gate to meet him.

All around him, Paul could hear the reunions of runners with loved ones waiting to meet them. Cheery words, the telltale sounds of kisses, a happy letdown from strenuous physical activity countered by a pick-me-up of tenderness and caring.

Ben wasn't there, and suddenly he felt lonely. Then he felt a soft hand on his shoulder. Not daring to believe what his senses told him, he turned—to face Elaine.

Her hand passed over his wet, matted hair in a gesture of tenderness. "I traded in the return ticket you gave me for an earlier date. I had to see you cross that Finish line. The sight was worth the trip of thousands of miles. Mr. Republican battling it out with Mr. Democrat. You were magnificent, Paul!''

Elaine definitely sounded different. What had happened in Seattle, anyway? Paul forgot Hawley, he forgot Keith, forgot his fatigue. All he could think of was Elaine. Her fingers brushed his temples and then his face.

He resisted the urge to crush her to his wet body, but found himself being kissed by her instead. ''I called Mary from the airport—I kept her home phone number in case of an emergency—and she headed off Ben. I'll take you downtown. We might be able to catch part of the memorial service. Jan told me the band concert is supposed to start at eleven and the service about noon.''

''You talked to Jan?''

''I called her at work right after I talked with Mary. My tickets for the Queen's Ball came in. Jan is holding them in her desk. After I drop you off at your car, I'll run up to my office and pick them up. Did you remember to reserve a rental tux?'' she asked, sounding worried.

''Don't have to. I already own one,'' Paul told her.

''Jeez. I might have known.'' She seemed pleased. ''I hope you don't think me sadistic, dragging you off to a dinner dance after you've run thirteen miles in this heat. You're probably bone-tired.''

Paul knew he should tell Elaine about Keith's disappearance, but couldn't bear the thought of seeing the glow in her face fade. He kissed her instead. He wanted this moment in the sun, the most beautiful moment he had ever known, to last forever. He didn't want anything to spoil it.

Yet minutes later he knew he had no choice. "The Channings are going to the Queen's Ball," he told her. "So is Alex Rande. Garry told me one of their sponsors invited them."

She sighed. "And you think that my brother might take a shot at Garry, right?" The cheery tone was gone. "If he does, he'll miss on purpose."

"I'm not sure Keith can hit the mark on purpose. He might hit his target by pure accident."

"Don't worry. Garry Channing is safe tonight," Elaine declared as she slid behind the steering wheel of her car.

"How can you be so sure?" Paul asked, half of him wishing she had remained safe in Seattle, the other half delighted she was back with him.

"I know my brother. This is a black-tie, formal occasion. Keith refuses to wear a penguin suit. I couldn't even get him to wear one to his senior prom. I felt so sorry for his date that night. So unless he comes dressed as a waiter, Keith won't be able to get in the door," Elaine declared as she pulled out of the parking area and joined the long line of waiting cars.

Paul wished he could be as certain as she seemed to be. If Keith had gone with Hawley against his will, Elaine was no safer than Garry Channing.

She was Brett Hawley's wild card in this deadly game of poker.

CHAPTER THIRTEEN

THE LEBARON EASED UP the curved driveway in front of the convention center in downtown Indianapolis, in line behind a half-dozen other cars. Paul sat behind the steering wheel, clad in black tuxedo with black cummerbund, black tie and white shirt. *Distinguished. Dignified,* Elaine thought as she gazed at him from the passenger seat.

Also impassioned. His nostrils were flaring and his azure eyes flashing dangerously.

"I won't do it! What you're asking is impossible. Crazy! I could be sentenced to a year in jail for contempt of court if I refused to tell the judge my source. Uh-uh. Not even for you." He moved the car forward.

"But you're a journalist. I didn't think you had to reveal the sources of your information."

"Put yourself in the president's place. I'd look ridiculous. What would he think of my explanation?" Paul was speaking rapidly, betraying his agitation. "'I'm a journalist. George Stamm sent me. He really isn't dead, after all. He didn't really mean to rob you. It was all a mistake. Here's your money back—without interest. He's sorry and asks your forgiveness.'

"Come on, Elaine! They'd have the cops on me before I could get out of the building."

Quickly Elaine reached into her sequined handbag and pulled out the Queen's Ball ticket. She handed it to him. "I'll go on inside," she said coolly, hoping his disposition would improve by the time he'd parked his car. Obviously it had been a mistake to spring this matter on him now.

The LeBaron advanced, and a uniformed doorman reached out a gloved hand to open the door for Elaine.

"I apologize for suggesting it. I'll take the money to Cincinnati myself." Ada had entrusted it to her. Elaine had brought the suitcases back on the plane, paying extra, terrified a baggage mishap might occur before they reached Indianapolis.

Paul was silent as she alighted and walked up the sidewalk with the bearing of a queen. If she took the money back, it would all come out. Commercial Bank officials would learn about it through the informal institutional network. Marked as George Stamm's daughter, his sins would fall upon her. They'd find some reason to dismiss her.

Elaine's worst fears were being realized. The wide, well-lighted hallway before her shimmered in a mist of tears as she made her way to the exhibition hall and showed her ticket at the door with a practiced smile.

The Indianapolis Symphony was playing a Broadway show tune in a rich, full-bodied sound that filled the huge, high-ceilinged room. The vast area was in shadow, only pinpoints of candlelight flickering from each dining table. The ambience was dreamlike and ethereal, Elaine felt, the effect heightened by the delicate archways and tiny electric lights over the orchestra's music stands. Her gaze lingered for a moment on the rainbow-hued chiffon wall hangings, but the beauty around her failed to distract her from the problem at hand.

Paul had every right to get upset. We've known each other only five weeks. I asked too much of him, she thought. She took a place in the line before the portable bar so as to have a drink ready for him when he rejoined her.

When Paul stepped into the ballroom, Elaine was waiting for him, a Scotch and soda in one hand, a glass of white wine for herself in the other. He looked grateful. Shadows of fatigue from his run still lingered on his face.

"Did you get some rest this afternoon?" she asked, concerned.

"Yes, three hours after a warm shower. You can tell I showered, can't you?" he teased as his arm reached for her waist, encircling it and bringing her close. "I like your dress. Very sexy in a demure way," he murmured, the agitation he had displayed in the car totally absent.

"Ada made it for me after I told her about having tickets for the ball. She wanted to do it. She insisted."

Elaine had been astonished when she had walked into the sewing room to find the finished garment on the dress form standing next to the sewing machine. Ada had taken her measurement two days before, telling her she would have a birthday present for her, but Elaine had not been prepared for the vision in lovely white lace over a long-sleeved satin sheath. Ada proved to be a master craftsperson.

"That would be a fine wedding dress," Paul whispered into her ear. Her heart skipped a beat.

The scent of his cologne, subtle and masculine, brought another leap to her pulse. She rested her head on his shoulder for a moment, then felt the arm around her suddenly stiffen. "I see Garry and Alex Rande. Garry's waving at us. Let's go speak to them before we find the bank's table," Paul suggested. He dropped his arm from her waist and took her hand as he cut a path through the crowd.

Elaine extended her hand to the Channings and Alex Rande, who rose to greet them. Garry Channing looked less genial, less western in his black tux and burgundy cummerbund. He was strikingly handsome, yet despite their similar dress, he looked very different from the CEO of BMQ/OXO. Rande possessed sophisticated ease surpassing even that of Elaine's trust department clients. The sight of him sent a thrill racing through her limbs. The tilt of his head, the gestures of his hands—everything was controlled and deliberate—effective.

Laura Channing, her slim figure enhanced to perfection in sleek black with an off-the-shoulder neckline, seemed entranced by the man. Elaine felt instant sympathy for Garry Channing, even a bizarre sense of loyalty. *This is the man my brother has been paid to murder.*

As Paul and Elaine joined the group, Laura tore her attention away from Alex Rande and directed a cool smile toward them.

"Sure sorry you couldn't join us at the mechanics recognition party yesterday," Garry Channing was saying.

What was the man talking about? Elaine exchanged a swift glance with Paul.

"I explained that you were tied up on bank business and couldn't get away," Paul told her.

Elaine smiled, suddenly uncomfortable; Alex Rande's stare was downright insolent! She had sensed his surprise at seeing her here tonight, but his almost-imperceptible reaction puzzled her, to say the least.

"We'll be watching the race from the Hulmans' suite," Rande announced. "Would you be interested in joining us?" he asked Elaine. The manner, the tone of voice would make any woman melt, she thought and felt instant hostility from Laura as the ex-model's eyes flashed.

She's hooked, Elaine decided. "Thank you, but I can't. I'm serving as hostess in the bank's hospitality suite during the race."

"Then may I have a dance later this evening?" Rande persisted. "Or does Paul have exclusive rights?" Alex Rande seemed almost amused as his glance shifted to Paul, who stiffened, an inscrutable look on his face.

This man is accustomed to getting whatever he wants, she realized, wanting to keep her distance. Her glance flicked quickly to Laura, who stood staring absently at the orchestra.

"Yes. Paul has exclusive rights." Elaine smiled gently. "Stop in at the bank suite after the race, Garry. We'll help you celebrate."

Laura is so lucky, she thought as Channing's face eased into a shining smile. *Does she even realize it?*

"I'll do that. Thank you kindly, ma'am."

"We'd better go find our table," Elaine said, taking Paul's arm.

"Do I really have exclusive rights with you?" Paul asked in a low voice as they threaded their way through the crowd, searching for the table number that was printed on their tickets. "Even after the argument we had in the car?"

"I was being unreasonable. I'm sorry. I had no right to ask you to jeopardize yourself for my father's sake. Actually it's my stepmother who discussed it with me. My father is too proud to ask anyone for anything. In some ways he reminds me of you."

They moved on to the table whose seats were filled with Commercial Bank officers, including the president and his wife. Elaine introduced Paul. The name of his magazine met with instant recognition.

A fanfare preceded the program, which began with the presentation of the "500" festival queen and her court, who were dressed in floor-length ball gowns.

All the celebrities who would ride in the parade were introduced next. Dinner followed, presented with a flourish by an army of servers. The chicken breast, broccoli, carrots, rice pilaf and baked Alaska were as fine a feast as Elaine had ever enjoyed.

The Indianapolis Symphony yielded to a smaller group, the Indianapolis Jazz Rock Ensemble.

"I'll take advantage of my exclusive right to a dance," Paul joked.

"Sure you feel up to it?" Elaine asked, but the look he gave her silenced her. She stood and they walked onto the crowded dance floor, Elaine moved into the circle of Paul's arm, and they began to dance to the moderate tempo. The sixteen hundred people in the vast room—many of them on the dance floor—faded into the background as Elaine moved closer to Paul. She sighed contentedly as the side of his chin moved slowly back and forth in a subtle caress along the side of her head.

"I'm not so worried about Garry tonight," Paul whispered into her ear.

"Why not?" she whispered back.

"Remember I told you about Jim Dickerson? He's seated at a table next to him. And one of the men stationed at the door here tonight was present at the police conference when Keith was interrogated. I recognized him when I walked in. There are probably others in the crowd, too.''

Elaine felt him relax against her. ''You were worried about tonight, weren't you?''

''Under the circumstances, do you blame me?''

''Then you think Keith may not be the only one involved in this plot against Channing.''

''It's a possibility.'' His voice was tight, but his lean body was supple as it moved in time with the music. He was so easy to follow.

''Darling, where is my brother?'' she asked, and felt Paul's body suddenly go rigid, even the arm braced against her back. ''I left a message on his answering machine as soon as I reached Indianapolis. I called from the airport. The machine is still on and he hasn't called me back. That isn't like him. Paul... what is it you aren't telling me?'' she whispered hoarsely, gazing up at him.

Paul clearly looked distressed, confirming her worst fears.

''Has something happened to him? What—?''

Both Paul's arms went around her and they stood motionless while other couples moved around them. He rested his face against her cheek. They stood in this embrace in full public view, and Elaine didn't even care.

''He disappeared from the house Tuesday morning, leaving the car with the transmitter in the driveway. We think Hawley came and got him,'' he told her quietly.

Her hands tightened on his shoulders. Now Paul was literally holding her up as her mind spun with the implications. "Do you think Hawley suspects Keith told the police?'' she whispered.

"I don't know. We'll find him. Don't worry.''

"Don't worry!'' Her head fell back. Elaine was about to explode when she became aware of someone approaching, threading his way through the moving couples. She said no more.

Alex Rande appeared behind Paul's back. His manicured hand fell upon Paul's shoulder. "I'm cutting in. I'd like a dance with Elaine. You don't mind, do you?''

Reluctantly Paul stepped to one side. Dazed, Elaine felt the arms of Alex Rande surrounding her, pulling her close in a gesture of instant intimacy to which she was not accustomed. The lower curve of his jaw settled against her cheek with the intensity of a kiss, making her skin burn. The dynamic authority she had sensed in the man settled upon her with undiluted force.

He led masterfully. She had no choice but to follow. Alex Rande didn't say a word, but his presence was so compelling, Elaine wondered how Laura ever resisted it. How Garry Channing could be so blind as not to sense it.

This man is Garry's close friend, she had to remind herself, her heartbeat quickening at his closeness. Here was a man who remained an enigma to the media, whose wealth had only been estimated, known only to the Internal Revenue Service, who charted the course of a variety of companies. He was divorced, on the list of the ten most eligible bachelors in the U.S., and even better looking than Paul Newman. Now he was dancing with her, his lips only inches away from hers. She felt herself growing weak, her legs unsteady.

"We have an invitation from our hosts to join them afterward. I'm sure there is room for two more. Would you—and Paul, of course—care to join us? I'd like a chance to learn more about you, Elaine." His voice had lost the harder quality she heard before; now it sounded like a lover's.

Elaine swallowed hard. "I think Paul is still tired from running this morning. The heat was pretty bad."

"Then I'll take full responsibility for you. I'll take you home afterward. It will give us a chance to be alone, to get to know one another better. I'd like that. Wouldn't you?" The smooth voice was a caress, making her tingle despite her feelings for Paul. His arm was pulling her closer against him, delivering a message that was subtle yet impossible to ignore. The room suddenly seemed warm.

"You look like a bride, innocent, pure, virginal," he whispered into her ear. She felt the self-assured pressure of Alex Rande's lips against her temple.

The music stopped. As others in the room applauded, Rande reluctantly released her. Elaine felt dizzy; she couldn't speak. She held out her hand to Paul instead. He took the cue. Standing dourly at the edge of the dance floor, he came immediately to her and took her hand, grasping it firmly.

Rande repeated the invitation to Paul, his tone much different now, one man to another, not forgetting the offer to take Elaine home if Paul was too tired to stay.

"That's up to her. Is that what you want?" Paul asked her stiffly. She was beseeching him with her eyes. She shook her head slightly, mute.

"We have other plans, Alex," Paul said briskly. "Thank you, anyway." The band broke into a rumba. "Come on, honey. Let's go back to the table. That's out of my league." He took Elaine firmly by the waist and they walked away.

A few minutes later they looked at the dance floor again. Alex Rande and Laura were doing the rumba with the expertise of professionals. Laura looked flushed and pleased.

"Poor girl. She doesn't stand a chance," muttered Elaine, unable to take her eyes off the couple.

"You had your chance. Good prospect. An estate in California. Another in Hawaii. A place in Maine. An apartment in New York City." Paul's tone was dry.

She laughed. "I'd forget what my address was. Not to mention my telephone number. No, Paul, that guy comes on too strong. Makes me feel uncomfortable. With you I feel comfortable. That means a lot."

They held hands openly, staring into each other's eyes. "You're not like Madeline," he said softly, gleams from the flickering candles bright in the depths of his eyes.

Was it a compliment? An expression of regret? Elaine couldn't be sure. She imagined Madeline to be the perfect woman—intelligent, cultured, beautiful. After all, wasn't she the director of one of the largest private art museums in the nation and fluent in three languages?

What can Paul see in me? The daughter of a thief? Elaine wondered, and thereafter much of the magic of the Queen's Ball was lost.

They danced every dance until midnight. Garry, Laura and Alex Rande didn't approach them again. At twelve, Elaine and Paul stole away, and Paul invited her to go home with him. Was the invitation an impulse? Was it planned?

After thinking it over a few minutes, she agreed, because spending the night with him was something she really wanted to do.

She loved Paul Cooper as she had loved no other man before.

THE FIRST THING Paul did when they walked into the living room was to check the answering machine in the office/guest room. Elaine stood in the doorway, hoping to hear Keith's voice on the tape. There was a certain intimacy in hearing the half-dozen messages callers had left for Paul. None were from women, she noted with a sense of relief. None were from Keith.

She turned her forehead against the wooden molding, fighting panic. Keith was missing—where was he? Paul was there instantly. He seemed to understand what she was feeling. She welcomed the comfort of his arms.

"He's all right. He can take care of himself," Paul said, holding her tightly. His arms were a warm, safe haven. She held him tightly in return, wanting to show her affection.

Elaine felt his lips press against her head, lingering there until she got control of herself. "I'm coming unglued. If Keith called Dickerson, would Dickerson call you right away to let you know?"

"I think so. Just hang on, honey! Everything about this mess will turn out all right." His azure eyes brimmed with compassion.

"What if Hawley found out Keith talked to the police?" She looked up at Paul's serious face. He ran the fingers of one hand tenderly through her hair at the temple. A pleasant tingle danced along her face. A sigh betrayed her pleasure.

"How would he find out? Keith won't tell him. They're probably holed up somewhere until race day. Or maybe the whole unholy project's been called off," Paul suggested.

"You think so?" Hope flared bright and hot.

"If Garry's ex-wife Marian and her son Todd are involved, perhaps a few questions by the police in California have persuaded them to scrub the plan."

"Then why *kidnap* Keith?"

"I don't know. I can't think the way these guys do, Elaine. Maybe Keith . . . ran off . . . took off for Canada or Mexico. After all, that's what you wanted him to do in the first place."

"You really think—?"

"He could be in Toronto or Mexico City right now. Washing dishes for a living." A wry grin crept over Paul's face. "It'd make a great novel." He waved a hand dramatically in the air. "*The Confessions of an Undercover Dishwasher.* The secret bacterial count on restaurant plates all over the U.S. Ought to sell a million copies to health-conscious readers."

Elaine gasped, coughed, then started laughing. He was doing his best to make her feel better.

"Nuttier things than that happen in the publishing business, hon." Paul's hand cupped her face. Such tenderness was in the touch, reflected in his eyes that Elaine's chest ached with a tumult of feelings. "He'll be all right, honey. Sometimes one has to have faith. Faith." He repeated the word softly. "Sometimes you have to believe in rainbows."

Something almost mystical was in his face, softening his features. "Rainbows?" she asked. What was he talking about? Usually every word Paul uttered had a purpose.

"Once I did. Rainbows to me were the bridge to heaven. The road to dreams. Rainbows were the sign that every good dream was possible if one had faith and worked hard, a sign that people who shared my world were basically good. Then, when I was twelve, my father decided no real man should believe in rainbows. Dreams had no place in a man's life, only harsh reality. He persuaded me. After all, he knew everything. He was a success. He was my father. So I plunged into the world, worked hard in my profession, rose to the top. Yet I wasn't happy. Often I saw people at their worst. I became cynical. I lost my faith in people during that competitive scramble to be first. I lost touch with who I am *inside*.

"My father was wrong. Rainbows are real," he said softly, his warm breath falling upon her ear.

"What makes you think so?"

"I found out who I am. I went in search of my own dream. I have my own magazine and it's one to be proud of. And I found you."

Now both hands cupped her face. His lips touched her lips, then her cheeks, the tip of her nose, both closed eyelids. He was so tender that the passion she sensed deep within him and the tumult of sensation welling up within herself were causing her no apprehension. Only excitement.

She wanted to bring him happiness.

Yet she wanted to be honest. For twenty years Elaine had been reticent, hiding vital parts of her inner self and her life from others. The words did not come easily.

"I was...raped...when I was fourteen. It...was evening...on high school property...I was going into the school for a play practice. Three boys...dragged me to a shed...." Elaine couldn't finish. She felt suddenly depleted, wanting to cry, yet not yielding to the impulse. Paul would reject her now, she was certain of it.

"I know." The arms around her tightened as if to reassure her that she was safe.

"You know? Your detective—found *that* out, too?" she stammered, shocked.

"Mick is a thorough guy. What happened wasn't your fault. You've been carrying around a guilt trip that you don't deserve." His hand was rubbing her back soothingly. "You didn't do anything to bring it on, Elaine. You need to forgive yourself. What happened to you was an act of violence. The immature creeps were getting back at your father through you, by humiliating you."

"You want me now, don't you?" Her voice trembled.

"Yes. But only if you want it as much as I do. I'll be content just to sit on the couch and hold you, if you'll let me. Tomorrow night, too. Until the '500' race is over and this damnable deal your brother's got himself into is resolved."

The gentle pressure of his arms confirmed his words. They enfolded her as if to attempt to compensate for the thoughtless pain others had inflicted on her years before. Elaine felt protected, secure, accepted, surrounded by a warm caring unlike any she had ever experienced.

Suddenly her pent-up tears burst forth. Elaine was powerless to restrain them. Paul's hand cradled the back of her head, pressing her forehead against his shoulder while he kissed the top of her head. His body was molding itself to fit hers, and she became aware of a soothing, rocking motion as she clung to him.

He moved his head and she noticed that Paul's cheeks were wet too.

"I love you." The confession was torn out of her, leaving a gaping hole in her soul. Did he pity her? Did he regard her as a hopeless neurotic who needed his help? Was she about to be hurt again, in a different way?

In answer, he pressed his lips against her forehead and his tenderness was exactly what Elaine needed now as her fears for Keith's safety—and Garry Channing's, too—obscured the horrors of her own past. She realized, to her amazement, how much she needed Paul Cooper—she, who'd always prided herself on needing no one.

"I want to stay with you tonight," she murmured, turning her face toward his. His cheek was scratchy with new beard growth.

"I'm glad. I want you here with me." His resonant baritone voice had grown husky. She could feel desire welling within him, yet he was waiting for her to make the first move. He was putting her wishes, her wants, her needs ahead of his own.

Elaine stood on her toes and kissed him full on the lips. She was filled with a passion so intense that she felt ready to explode. She felt him gasp and his lips opened to accept her kiss. As his body responded, she was aware of the strength of lean, trained muscle.

Not another word was necessary as they clung to each other, kissing long and deep, their hands memorizing each curve and fold of the other's body. The sounds of their breathing and the thudding of their heartbeats provided all the music Elaine needed. She was encountering herself for the first time, and Paul was making it happen.

"Are you ready?" he asked, his breathing coming harder.

She nodded and they walked, arms around each other's waist, into the master bedroom. He released the buttons and the long zipper at the back of the smooth satin sheath. She stepped free of the treasured garment and laid it carefully over the back of a chair.

Still clad in bra, teddy and hose, she helped Paul to undress, too. His hands caressed her shoulders, moving over her with the slowness of wonder. Before divesting himself of his trousers he stooped to kiss her shoulders, her breasts, right through the lingerie that shielded them. They were kisses of reverence.

The memory of Paul pressing toward the Finish line at the track, sun-drenched body glistening with sweat, leaning into the wind, muscles straining, an expression of intensity on his face, flashed before her eyes. Then he had belonged to the task at hand. At this moment he belonged to her.

His hands slipped the shoulder straps of her bra down over her shoulders. Consumed by the need to merge with him, her lips went to his neck, her tongue tasting the salt of his skin. She felt him smile. He pulled her teddy over her head and removed her bra. She felt as if she were on the edge of a precipice, and realized she was about to lose herself in him. A trembling seized her; she was hot and cold at the same time.

Elaine slid her fingertips through his soft hair, outlining the hairline above the wide forehead, caressing the temples just beginning to gray, the fullness of the square jaw and the stubborn chin. His eyes were closed as he savored the feel of her hands on his face. His hands captured hers, and he pressed kisses into her palms, his warm tongue licking the sensitive area of her inner wrists.

They sank onto the bed in one fluid motion. He was still touching her, every stroke stirring the intensity of Elaine's desire for him. She was totally without fear as his lips and hands caressed her as only the hands of a lover can, lifting her to an ecstasy of contentment and release.

His body gave a tiny shudder and relaxed. They lay in each other's arms, unwilling to release each other.

The same floating peace Elaine had experienced before settled over her now.

The telephone rang twice, breaking the stillness. Before Paul could roll over to answer, Elaine heard her brother's voice, strained and harsh, come over the speaker of the answering machine in the office.

"Paul, help me! I'm in trouble!"

There was a loud click. Nothing more.

CHAPTER FOURTEEN

THE CEILING LIGHT flashed on, harsh and bright, a physical blow to closed eyelids. "Everybody up! We're moving out. It's Saturday morning! We'll catch breakfast on the way!" announced Brett Hawley's grating voice.

Keith struggled up through the cotton batting of troubled sleep. He opened bleary eyes. When the window took on a sharper focus, he perceived the faint blue light of dawn. His jaw was aching.

"About time! I can't stand another meal in this place," muttered Lucky, sitting up in his sleeping bag and yawning and stretching as he looked about the furnished efficiency suite.

"Yeah, pancakes and sausages at McDonald's sound good to me." Jed, in jeans and cotton pullover, was already out of his sleeping bag and rolling it up.

Quickly the men shaved, Hawley and Jed using the bathroom mirror, Lucky and Keith the cracked one next to the kitchenette sink. Keith's hand was unsteady; he nicked himself twice, bright red blood welling to the surface and trickling over his chin and neck. He swore softly under his breath at the bites of pain, making Lucky laugh.

Keith could see that his swollen jaw was giving his round face a slightly lopsided appearance; a bluish-red bruise was spreading upward toward his ear. Lucky looked curiously at the result of Hawley's blow but said nothing.

They finished rolling up the sleeping bags, hefted their duffel bags and stole down the stairway in commando style, making no sound. Keith rode in Lucky's pickup, wedged between Jed and Lucky, the rifle hidden behind the seat. Brett followed in the Dodge.

They drove to the nearest McDonald's. Keith could tell from the street signs that they were on the west side of Indianapolis. He swallowed hard as he got out of the truck and walked to the Dodge. They had to wait a few minutes for the fast-food restaurant to open. "Is it . . . going to happen today?" he asked.

Brett Hawley, in denims and dark blue shirt, seemed in a rare good mood. He gripped Keith's shoulder in comradely fashion. "Today you do your stuff, kid. We have to be at the new place before nine and get in without being noticed. Downtown will be crawling, people swarming all over the place. Cops, too, but it'll all be over by two-thirty."

A steely gaze devoid of expression fastened on Keith's face. "You getting a case of nerves?" For a second Keith thought he saw a look of regret flicker deep in the former boxer's eyes. Had he imagined it?

"I'm sorry I had to slug you, when I found you using the pay phone at the bar." A beefy hand reached up and seized his chin as Hawley peered with a squint at the younger man's bruises. "Your jaw's probably not broken." The big hand released Keith's face. "You shoulda had more goddamn sense than to try to call your girlfriend before this job! You know my rules. No contact with anybody on the outside!"

"I miss her!" Keith lied, terrified that Hawley would go after Paul Cooper next. "All I got was her answering machine, anyway." At least that was the truth. The misery Keith was experiencing was no act. He felt Paul had let him down by not being there when he needed him.

"She's probably out with another guy. Out of sight, out of mind. Ever hear that old saying? You almost got yourself killed, too. I've killed men in the ring during a fight when I was in top form. I held back on that punch I threw you."

"Gee, thanks," Keith muttered, trying to control the panic that threatened to overwhelm him. If only Paul had answered his telephone! He might never get another chance to warn him of the move against Channing.

"I still don't understand what those guys are doing here," Keith went on, aware that he sounded surly. He jerked a thumb toward Jed and Lucky, who were leaning against a fender of the truck, sharing a cigarette. When Hawley had dragged him up to the old apartment building, Lucky and Jed had already been there, hunched over a card table, playing gin rummy. They had barely spoken a word to him in more than three days. They were armed to the teeth, too. Jed had a pistol with a silencer—the handgun seemed made of the same material as the rifle—and Lucky carried a wicked knife with a five-inch blade in a leather sheath inside his belt.

"If I'm the hit man, the least you can do is let me in on the plan." Keith made no attempt to hide his resentment.

"I guess it won't hurt to tell you now," Hawley answered, his mood appearing almost congenial for once. "The boss made arrangements for a place overlooking North Meridian Street. Hired a yuppy-type couple to lease it nine months ago, had furniture sent up and hired a decorator to make it look like somebody was living there. Course, the name on the lease is phony—can't be traced later. The boss sure thinks of everything!"

Hawley looked pleased, but Keith suddenly felt sick; his heart seemed to stop momentarily. "Where on North Meridian?" he asked.

Hawley's eyes squinted. "South of the public library. We'll be going there after we eat."

"Then you know who the boss is?"

Hawley looked at him sharply. "Sure, I know."

"Who? A man or a woman?" Keith inquired, still hoping he could get a message to Paul in some way. He was also remembering the possible suspects mentioned during the meeting with Channing and the police in the hospitality suite.

A harsh grunt rolled from Hawley's lips. "I'd be nuts to tell you *or* them." He nodded at the two men beside the truck. He saw the counter person unlock the door from the inside, "Let's go eat. I'm starved."

The three of them ordered pancakes, sausages, biscuits and coffee. Keith studied the two uniformed counter persons. One of them was a gray-haired woman. She reminded Keith of his mother; she smiled a lot, looked kind. *Could I slip a note to her?* he wondered.

On what? The thought jerked Keith back to reality. Hawley had even refused to accept paper-covered trays when their orders were ready, so each man carried his food in plastic containers. Keith led the way to a table at the rear, next to a window, and for once, the other men allowed him to choose.

But the delicious aroma of the pancakes and sausages drifting up to his nostrils didn't even tempt him. For the past three days he had been praying, driven by a desperation he had never felt before in his life. He didn't want to kill Garry Channing, nor did he want Elaine to die, and now there was a third possibility: he might be killed himself. One of these outcomes seemed inevitable.

"Eat. Whatcha waiting on?" Hawley grunted, eyeing Keith before he returned his attention to the sports section of the *Indianapolis Star* that lay folded in front of him. Jed and Lucky were talking in low voices as they leaned over the table, heads toward each other while they ate. For the moment, no one was paying attention to their unwilling partner in murder.

As Keith shoved his coffee cup to one side, he accidentally pushed two paper packets containing sugar over the table edge, so that they dropped to the shiny floor beneath. Seated closest to the window, he scooted his chair back to retrieve them, barely drawing a glance from the others. With his head under the table he spotted something green. A small piece of paper lay crumpled next to the foot of the pedestal table. The stub of a small yellow pencil, the kind often used for marking golf scores, lay beside it as if left behind after a hasty cleanup job.

Keith's heart skipped a beat. He snatched up his windfall and jammed it inside the top of his white tube sock, pulling down the leg of his jeans to cover the bulge.

"What the hell are you doin' down there?" Hawley rasped. Keith's heart leaped against his ribs. He came up quickly, hitting his head against the table. The pain brought tears to his eyes, making him blink. With a furtive glance toward the counter, Keith noticed the motherly woman staring at him.

Jed gave a coarse snicker when Keith, unable to speak, held up the two packets of sugar he had retrieved from the floor. Hawley shot a withering glance at all of them and returned to his reading.

The color of the paper reminded Keith of Garry Channing's words on the balcony overlooking the track the day of the police meeting: *"The green flag is out."* For the first time since Hawley had taken him captive, hope flared high. He stirred his coffee and forced himself to eat.

Jed and Lucky finished first. They left the table without excusing themselves and, after a few minutes, emerged from the men's rest room. Hawley stood, pushing his chair back with a scuffing sound. "Let's go!" he ordered.

Keith bent over, one hand on his abdomen. "I think I've got diarrhea. I felt bum all day yesterday. Just a minute, okay?" He gestured toward the rest rooms. Hawley scowled.

"No windows in there. It's safe. He can't run," Jed assured the boss.

No one followed Keith. He locked himself in a stall, pulled the wad of green paper from his sock and smoothed it with trembling hands. It was an announcement for a church's summer Bible school. The letters had been obscured by wide, random circles of graphite, motions a preschooler might make while being kept busy by a mother or father trying to finish a meal.

Placing the paper against the metal partition that surrounded the stall, Keith printed on the blank side in small letters with the stub of pencil, hands trembling, heart beating wildly.

This is life or death! Please call Paul Cooper—he wrote the home telephone number—and Jim Dickerson, Indiana state police. Tell them green flag today! N. Meridian St. S. of public library. All over by 2:30 p.m. Help! Keith Malden.

He folded the paper neatly, then lined up the message with a dollar bill he took from his jeans pocket, folding them into his closed fist. Then he left the men's room and went to the counter, feeling Hawley's eyes on him all the way. "A small iced tea to go, please, ma'am," he said to the older woman. She smiled and set the paper cup on the counter.

He paid her, handing her the folded dollar bill and pressing it firmly into her outstretched hand, his other hand beneath hers. He watched her smile fade at this unusual action and beseeched her with a look to remain silent. Her gaze was troubled, clearly fastened on the angry bruise on his face.

"Come on, time's up!" Hawley called sharply.

She popped open the register drawer and looked down at her hand to put in the dollar bill and give Keith his change. At that moment he bolted, hoping to draw Hawley's attention away from what the woman's hand contained. Not waiting for the change, he snatched up the cup and made for the door. He could see Jed and Lucky outside, waiting beside the truck. Hawley followed him out.

Please, God, let her read it and follow through!

Morning sun glinted on the windshield as Keith silently climbed back into the pickup.

THE NOON SUN was at its zenith, the breeze light, the temperature 76° Fahrenheit by the time Paul and Elaine made their way to North Pennsylvania Street.

After a leisurely breakfast seasoned with kisses in Paul's apartment, they had driven to her home, where she had changed into culottes, cotton blouse and walking shoes.

Now they joined the crowd of spectators headed for the downtown memorial parade route. Paul knew it began on North Street near the Federal Office Building, moved south on Pennsylvania Street, west on Ohio, then north on Meridian to 16th Street, where it terminated.

As they passed a crowd of spectators headed in the same direction, Paul was reminded of the old saying, All Roads Lead to Rome. Today all roads led to Monument Circle.

The sounds of college and high school bands in energetic practice danced in the air from different locations, a cacophony of brass and drums, cymbals, clarinets, trumpets and oboes. The sound was strangely pleasing to Paul's ears.

"I would never—have been able—to make this run—in those white pumps I wore last night," Elaine said breathlessly, panting in her attempt to keep up with Paul's rapid stride.

Instantly he slowed. "I'm sorry. I didn't mean to go so fast. I put in a call to Dickerson while you were dressing to tell him Keith tried to make contact early this morning... and we missed him." Guilt weighed heavily on Paul.

"He hung up before you had time to pick up the telephone. Why did he do that, Paul?" Elaine's voice was tense; her lovely face showed the signs of strain, he noted.

All the sympathy he felt for her rose to the surface. He was also angry—angry with the man named Brett Hawley, angry with the unknown person who was responsible for the ad that had drawn Keith into this deadly drama. He took Elaine's hand, trying to reassure her with a gentle pressure. "We know he's alive. That's important. We'll find him." He wanted to comfort her, yet his words rang hollow. Indianapolis and Marion County had more than 700,000 inhabitants. Finding a needle in a haystack would be easier.

"Jim may be at the reviewing stand. We have half an hour until the parade starts. Maybe he's heard something since I called him. Something's bound to happen soon. Garry's due to leave for California on Tuesday."

"So there are only three events left—today, the race tomorrow and the banquet on Monday. Are Garry and Laura flying back to California on Alex Rande's jet?" asked Elaine.

"I don't know. Garry didn't say."

"I still think Rande is attracted to Laura," Elaine said thoughtfully. "That invitation to take me to a party after the ball last night was a smoke screen for somebody's benefit. I can't figure out why. Maybe he was trying to make Laura jealous." She looked puzzled.

"Don't underestimate yourself!" said Paul grimly, remembering the hot burst of jealousy he had felt when he had seen Elaine dancing in Rande's arms.

To his surprise, Elaine flashed him a mysterious smile, pulled her hand free and broke into a jog as they headed south along the curb on North Pennsylvania Street. Already the area was crowded with spectators; 300,000 had been predicted in the morning's newspaper. Lawn chairs and blankets, strollers and lunch coolers dotted the grassy strips and sidewalks. A party atmosphere prevailed. "What are you waiting for?" she called back in challenge as she stepped onto the black-and-white checkered carpeting laid over the street for the parade.

Paul broke into an easy running stride beside her. He grinned despite his concern for Garry and Keith.

At the reviewing stand they saw Jim Dickerson, wearing a short-sleeved white shirt, dark trousers and sunglasses, scanning the sea of faces. He carried a police radio in one hand. As soon as he spotted Paul and Elaine, he began to move toward them.

"I may have been wrong about the kid. He *is* being held against his will and he's eager to cooperate with us." Dickerson held out a small piece of crumpled green paper. "A dispatcher received a call at eight this morning from a McDonald's on the west side. This note was slipped to a counter person by someone who matches Keith's description. He was with three older males and apparently showed signs of an assault. The facial area was badly bruised. He acted fearful and was being watched closely by the others. Is this your brother's writing, Ms. Malden?"

Elaine took the note, her face suddenly drained of color, and read it while Paul looked at it over her shoulder. Her hand was trembling slightly. "Yes, this is Keith's writing. Thank God he's still alive! Do something!" she begged, her eyes misting with tears as she looked into Dickerson's face.

"Ma'am, do you realize how many commercial and residential buildings are on the North Meridian Street south of Central Library? Why couldn't he have been more specific?" Dickerson looked upset. "You know how many men it would take to search every single unit with access to Meridian Street, even if we used every officer on duty in the downtown area? The parade starts in twenty minutes. Why in hell did Channing agree to appear in the parade? Considering the circumstances, the guy's just plain nuts!"

"Garry's in the parade?" Paul inquired, staring at his friend's face. This was news to him.

"That's what the parade marshal informed me when I double-checked. Oh, the man isn't listed by name on the program, only as a celebrity, but he's going through with the original plan despite our warnings. I don't think he takes this damned thing seriously.''

Jim was looking into the distance, his attention snared by the sounds of two men arguing in the crowd. A police officer, stationed along the curb with a walkie-talkie in hand, was moving toward the minor disturbance with a quick stride.

"We've got the problem taken care of, anyway," Jim declared, still staring at the scene of the argument.

"How?" asked Paul in disbelief.

"We took the rifle and ammo in for a lab check, the day of the meeting, remember? I returned the equipment to Keith a week later."

Paul nodded.

"The ammunition I returned was blank cartridges," Jim told him. "Of course, neither Keith nor Hawley knows that." A satisfied smile spread over Dickerson's face.

"What happens when Hawley finds out the bullets have been changed?" asked Paul quietly. "He'll know Keith has crossed him up, that he's working with you."

The smile vanished. Dickerson glanced quickly at Elaine. Tears were brimming in her eyes. "I'll divert what men I can for a search of the North Meridian area. I'll do everything I can to find the kid, Paul. But the fact is, he should never have gotten mixed up in a rotten deal like this to begin with. *That* was where he made his big mistake." The static of a voice on the handset snagged Jim's attention. The voice was speaking in a type of number-spiced jargon that neither Paul nor Elaine could understand. Jim murmured into the unit in reply.

Paul and Elaine moved away.

"Hawley will kill Keith," she said in a tone of quiet despair. Paul took her hand; it was cool, despite the warmth of the sun.

"Let's try to find a piece of curb to call our own," Paul suggested. "Then maybe we can figure something out."

As they walked north on Pennsylvania, headed toward the American Legion's headquarters, he searched his mind for a way to help Keith. The parade started at twelve-thirty. He had up to two hours to come up with a solution.

They passed adults and children sprawled on blankets beside the curb, finishing picnic lunches, people sitting on folding lawn chairs, children carrying skateboards in their arms. There were even temporary bleachers set up on a sidewalk thick with spectators. More than forty thousand bleacher seats had been sold in advance.

Police and volunteers were motioning people to clear out of the street. Ahead Elaine could see band personnel in uniform lounging on Central Library's green lawn, taking a last-minute rest before the march in the sun began.

Finally they spotted a few feet of unclaimed curb and rushed to occupy it. "Keith must be going through hell right now." Elaine's lower lip quivered; she was blinking hard.

She'll feel like Keith's mother for the rest of her life, thought Paul. *Her promise to look after him will take precedence over her own marriage, even if she did make peace with her father. What man would want to walk into an arrangement like that?* His sadness was made bitter with irritation and fear for the kid.

Why hadn't Elaine told him about the days she had spent with her father and stepmother? Why wasn't she willing to share her feelings? Was she angry with him for refusing to return the cash to the savings and loan headquarters in Cincinnati? *I could have phrased my refusal in more polite terms,* he admitted to himself.

Paul spotted a festival volunteer in the standard black jacket and white trousers. The man was walking along the curb, selling souvenir program books. Paul rushed forward to buy one. As he and Elaine waited for the parade to begin, he turned to the middle of the book, where the many units in the parade were listed.

They were reading the names of the bands and floats and noting the order of the celebrity cars in the lineup when they heard the Indianapolis motorcycle drill team begin the parade, followed by the full-bodied sound of the Purdue University marching band. The band was headed by a girl in a glittering one-piece bodysuit who twirled her baton high in the air. Brass tubas swayed from side to side in time with feet stepping in military precision. The living wave of black, white and gold moved briskly past.

Paul's eyes swept the street and the crowd. Police department patrol officers were standing quietly, radios in hand. So were sheriff's deputies and officers of the state police. All had been quietly absorbed by the orderly crowd, attracting no attention, but watching, ready, alert.

The crowd was entranced as the governor of Indiana and his wife rolled past in an antique car loaned by the speedway's Hall of Fame Museum. Then came the festival queen and her court on floats and the mayor of Indianapolis, smiling and waving from another antique car.

"Oh, look!" Elaine actually smiled as she tugged at the tail on Paul's pullover to catch his eye.

A seventy-two-foot balloon floated above the checkered carpet, anchored by guy ropes in the hands of a team of volunteers who were walking in time to the rhythm of the 74th army band. The balloon represented the infamous Deputy Dan. A tall white cowboy hat was jammed on to a bulbous nose, under which a huge black handlebar mustache swayed with the balloon's undulations. Red jacket and chaps with fluttered fringe completed this jaunty figure from the Old West.

Something about the towering, arrogant figure reminded Paul of Alex Rande. He leaned close to Elaine, shouting to make himself heard. "Did I tell you that Alex Rande tried to take over both of Garry Channing's companies, including the plastics company that will manufacture the new polymer battery Garry patented?''

Elaine looked up, puzzled. "A takeover attempt? Are you sure? When?''

"Six months ago. I saw it in one of the business journals at the public library when you were in Seattle. Garry beat him, though. Topped Rande's offer to the stockholders. I bet Garry went to an investment banker to accomplish that.''

"And they're still friends?'' Elaine had to yell over the trumpets and brass drums of the band.

"In matters of business, people often keep their professional and personal lives separate. Garry and Rande became friends in college more than twenty years ago. Garry's not the kind to let a competitive spirit on Rande's part kill the friendship, I guess. He feels he can handle him,'' said Paul.

"I just hope Garry can handle his wife,'' muttered Elaine, craning her neck to see the following units. Paul could tell she was not enjoying the parade. There was a haunted expression in her eyes.

Gradually he became aware of a subtle stop-start cadence to the roll of the procession. It formed a rhythm that flowed through the street. The ground itself pulsed with the heartbeat of all the military, college and high school bands as they peeled into formation on North Street, each playing a different tune.

Paul heard a familiar hum. He looked up at the clear, pale sky. Far overhead was the Goodyear dirigible, a regular sight at each parade, and much lower, skimming just above the rooftops, was a state police helicopter, monitoring the crowd as it moved in slow, wide circles.

A FEW BLOCKS AWAY Keith sat with his back propped against a wall, knees bent, sock feet resting on expensive plush carpet. His aching head rested on his forearms; drums pounded inside his skull as well as on the street below the opened window.

"Jed didn't need to do that," he mumbled, barely able to speak. His jaw did feel broken this time. Nothing had ever hurt as badly, not even the football tackle during his senior year that had put him out of commission for the rest of the season.

"You shouldn't have given Jed the smart mouth," answered Hawley.

"All I did was ask him where the hell he and Lucky thought they were going when they took off out of here at eleven. Is that any reason to punch me? What time is it now? My watch's stopped. It probably broke when I fell." Keith tried to wind it.

"You tried to look in his bag, kid. It's his."

"He carries that gym bag around with him like it was gold from Fort Knox," Keith complained. "So he's got a gun in it. Big deal!"

"You saw the handgun?"

"Yeah. In the other apartment. He took it out to check it over. He thought I was asleep."

"Here's two aspirin. Take 'em." Hawley held out two tablets with a glass of water from the kitchenette.

Keith did as ordered, then leaned back against the papered wall. Through the fringe of his eyelashes he watched Hawley assemble the strange rifle, screwing on the barrel, attaching the scope, loading the ammunition.

"Where *did* Jed and Lucky go?" Keith asked.

Hawley looked up. His face took on a hard look. "Out to find your sister maybe, smart mouth. The boss says she's back in town. If the guy who's your target doesn't get his head blown off soon, your sister will. It's all up to you. You've been paid to do a job. You go through with it ... or else."

"I've been paid *half*. When do I collect the other half?"

Hawley looked up, surprised. "Now you're talking money? That's real sensible. You get the rest of the payment after it's all over. Come here." He motioned to the window.

Keith forced himself to stand. He walked to the window, pulled the curtain aside, and found himself staring at the crown of a white rubberized hat on the head of a towering balloon figure. In the distance, at an oblique angle across the street, loomed the Central Public Library.

Hawley stood beside Keith and pointed. "See that light post? When the target's car comes by, he'll be standing up through the sunroof opening. Wait till the car passes the light post. Take careful aim for the *back* of his head. *After* the car passes *that* lamppost. Understand?"

"What if I miss?" Keith licked his lips. "What if I hit somebody in the crowd instead?"

Hawley's lips drew into a thin line. He said nothing. He turned away from the window, let the curtain fall. The rubberized hat with the tall crown floated past.

"I'm . . . rusty. I haven't fired a rifle very m-many times since I got out of the s-service," Keith stammered.

"You were never *in* the service. Whoever forged that set of discharge papers and did the dog tag for you did a pretty good job, though."

"You know?" Keith stared at him.

"Who did you think you were playing with, kid? Amateurs? I bet I even know the guy in Chicago who furnished you with the stuff. Jed didn't like it when he found out you'd presented yourself as a veteran, when you're not. Kinda rubbed him the wrong way."

"Then why did you give *me* the job?"

Hawley pursed his lips. He tried to look genial. "I liked you. I was always a sucker for football players. You needed the money. So...I gave you a break. Then you got cold feet and tried to weasel out on me after you accepted the money. That put me in bad with the boss." He shook his head and walked to the door leading from the living room to the hallway of the apartment building. He opened the door.

"What's the man's name? The man I'm supposed to 'ice.' You never even told me his name." Keith was trying to find out how much Hawley knew.

"Names don't matter. Who he is don't matter. You just do your job, and your sister will get to go to work Monday.

"The car will be coming around soon. Be ready. You aim real careful, line up the back of his head in the cross hairs in the scope, and press that trigger. If you don't, your sister's as good as dead. Jed will see to it. Sorry, kid, but that's the way it is." He walked out, closed the door and locked the dead bolt from the outside.

With a sinking feeling, Keith realized he was still a prisoner, and time was growing short.

He had only one decision to make: would it be Garry Channing or Elaine?

CHAPTER FIFTEEN

THERE WAS NO LACK of celebrities in the parade, including television stars, Paul noted. All thirty-three qualified race drivers passed in review, accompanied by wives and children. But no tall, lean, suntanned Garry Channing—yet.

"How do they do that?" asked Elaine.

She was pointing to an approaching float. A Goliath of a Texas steer with massive horns was chasing the diminutive figure of a cowboy on a horse. The cowboy's arms and legs were in constant motion, rising and falling in a comical reaction to the rush of the massive steer.

"Is there a man hidden inside the float to make the cowboy's arms and legs move?" she wanted to know.

"There's a man hidden inside the tow unit below the floor level to pull the float. A raised lid over the opening allows room for the man's head and enables the driver to see out, but it's disguised well enough that spectators don't see him," he answered.

Paul had done an article for the magazine's May issue on festival parade floats under construction.

"Then what makes the figure move?" Elaine insisted.

"That's a good question. I don't know."

"Look. The figure on the next float is moving, too," she pointed out.

An old-fashioned woodshed topped the tow unit, and behind it was a log cabin and the huge wood and fiberglass figure of a pioneer woman, a bonnet on her head to shield her oversized face. In her arms she held an infant wrapped in a blanket. Two barefoot children and a mangy dog completed the Western frontier theme. The figures stood in front of the cabin, which appeared to be made of real logs. Fringed leather strips hung over the cabin's window like a curtain, swaying gently with the vehicle's motion.

"That float's a real work of art. Who's paying the bill?" Paul glanced but didn't need to look at the souvenir program. To his surprise, the name of a building manufacturing company owned by BMQ/OXO Corporation was painted on the side of the float.

"Rande never mentioned he was sponsoring one of the floats this year," he muttered, puzzled.

"That's Garry in the car behind it," said Elaine. Her voice was tense. "Laura's not with him."

Garry Channing sported a Stetson hat and a cowboy shirt. With his Marlboro man's craggy face, Channing would have looked right at home astride a horse. Instead, he stood upright through the sunroof of a black sports car, waving at the crowd.

For a few seconds the procession halted, band members down the line marching in place in the stop-start rhythm Paul had noticed earlier. Suddenly the pioneer swung about to face the smiling Garry Channing. A few seconds later she turned again, to face the cabin. Overhead, the droning hum of the police helicopter making its routine surveillance of the crowd could be heard.

Paul stared at his friend, but Channing took no notice of him. His car continued to follow the pioneer float. Paul gazed after them, watching them move south on Pennsylvania over the checkered carpet, then turn west on Ohio and disappear from sight.

Suddenly the pieces of the puzzle fell into place, making him gasp in disbelief. Why hadn't he been able to see it before? The plan was ingenious, yet so simple.

Paul grabbed Elaine's arm, startling her. "Keith's been set up to take the blame. The *real* killer's on that float!"

He looked about wildly for the nearest police officer with a radio. Abandoning Elaine without further explanation, he took off at a run, grabbing the officer by the forearm. The man reacted automatically, his free hand reaching for his gun holster.

"I'm Paul Cooper. Contact Jim Dickerson, state police, at the review stand. Advise him that Channing's killer is on the pioneer mother float just ahead of Channing's car and the guy's armed with *real* ammunition. Tell Jim!"

The officer, who didn't recognize Paul, kept a bland expression, but in his eyes Paul read his disbelief. Nevertheless, he put the radio to his lips. Paul heard Dickerson's name mentioned, then his own. He had gotten through.

Paul didn't wait. He ran north on Pennsylvania, staying close to the curb, and headed toward the stately public library building and Saint Claire Street, barricaded to traffic for the day's event. He ran past Memorial Plaza, almost colliding with a boy sailing along on a skateboard. He played dodge'em with a Popsicle pushcart and earned a profane greeting from the vendor. Paul didn't apologize—there wasn't time.

He reached Meridian Street and headed south toward the approaching float that bore the pioneer mother and her child. He heard a pulsing beat and glanced up. The state police helicopter had dropped lower, moving in a tight circle over Meridian Street. City police officers, county sheriff's deputies and several state troopers were coming out of the crowd, all converging on the float.

Jim got the message. Thank God!

Yet to Paul's despair, the float continued to roll on, drawing close to the intersection with 9th Street.

His mouth aching with dryness, chest ready to burst, Paul pushed ahead. He yelled Channing's name as loudly as he could, trying to make himself heard over the sound of the music. He waved his arms wildly.

When Channing's startled gaze fixed on him, he made vigorous downward motions with outstretched arms, but Channing continued to stare at him, as if trying to figure out the sign language.

A shot rang out.

At that moment Garry Channing collapsed like a rag doll into the interior of the car. A woman in the crowd screamed. The parade procession slowed to a halt.

A man's voice called out. It was a powerful voice with a husky quality that soared over the stunned silence of the spectators, making itself heard even above the blare of the nearest band.

"Up there! I saw a rifle up there in the window! He's up there!" The speaker was pointing at an upper window in a building that faced onto Meridian Street. Paul saw him clearly as several policemen halted, looked up and ran toward the building.

The man who had called the warning melted into the crowd and disappeared while the helicopter droned louder. The aircraft hovered, then went off in another direction.

EPILOGUE

THE GENTLE WIND felt good against Elaine's damp face, against the skin of her bare thighs. The grass and earth at the shoulder of the road felt good beneath her feet. Her heart was pumping hard, her breath coming fast.

The startling events of the festival parade seemed unreal, like the scenes of an old movie, far away in time. As the memories of that eventful day intruded now, Elaine shut them out, unwilling to think of the trial that lay ahead for Keith, and for herself. Keith was her brother—what happened to him affected her, too.

"You've run far enough. Kessler Boulevard is just ahead. Better slow down to a walk."

Paul didn't even sound breathless. He didn't look tired. He moved beside her with little effort as she obeyed. Like her, he was wearing running shorts, pullover shirt and running shoes. Her clothes were new; his bore the signs of wear and frequent washings.

They turned onto Kessler Boulevard just west of Elaine's home. Since Elaine was a beginner, Paul had paced her on a three-mile circuit of her neighborhood. Traffic was light at eight o'clock in the morning on the Fourth of July, though the neighborhood was already gearing up for the holiday, with outdoor grills and patio furniture featured prominently on the lush green lawns.

Elaine's skin was slick with sweat. Her pulse was pounding but beginning to slow now. She was pleasantly tired, and felt drained of tension. The exhilaration was exactly as Paul had described it; he was proving a good coach.

Paul had insisted that Elaine have a complete physical before he would agree to go out running with her. She had argued with him, but he had won, of course. As always he had been firm but fair, qualities she had come to appreciate more and more since their first meeting. Now Paul had become so much a part of her life that she could not imagine a day without either seeing him or hearing his voice on the telephone.

"Can we sit on the patio and talk a minute before we go in?" he asked, running his fingers through damp hair.

He's had something on his mind for the past week, Elaine reflected. *It must be something to do with the trial.* She experienced the sinking feeling that came whenever she thought about what lay ahead for her brother.

"Sure," she answered. "But Keith promised he'd have pancakes ready for breakfast when we came back. Cooking is a new hobby for him. I don't want to disappoint him by showing up late."

"This won't take long," Paul assured her.

They walked around the house to the flagstone patio at the rear. It was cooler there and fragrant with red geraniums, purple and white petunias, and two rosebushes. Elaine dropped onto the love seat, leaving space for him beside her. Paul leaned back on the floral cushions, stretching his long frame to its full length as his arm went around her.

"I bet I lose ten pounds by next month," she declared. "Now I know why you can eat anything you want and never gain weight."

"You'll be burning calories fast," he agreed.

"What's on your mind, darling?" Elaine asked.

Paul surprised her. "I'm going to offer Keith a position on the magazine as a staff writer. Do you think he'll accept?"

Elaine felt a leap of joy within her. Ever since she had put up the stiff bail to get Keith released from jail and guaranteed he would live with her under her supervision until the date of the trial, Keith had been depressed and quiet. Her zany, fun-loving brother had disappeared.

"That would be wonderful! Keith needs to work, but he's been scared no one will hire him after the article about the attempt on Channing's life hit the newspapers. This could be the answer. Writing is his life, Paul. The novel is half-finished, but he won't let me read the draft yet."

"I can be tough on the job—ask Ben. Keith may end up hating me as an employer."

"Ben loves you. He also respects you. Keith will, too. He's already beginning to understand what you've done for us. He'll learn a lot with you as his mentor." Elaine felt an overwhelming gratitude to this man, but the love she felt for him was so much more than that—it was tender caring, affection, admiration and respect mingled with a passion that amazed her.

"When are you going to tell Keith his father's still alive?" Paul asked in a low voice. He glanced up at the glass patio doors to make sure Keith was not nearby.

Elaine took a tortured breath. The old panic was back. She had been fighting it since the day of the parade. "I...can't. I don't want to hurt Keith further, with all that lies ahead of him. How would he react if he knew our father was still alive?"

"He's cooperating with the prosecutor by testifying against Brett Hawley. Keith's been offered a plea bargain. He could draw a suspended sentence...."

"Thank God the police caught Jed before he could escape from the float...." Elaine shuddered despite the warm morning air.

Paul grinned. He seemed amused. "Caught with the handgun in his gym bag. And a police record as long as his arm. The guy's been in trouble all his life. Lucky didn't get far, either. It was fortunate that I could identify him as the man who tried to finger Keith."

"What if Garry Channing hadn't seen your warning for him to duck?" She shivered again and Paul's arm tightened around her.

"He'd be dead, and his son would be spending his inheritance about now," Paul answered.

"And what if that horrible Hawley had kept his mouth shut and hadn't implicated Alex Rande as the man who hired him?"

"Hawley was too smart to take the blame for masterminding this plot. That was the biggest thing we had going for us. Alex Rande didn't intimidate him."

"They're two of a kind, that's why. The difference is that one looks good in a tuxedo and has a better golf score," Elaine declared.

Paul leaned his head back and let out a boisterous laugh. Elaine smiled. Paul pushed his glasses upward with a bony knuckle and wiped away the trace of a tear.

"If you had decided to go with Rande the night of the Queen's Ball..."

"I probably wouldn't be sitting here now. I would have—disappeared, right?" Her voice wavered. Paul's arm squeezed her warmly. She settled her head into the warm hollow between his neck and shoulder, luxuriating in the comfort of his physical presence.

"You were his trump card, honey, to guarantee your brother's cooperation. Thank God you're the right kind of woman. If you had dumped me that night because you thought you had a chance with Mr. Moneybags . . .''

Her finger settled over his lips to silence them. "No chance of that."

He reached up, took her hand, pressed the palm against his lips. "Madeline did."

"Madeline was crazy!" Elaine declared.

A slow grin spread over his face, lighting his eyes. Candles of pure joy, or of mischief, burned deeply within the dark pupils. "Let's get married. Will you agree to become my wife?" Paul asked softly.

Elaine blinked, staring at the face that was mere inches from hers. This was not the way she had fantasized he would propose. They had been to dinner at every fabulous restaurant in town, and Elaine had daydreamed about hearing those magic words in the glow of candlelight, in a room overlooking a twilight vista of twinkling lights, perhaps with some soft music in the background.

"What . . . did you say?" She could hardly speak.

His arm pulled her snugly against him. One hand stroked her hair. His voice was like a kiss, tender, caressing. "I'm saying I love you and I want to share the rest of my life with you. I'll be the best husband I can."

Elaine reached for his hand and pressed it to her lips, hard. She was so filled with emotion that she feared her chest would shatter, spilling her heart all over him. She couldn't speak.

"The magazine is in good shape. Subscription orders have been pouring in—new ads, too, since I hired an advertising manager—and retail store sales have jumped. I'm not asking you to support me on the interest from your trust account," he added.

This time it was her turn to laugh. She lifted her head to give him her answer—a long, passionate kiss. He understood, as he usually did, and responded with a dazzling smile.

Suddenly Elaine heard the whisper of the patio doors.

"Out here, in front of the neighbors?" Keith asked. "You'll have to order a privacy fence."

They turned to look at Keith, who stood in the doorway, clutching a plastic spatula like a baseball bat.

"Paul's going to be your brother-in-law," Elaine announced proudly.

"Shoot, I knew that, but if I keep the pancakes warm in the oven much longer, we'll be eating shoe leather," Keith complained. His voice was husky, though, betraying his happiness for his sister.

"Congratulations, Paul! Put her here!" he said, extending his hand.

Paul rose from the love seat, giving Keith's hand a mock slap, then grabbing it in a salute of brotherly affection.

"Always wanted a brother!" Keith said in a low voice.

"Paul has a position open on the magazine he wants you to fill, too. Real money," added Elaine, pleased by Keith's look of astonishment.

"You kidding me?" The young man seemed animated for the first time in weeks.

THE PANCAKES were still moist and tender and the biscuits flaky after Keith pulled them from the oven. There were sausages and fresh fruit and, of course, strawberry jam. It was not exactly a low-calorie meal, but after running, Elaine didn't feel too guilty. She praised Keith's culinary triumph.

He was glad to accept Paul's offer of a job and was soon asking pertinent questions about Mary, Paul's blond secretary, whom he'd already seen several times. She had accompanied Paul to the arraignment, and once the four of them had gone to dinner and the movies.

By the time Keith had cleared the dishes off the kitchen table and was stuffing them into the dishwasher, Elaine knew her brother's spirits had lifted considerably. She heard the portable TV on the kitchen counter click on, the murmur of music and voices.

She and Paul walked into the family room, arms around each other. They had showered and changed before breakfast, and the sweet peace brought by full stomachs, clean bodies and pleasantly tired muscles was just right for a lazy holiday Sunday.

"I'd like to call Dad and Ada. Tell them about us," she told Paul.

The smile he gave her was a gentle one, and she could see something almost triumphant in his expression. He stood up, shoving his thumbs into the pockets of his jeans. "Tell your stepmother I'll take the money to Cincinnati. I'll tell the bank I came across the money when I was running down another story and I can't reveal my sources. A journalist's prerogative." He shrugged his shoulders. "I'll say... your father regrets what he did and wants to make restitution before he dies."

Elaine gasped. "You'd do that for *me?*"

"You can bet there isn't anybody *else* I'd do it for!" Paul declared. "I'll keep your name out of it completely. Nobody at Commercial Bank will ever know your connection with George Stamm. Consider it a wedding present." His arms went around her and he kissed her deeply.

Elaine started to cry from pure joy.

"Come on, none of that," Paul urged. "Your father did a foolish thing, but it wasn't for greed. He's proved that. He was trying to make a point—that security concerning the vault was lax, that the manager's policies were in error. I'll try to get that message across."

Elaine embraced Paul so tightly he gasped. "I love you!" she whispered ardently.

"I know!" he answered softly, lights shimmering in his eyes and a haunting half smile touching his lips.

The feeling inside Elaine was so immense that it was no longer subject to caution or fear. She released Paul reluctantly and went to the telephone in the family room, picked up the receiver and punched in a long-distance number. After a dozen rings, Ada answered.

"Ada? This is Elaine. I had to call you. Paul has agreed to take the . . . the suitcases to the proper person."

She heard Ada gasp. "He has?"

"It's all in the family now. Paul asked me to marry him. I said yes. We haven't set the date yet."

Elaine heard a squeal of excitement at the other end of the line. "Oh, my dear, I am so happy for you! He sounds like such a fine man."

"He certainly is. Is Dad awake?"

"Yes. He's in the other room. Do you want to talk to him?"

"Yes. Keith's birthday is next week. He'll be twenty-three. Would Dad be willing to talk with him?"

"I'll get him. Hold on. Hold on!" Ada moved away from the telephone.

"Keith. Come in here, honey. Hurry," Elaine called, wishing she had informed her brother that their father was still alive. She hoped she was doing the right thing. She glanced at Paul for moral support. His expression was encouraging, imparting strength.

Keith appeared in the doorway. "I didn't hear the phone ring. Is it for me?" He walked across the room toward Elaine, wearing the gray sweatpants and white cotton T-shirt that had become his uniform since the weather had turned warm. "Who is it?" he asked, reaching for the telephone receiver she was holding out toward him.

"It's Dad. He's alive, living in Seattle. He loves you. He wants to wish you a happy birthday." The words were coming out, after all. She felt breathless, excited. "His wife is named Ada. You have two step-brothers dying to meet you. They want to play football when they get into high school and be just like you."

Keith looked stunned. He blinked hard several times. "Dad? My father's alive? He's concerned about me?" The hand raising the receiver to his ear was unsteady. The other hand cupped the mouth-piece.

"Dad . . . ? Is it really you?" Tears sprang into his dark eyes, and his face was radiant.

"Well, I can't come to Seattle just now . . . I'm not allowed to leave the state. But just as soon as some things I've . . . got to take care of . . . are over . . . sure, I'll come to see you.

"Gee, Dad . . . you sure sound great!

"I've missed you."

Listening, Paul and Elaine embraced tenderly. If you believed, there were rainbows after all.

Six exciting series for you every month... from Harlequin

HARLEQUIN Romance®

The series that started it all

Tender, captivating and heartwarming...
love stories that sweep you off to faraway places
and delight you with the magic of love.

◆

Harlequin Presents®

Powerful contemporary love stories...as individual as the women who read them

The No. 1 romance series...
exciting love stories for you, the woman of today...
a rare blend of passion and dramatic realism.

◆

Harlequin Superromance®

It's more than romance... it's Harlequin Superromance

A sophisticated, contemporary romance-fiction
series, providing you with a longer,
more involving read...a richer mix of complex plots,
realism and adventure.

HARLEQUIN
American Romance®
Harlequin celebrates the American woman...

...by offering you romance stories written about American women, by American women for American women. This series offers you contemporary romances uniquely North American in flavor and appeal.

◆

HARLEQUIN
Temptation®

Passionate stories for today's woman

An exciting series of sensual, mature stories of love...dilemmas, choices, resolutions... all contemporary issues dealt with in a true-to-life fashion by some of your favorite authors.

◆

Harlequin Intrigue®
Because romance can be quite an adventure

Harlequin Intrigue, an innovative series that blends the romance you expect... with the unexpected. Each story has an added element of intrigue that provides a new twist to the Harlequin tradition of romance excellence.

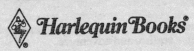 *Harlequin Books*®

Harlequin Superromance®

Here are the longer, more involving stories you have been waiting for . . . Superromance.

Modern, believable novels of love, full of the complex joys and heartaches of real people.

Intriguing conflicts based on today's constantly changing life-styles.

Four new titles every month.